A Deadly Coincidence

A Lipton St Faith Mystery

A Deadly Coincidence

KEITH FINNEY

LUME BOOKS

LUME BOOKS

Published in 2021 by Lume Books
30 Great Guildford Street,
Borough, SE1 0HS

ISBN 978-1-83901-222-8

Typeset using Atomik ePublisher from Easypress Technologies

www.lumebooks.co.uk

For Joan

Chapter 1: A Hard Fall

'The police said Ted Fleming must have been thrown from his bicycle after hitting something on the road during the blackout. It seems he then had the misfortune of getting tangled on barbed wire in the ditch.'

Reverend Charles Grix let out a sigh as he recounted being called out overnight to attend the sad scene. Joining him for lunch after he had taken Sunday worship were his wife Helen and daughter Anna.

'So that's why you look so worn out, Dad. I assumed that your flock was a little more demanding than usual this morning and you needed one of Mum's Sunday roasts to put you right.'

The vicar gave Anna a weary smile as he looked towards his wife approaching the table.

'Not so much a feast this week; we might live in the country, but I've had trouble getting a decent joint of beef for us.'

Anna reflected on the amount of food available to them compared with most people as rationing was beginning to bite all over the country. 'I think we've plenty to be thankful for. What do you say, Dad?'

Charles Grix nodded, held a hand out to his wife and smiled at Anna. 'It's so cruel everyone has to go through this again within a single generation of the Great War.'

Anna caught her parents exchanging a furtive glance, sadness etched momentarily into their faces. Attempting to move the conversation on, she turned her attention to her mother. 'How's the village thrift store doing, Mum?'

Helen Grix glanced at her daughter and smiled. 'Well, we're fortunate to have plenty of volunteers ready to step in at a moment's notice. Our real problem is having enough good quality items to sell. Most people nowadays are hanging on to anything that can be repaired or reused, like last time. If it goes on like this, we shall never get anywhere near the £5,000 needed to buy our Spitfire for the RAF.'

Anna helped herself to a small portion of potatoes, carrots and cauliflower before pouring a liberal covering of beef stock gravy over her meal. 'Do you think you're being a little ambitious, perhaps, in aiming for a whole fighter plane?'

Her mother offered the slightest of frowns as she, too, allowed herself a small portion of food. 'Well, apparently you can buy just a gun, which costs £200, so maybe that's a more realistic ambition for our small community. What do you think, Charles?'

Anna smiled as she watched her father's eyes drooping while trying to keep up with the conversation.

'Yes, yes. Of course.'

Helen tapped the back of her husband's hand with her index finger to gain his full attention. 'What you need, my darling, is your bed.'

The vicar attempted to stifle a yawn. 'Of course, you're correct.

However, I cannot get Ted Fleming out of my mind. Such a sad sight and a terrible way in which to leave our little paradise.'

Anna was struck by how deeply her father was taking the postman's death, given that it was such a routine part of his ministry. 'Was he still alive when you reached him, Dad?'

Her father nodded. 'Barely. In fact, within a minute of me getting to him, he breathed his last. Such a tragedy teaches us how fragile life is. I imagine Ted had ridden down that road every morning for the last twenty years to sort the first post ready for his morning delivery. What made today any different from all the others?'

'The thing is, Dad, at least you were there to offer him comfort. That's got to count for something.'

He pushed several sliced carrots around his plate. 'Do you know what always strikes me? It's the seemingly odd things those who are dying say in the minutes before they expire.'

Anna looked quizzical. 'I imagine most would say how much they loved those nearest to them, or perhaps offer regret for ambitions unfulfilled, or words to a loved one left unsaid?'

'Of course, that's true much of the time. But in other instances, the dying will state their regret about something so mundane that, in other circumstances, it might pass without the need for comment. Yet, in that instant, it's as if this trifle is the most important thing in the universe.'

Helen took hold of her husband's hand. 'To your bed.'

Anna was keen to continue the conversation but felt guilty at insisting her father spoke about a subject he found painful. 'Mum's right. You need to sleep.'

The vicar rose wearily from the dining table and began to turn towards the hallway stairs. 'The only thing Ted Fleming said to me was, "letter". Not a word about his wife or all the other things we might ordinarily consider necessary in our lives. Just his job of delivering letters…'

Springing to her feet, Anna put her arm around her father. 'Let me turn the bed down for you while you get yourself ready.' Without waiting for a reply, she stepped ahead of her father and hurried up a dark, narrow flight of stairs before disappearing into her parent's bedroom.

Within minutes, the Reverend Grix left his dressing room behind and entered the bedroom. 'Thank you so much, that's most kind.'

Anna hesitated before leaving. 'Why do you think poor Ted was so concerned about his letters?'

'Come here, my child.' The vicar patted the flock eiderdown as he made himself comfortable in the iron-framed bed.

Accepting her father's invitation, Anna perched on the edge of the bed.

'The only explanation I can offer is that in those final few seconds, the unfortunate soul says what is most important to him or her at that moment. They may utter words that make no sense to us or do not mean to us what is meant by the person uttering them. Who is to say what Ted Fleming really meant?'

Anna smiled, leant forward and gave her father an affectionate peck on his forehead.

Standing in the old stables of the nineteenth-century vicarage, Anna fixed her gaze on the black post office bicycle that the police had delivered to her father earlier that morning.

What tales you could tell of the last twenty-four hours.

She stepped across the cobbled floor and entered one of two

stalls, which had previously stabled the horses of her father's predecessors. Leaning lazily against a stone water trough, Anna inspected every inch of the old bike. Moving methodically from the front wheel across the iron frame before examining the rear wheel, she paid particular attention to the well-oiled chain.

Nothing wrong with it, so that can't have caused Ted to take a tumble.

Holding the handlebar and seat, she turned the bike through 180 degrees and was surprised by its heavy weight.

I expect these were made to last, but this is ridiculous.

Leaning the bicycle back against the trough, Anna once again undertook a diligent inspection, covering every component. She found no sign of damage, having paid particular attention to the front wheel to identify any twist or misalignment due to sudden contact with an obstacle.

Why no damage?

It was only when she stood back that she noticed the rear mudguard was misshapen. Adding to her curiosity, Anna discovered a small patch of colour, which could just be made out against the pitch-black paint and spattering of mud covering the metal guard.

She bent forward and lightly touched the peculiar patch.

It's blood. The poor man must have tumbled backwards, hit his head and rolled into the ditch.

Determining there was nothing more to be gained from her inspection, Anna decided to visit Ted's widow, Peggy. She made her way to what constituted the main road through Lipton St Faith, the village she had called home for all her twenty-five years.

Anna smiled contentedly as she viewed the quiet streetscape

of half-timbered houses. Many retained their reed thatching and small-paned windows with the occasional glass bullseye adding to their attraction.

In the middle distance stood the village green with some of the village's larger houses clustered around its circumference. At one edge, where High Street and New Road intersected, an ancient sandstone cross sat on top of a layered step platform. Anna conjured up an image of riders down the millennia using the steps as an aid to mount their horses.

The tranquillity was not to last. Out of the corner of her eye, Anna caught sight of Beatrice Flowers, well known as the village gossip with an opinion on all things, whether asked for or not.

Here we go.

'I see you have your hair done up like those American actresses you see at the pictures. Don't you think that's a little brash for a vicar's daughter?'

Anna offered the elderly spinster a wide smile. 'Now, Miss Flowers, you well know my hairstyle is nothing like the Betty Grables of this world, not least with shampoo so hard to get hold of.'

She watched as the old woman eyed her from tip to toe, shaking her head and offering an occasional 'tut-tut'.

'Anyway, Miss Flowers, I see you're wearing a fine silk scarf this morning. Don't you think it might contribute to the making of a parachute for one of our fine young fighting men?'

Anna's rebuke was sufficient to cause Beatrice Flowers to beat a hasty retreat.

'What's that you said, Miss Flowers?' She knew her question would go unanswered as the old lady muttered under her breath before disappearing into the milliners.

The remainder of Anna's short journey to Peggy Fleming's small painted brick cottage concluded without further incident. Lightly tapping on the heavy wooden door with its cast-iron dolphin-shaped door knocker, Anna took a step back. A few seconds later, the door began to slowly open, at first only enough for Peggy Fleming to show one side of her face. Recognising her visitor, she held open the door and gestured for Anna to step into the tiny lounge.

'I wanted to pop in to offer you my condolences. Ted was a wonderful man, and he'll be sadly missed by us all.'

Peggy began to fill up. 'Will you thank your father for me? It gives me comfort to know the vicar was with my Ted at the end.'

Anna wanted to reach out and give the widow a hug but knew Peggy came from a generation that found physical contact with others difficult. 'So typical of you, Peggy, thinking of others when it's you that needs looking after, but thank you, I'll pass your kind words on to my father.'

'May I get you some tea, Anna?'

'If you're sure it's not too much trouble?'

'To be honest, I'm glad of the company. I know it's only been a few hours, but I can't tell you how empty I feel. Please, do take a seat.'

After Peggy left for the kitchen, Anna cast her eyes around a room kept spotlessly clean and which included several pictures of her unfortunate husband.

'Here we are. I'm sorry I've no sugar, and you may find the tea a little weak, but I'm sure we'll manage.'

Anna smiled. 'We most certainly shall, Peggy. Thank you, so kind.'

The two women sat in silence for a short while as they drank from the widow's best china cups. Before long, Anna noticed Peggy beginning to lean forward in her cottage chair.

'I realise that what I'm about to ask may sound odd, but I wonder if you'd mind?'

Intrigued, Anna mirrored Peggy's body language. 'Peggy, if there's anything I can do for you, please let me know.'

The widow fidgeted with her cup before standing up and placing it on what little space remained on the mantelpiece. 'What I don't understand is how my Ted ended up in a ditch at the side of the road. He's made the same journey every day at the same time for years and never so much as a puncture, never mind falling off the stupid thing.'

Anna sat back in her chair, trying to understand what Peggy was getting at. 'Peggy, the police think… no, are certain, it was an unfortunate accident…'

The widow shook her head. 'I told them he was so careful. Ted wouldn't have fallen off like that, but they wouldn't listen. They say there's nothing further to investigate, yet they want to cut him open and do a post-mortem. You tell me why they want to do that.'

Anna stood and walked the short distance to Peggy's side. Gently clasping one of the widow's hands, she offered a sympathetic smile. 'Although they're sure it was an accident, there were no witnesses. Until a post-mortem's completed, there can be no certainty how Ted died. I'm sorry if that sounds harsh, but I think what you need now is for people to speak truthfully to you. Don't you agree?' Anna maintained constant eye contact with the widow.

'You're right, of course. But all the same, it's a horrible thought.'

'Whatever you need, Peggy, the village will pull together for you. Now, what was it you wanted to ask?'

Peggy released her hand from Anna's, turned to the mantelpiece and picked up a portrait of her late husband. 'Anna Grix, I know you to be an independently minded woman who is the daughter of a good man. I know I can trust you. Will you try to find out what really happened to my Ted? If it was an accident, so be it. But I want to be sure no one deliberately hurt him.'

Anna tried hard to hide her surprise. 'So you think it wasn't an accident? Ted was universally liked; are you telling me some wished him harm?'

Peggy began to fill up again, but instead of welcoming Anna's embrace, she stepped back and once more reached for his photo. 'We all have skeletons in our cupboards, Anna. All I ask is that you find out what really happened and tell me the truth.'

'Anna Grix.'

Anna almost jumped out of her skin; such was her surprise at the officious tone coming from behind. As she turned on the spot, the firm retort she had intended to deploy melted away as she recognised who was barking at her. 'Tom Bradshaw, you may think you're the bee's knees now that you're a police constable. However, remember I always could run faster, punch harder and tell better fibs than you. You'd better watch out that I don't clout you one, whether you're wearing a bobby's helmet or not.'

Tom's smile matched Anna's as the two friends continued to exchange light-hearted insults.

'Are you going to tell me how Ted Fleming came to meet his maker?'

She knew such a direct question would throw Tom off balance and put him in a difficult position. Anna also knew that he had always been sweet on her and could rarely refuse her anything.

'I assume you found out about that through the vicar. If so, you probably know as much as I do about Ted's accident.'

Anna's eyes narrowed. 'Then the police are convinced it's an accident?'

'It's not for me to say whether it was or was not an accident. All I'm saying is your father was there. Ted Fleming appeared to have fallen into some barbed wire, causing an injury to his neck. No evidence to suggest anything other than an accident was found. You see, we in the police deal in facts, not supposition.'

Anna sauntered towards the constable, causing Tom to take a step back. 'Get you off that high horse, Constable. Dad was a bit vague on what and where it happened. Now, is it a state secret or are you going to say where Ted fell off his bike?'

Tom looked distinctly uneasy. 'Are you trying to get me in trouble with my sergeant? If he finds out I've given you any information, he'll have my guts for garters.'

Anna gave Tom one of those looks to which she knew he had no defence. 'That predisposes that Sergeant Dick Ilford finds out. I'll do you a deal. If you don't tell him, then neither will I. Agreed?'

She could see Tom was far from convinced about her logic. Nevertheless, she detected he was about to give in.

'It was on the Norwich road about two miles outside the village, just before that sharp right-hand bend. You know the place, not far from where we used to go climbing for conkers.'

Anna laughed. 'The less said about our tree climbing capers, the better. I know exactly where you mean.'

She raced back to the vicarage, collected her bicycle and made off to where Tom said the incident took place. Anna knew there was only around an hour of daylight left and didn't want to get caught cycling in the dark.

Within fifteen minutes, she stood on the spot where Ted Fleming had apparently tumbled off his bike. She surveyed the deathly quiet scene as the light began to fade. Anna failed to find any damage to the road surface other than a single scuff mark, which she presumed occurred when one of the pedals hit the tarmac as Ted fell.

Scrambling into the deep ditch nearest the scuff mark, Anna searched for any trace of the barbed wire which had led to the postie's death. There was nothing to be found and she assumed the police had collected anything they considered evidence that might assist in the post-mortem. All that remained of Ted Fleming's presence was a dark stain at the bottom of the ditch.

Anna concluded it was time to head home. Turning through 360 degrees, she took one last look at the scene and was about to scramble back up the bank when she noticed damage to the trunk of a large tree on the other side of the ditch, adjacent to where Ted had been found.

Fighting her inclination to leave before total darkness set in, she scurried to take a closer look. About five feet from ground level, she could clearly see a cut mark in the bark, which ran around the circumference of the tree.

This is where the barbed wire must've been attached when he got caught up in it as he tumbled into the ditch, poor chap.

Satisfied she had at least a partial picture of what may have happened, Anna began to cycle home along the narrow Norfolk

11

lane. The road was dangerous at the best of times, let alone in the dark.

A split second later, Anna heard the sound of a vehicle. The last thing she remembered was screaming.

Chapter 2: An Odd Meeting

'Are you OK, ma'am?'

Anna slowly opened her eyes to see an American serviceman crouching over her, his tall frame backlit by a new moon and star-filled Norfolk sky.

'What kind of a crazy American are you? Are you blind? The Luftwaffe can see clearly enough to drop bombs on us from 25,000 feet. How come you were having so much difficulty seeing what's twenty-five feet in front of you?'

She lay still, unsure which bit of her hurt, and watched with curiosity as the stranger slowly moved his eyeline from the tip of her toes to her head.

'There doesn't seem to be any damage, ma'am.'

'What, to me? Or that stupid Jeep you're driving? Anyway, I'll be the judge of whether anything's damaged. Perhaps you would like to assist a lady in getting up from a dirty road surface? Heaven knows what my father would think if he saw me now.'

'Lieutenant Eddie Elsner, US Army Special Observer Group at your service, ma'am.'

As Anna tried to bear her full weight, her left ankle gave way, and she cried out in pain. 'I think you've been of quite enough service for one night, put me down.'

'Forgive me, ma'am, I'm concerned another vehicle will drive up this track and hit us.'

Anna raised an eyebrow and shook her head at the American. 'What, two cars in one night? You haven't been in this part of Norfolk long, have you?' She stiffened as the stranger reached over to check her ankle. 'If you cause me any more pain, you won't know what's hit you, I promise.'

The officer's attempt to manipulate Anna's ankle quickly met resistance. 'OK, OK, I get it. Looks like a bad sprain. And to answer your question, yep, I'm new around these parts, and it's kinda taking time to find out how things work.'

Having let go of his collar on condition that he left her ankle alone, Anna gave him a dismissive glance. 'Let me guess: New England?'

The officer smiled. 'Southwest Colorado, ma'am. But I guess it's an easy mistake to make; you Brits all sound the same, too.'

Anna shuffled her bottom by supporting herself with both hands pressed firmly onto the tarmac to find a more comfortable position and ease the pain in her ankle. 'And what exactly are you doing driving around the Norfolk countryside after the blackout in an American uniform? For all I know, you could be a German spy.'

The lieutenant laughed. 'I can think of better places to spy than in the middle of nowhere. There seem to be more windmills than people.'

'For your information, most are windpumps, not mills. As for people, you'd be surprised at how many live here. We simply prefer to keep ourselves to ourselves, rather than race around the county, knocking people off bicycles.'

'Touché; I suppose I deserve that. All the same, need to get you off this track.'

Anna braced herself as the officer lifted her from behind. 'That's the second or third time you've said "track". In England, we call them lanes. Tracks don't have a tarmac surface, lanes do.'

Anna winced as she attempted to walk the few steps to her crumpled bicycle.

'Here, let me help you, there's no way you'll be able to ride that thing.'

Anna looked to the ditch where Ted had been found, then back at her bike. 'This is your fault, so I suppose the least you can do is give me a lift home.' She pointed to the twisted front wheel of the bicycle. 'My father's not going to be best pleased. Do you know how much a new one of these costs? That's if you can even get one, what with the rationing and all.'

Leaving the lieutenant to pick up her broken conveyance and place it in the back of his army issue Jeep, Anna hobbled to the passenger side and attempted to climb in. Within a split second, she felt a hand at her elbow. 'Leave me alone, you might be surprised to learn that even a woman can climb into one of these things.'

Taking the hint, he quickly withdrew, walked briskly around to the driver's side and heaved himself into his seat.

Surveying his hunched frame behind the wheel, Anna asked, 'Exactly how tall are you?'

Lieutenant Elsner grabbed the steering wheel to lever himself into a more comfortable driving position and fumbled in the moonlight for the ignition key. '6'2", ma'am, and in this little thing, I'm feeling every inch of it.'

Seconds later, the vehicle roared into life, emitting a noxious grey cloud from the exhaust. Above the sound of the Jeep's throaty engine, Anna became aware of a low humming sound. It was a noise she recognised.

Scanning the velvety blue-black sky, she looked south, then moved her head slowly left. 'There they are. I'd say about a hundred of the horrible things. I hate what they're doing to us.'

Eddie lifted his peaked cap as he glimpsed a swarm of black dots getting closer. 'We'll pay them back, mark my words.'

Anna detected a hard edge to his reply. 'Did you hear what they did to Coventry last November?' Her voice was tinged with anger.

'Yes, on the radio. The Germans invented a new word for what they'd done, didn't they.'

It was a sad face that returned the American's look. 'Coventrated.' She looked up once again to see the menacing swarm passing directly overhead as they remorselessly made their way northward.

The ten minutes it took to drive back to Lipton St Faith allowed enough time for Anna to explain why she had been out in the first place.

'Where the heck are we? Everything looks the same.'

Anna smiled and pointed to a church steeple. 'Head for that.'

Soon, the Jeep came to a halt adjacent to a gate set in a low cobblestone wall. 'Are you telling me you live in a church?'

Anna couldn't help laughing. 'Well, to be accurate, the vicarage. You see, that's what you do when you're a vicar's daughter.'

'This is one of your English jokes, yes?'

'Are you suggesting something is amusing about being a vicar's daughter?' Anna knew she now had him on the run.

'Er… no, I, well…'

'An American officer you may be, but you're so easy to hook. Now, get me out of this thing and don't think you're getting off so lightly. Since you almost crippled me, you can chauffeur me around for a few days while I look into the postie's death.'

Lieutenant Elsner frowned. 'Whose death? Anyway, I thought you didn't need any help getting in or out of Jeeps?'

Anna smiled. 'I forgot you Americans don't speak English – I mean the postman. As for whether I need help or not, let's say I decide the rules. You caused my injuries so owe me a favour, which I'm calling in immediately. Please collect me tomorrow at 9.00 am sharp.'

Opening the ancient, creaking gate to the vicarage, Anna began to hobble along the path to a side door.

'Do I have any choice?'

'No,' replied Anna without turning her head.

Reverend Grix looked up from tending his vegetable patch, which had until 1939 been his prized lawn. 'Ah, you must be the American officer who tried to kill my daughter last night?'

'I'm so sorry, sir, it was not my intention to cause your daughter any injury.' Eddie had a nervous look about him.

The reverend plunged his spade into the rich loam, which he'd spent almost three years cultivating, wiped a palm on his gardening apron and extended his hand. 'Don't worry, I haven't come across a man yet that can get the better of my daughter, so I wouldn't feel too guilty. Now, do come in and have some breakfast. Anna is getting ready, she told us you'd be calling.' The vicar lifted a finger to the side of his nose. 'A word of advice, don't let her bully you. I imagine you've noticed that she's somewhat assertive?'

Eddie offered an awkward smile, not quite sure how to respond.

'Good morning to you, do come in and sit yourself down at the table, breakfast will be ready in a couple of minutes.' The vicar's wife, Helen, offered her guest a broad smile which seemed to settle his nerves as he took his seat at the huge pine table.

'That's most kind of you, ma'am, but I've already—'

'You'll say you've had breakfast. The thing is, you haven't had one of *my* breakfasts, so let's have no more nonsense. Do take your jacket off, I can see you're sweating.'

Just then, Anna hobbled into the spacious kitchen. 'I doubt it's because it's warm in here. I suspect he's still nervous about almost killing me.' She limped to the table and took her seat opposite Eddie.

Her mother gave Anna a look of mild rebuke. 'Now, young lady, do stop playing games, or are you trying to scare this one off as well?'

Anna smiled at her mother and winked. Turning back to Eddie, she could see he didn't know what to make of the situation. 'Oh, don't be so stiff. I thought you Americans were supposed to be laid back and overfamiliar, so take your jacket off and stop with the little boy look. I've many ways of making you feel guilty for almost crippling me, so I suggest you enjoy Mum's cooking.'

As the family tucked into their egg, single slice of bacon and two sausages each, the lieutenant told the vicar and his wife a little of his background.

'So seeing as I'd heard so much about this place, you know, the broad rivers and all that, I thought I'd come and take a look.'

Anna was in like a shot. 'They are not broad rivers, in fact, they're universally known as the Norfolk Broads, although I do accept some are quite wide. All created centuries ago as peat diggings which, over time, filled with water.' She turned to her father. 'I've already asked him what he's doing here, but he won't tell me. I think he's a spy and we should hand him over to the police after we finish breakfast.'

The lieutenant froze. 'But—'

Her father grinned. 'Anna is doing what Anna does, Lieutenant Elsner. Don't take any notice of her, she's a very naughty girl.'

Anna smiled at her father before turning her attention back to the confused guest. 'Well, have you finished your breakfast? We need to get going.'

Eddie looked forlornly at what remained of his sausage and poached egg before turning to the knowing vicar and shrugging his shoulders.

Once they were outside, Eddie was helping Anna back into the Jeep when she pointed at an approaching figure. 'Look what the cat dragged in.'

'Are you OK?'

'He's an old boyfriend who doesn't know when to move on. If it weren't for his flat feet, he'd have been busy poisoning our boys with his naff cooking skills in a field kitchen somewhere .'

Walter Plowright flicked back his greasy hair, stretched himself to his full 5'6" and stopped less than three feet from Anna and Eddie. 'I see you've moved onto the Yanks now. What's the matter, Englishmen not good enough for you anymore?'

Anna gave him an icy stare. 'Get lost. How many times do I have to tell you I'm not interested?'

Walter took a step closer to Anna.

Eddie countered by moving between the two. He towered over her ex. 'Forgive me, sir, but I believe the lady asked you to leave?' The lieutenant's large chest touched the thwarted suitor's cheek, forcing Walter to tilt his head back at an awkward angle to see his would-be competitor. 'If I'm a Yank, that makes you a Limey. Now, are we to stand here trading insults, or are you going to act the gentleman I know you can be by leaving this lady alone?'

Anna noticed Walter beginning to make a fist and said, 'I wouldn't do that if I were you.'

Eddie nodded. 'I think you should take the lady's advice.'

Walter took the hint, relaxed his hand and withdrew, all the time giving Anna an angry look.

She turned her attention to the lieutenant and accepted his arm as she struggled into the vehicle.

He makes quite a knight in shining armour.

'So what do you think you'll discover by going back to where your postman was found?'

Anna hung on as Eddie launched the Jeep into Norfolk's meandering lanes as if he were on a racetrack. 'Well, if we ever get there alive, I want to check that I didn't miss anything last night; you know, before you ran over me.'

Eddie crunched his way through the Jeep's gears. 'How many times are you going to repeat that I nearly killed you? If you think it'll make me feel any more guilty than I already do, you're mistaken.'

Anna lifted her head contentedly to allow the breeze being forced over the aluminium framed windscreen to catch her hair. 'Good, and I should think so too. As for Ted Fleming, his wife is convinced it wasn't an accident and I promised to look into it. Nothing more complicated than that really.'

Eddie shrugged his shoulders as the sound of metal grating on metal signalled he was changing gear again. 'Can you at least show me a bit of the countryside as we drive, since you talk about it so much?'

She smiled as she pointed to a turn fifty yards ahead. 'Your wish is my command.' Instead of the journey back to the accident site taking ten minutes, the detour delayed arrival for a further twenty. Anna pointed left and right as she waxed lyrical about the delights of the Norfolk flatlands. 'See over there? That's Flaxen's grain mill, while in the distance you can see a windpump. See the difference?' She could see Eddie straining to look from one ancient landmark to the other. 'The grain windmill is much broader and taller, whereas windpumps are often smaller because of the job they do in draining the fields.'

She turned to see Eddie shaking his head and realised he couldn't see any difference at all, and thought it better to change the subject. 'I suppose you must have noticed the young women in the fields?'

Eddie struggled to keep control of the Jeep as he stretched to see where his companion was pointing to.

'Steady on, one accident in twenty-four hours is quite enough for me. They all belong to the Women's Land Army. Now that so many men are away fighting, there aren't enough left to plant and gather the crops. We all have to help by growing vegetables and keeping a pig or some chickens, but that's still not enough, so these women signed up to work the fields. So, don't tell me that women aren't up to the type of work men normally do. My mother tells me they did it in the Great War, and here we are again.'

Eddie pulled over onto a patch of grass to allow an ancient tractor coming the other way to pass. 'You don't see this at home; I guess we don't know how difficult it is for you all.'

So this man has a softer side to him.

Presently, they arrived at the spot with which Anna had become intimate. As Eddie pulled over to the right, allowing the passenger-side wheels to climb a steep bank, Anna gave him a sharp look.

'And how am I supposed to get out of this thing?'

Eddie scrambled into the back of the Jeep but still managed to clip the back of Anna's head as he clambered out of the vehicle.

'That's the second time in two days, Lieutenant Elsner.'

Eddie offered an awkward smile as he helped his companion onto the tarmac. 'I'm trying to make room on the track… er, lane, so that anything else that comes along can get past us.'

Anna flicked her right wrist to catch sight of her watch. 'Well, it's eleven o'clock, and the weekly bus to Norwich isn't due for another hour. That's if it arrives at all, since the bus company is having terrible trouble with spivs stealing petrol from their depot.'

'I thought you Brits adopted a bulldog spirit and all pulled together?'

'And I thought all you Americans lived in log cabins and ate stewed beans every day. So, you see, you can't always believe what you see at the pictures.' She watched as Eddie's face gave away his confusion.

'Pictures? You mean the movies?'

'No, I mean the pictures. You Americans can call them what you like, but if you want to be understood around here, you'll have to learn to speak properly.'

Anna didn't wait for his reply. Instead, she directed the lieutenant to scour the road to see if he could find anything she might have missed. She then moved to the ditch, where the dark stain she'd seen the previous evening was still visible.

'Did you say the postman got caught in some barbed wire?'

She turned to see Eddie gingerly holding a short strip of rusting metal with sharp spikes spaced every few inches.

'That's what they said. I assumed the police had taken it all away to use as evidence. Is there any blood on it?'

Eddie looked closely at the twisted metal and shook his head. 'Clean as a whistle, that's if a rusty bit of old metal can be clean, if you get my drift.'

Anna gave Eddie a resigned look. 'Is that what passes for American humour?'

The lieutenant smiled and threw the piece of metal into a thick line of hedges which bounded the ditch.

Her attention was drawn back to the mark on the tree she'd noticed the previous evening. In full daylight, she struggled to make the connection between the damaged bark and barbed wire. 'What do you think?'

Eddie scrambled up the bank and traced a finger along the mark which had bitten into the bark. 'Nope, barbed wire didn't cause this. Your postman may have fallen into a tangle of barbed wire, but it was never attached to this tree.'

Anna looked closely at the precise cut.

Then what did cause it?

Eddie's attention shifted to a telegraph pole on the opposite

23

side of the road. However, as he attempted to scramble out of the ditch, the loose bank caused him to slip back. It was then that Anna noticed an envelope brought to the surface by Eddie disturbing the ditch bottom.

'What's that?' She retrieved the envelope, which was sealed. Addressed to a man of the same surname as Ted, in Norwich, it carried a stamp, ready for posting. 'How did a stamped addressed envelope to a relative, perhaps his brother, end up in the exact spot that a postman was found dead before he'd picked up his morning post?'

Eddie held a corner of the envelope. 'I think you've answered your own question.'

She looked at Eddie, then back to the envelope. 'It must have belonged to Ted. Perhaps he was going to post it when he reached the sorting office.'

'As I said, I suggest you've answered your own question. I guess we should hand this over to the authorities, right?'

Anna knew it was the right thing to do and pondered whether reading its contents might push her investigation on. She thought better of the notion. 'You're right, I'll pop it in to the police station when we get back.'

Eddie turned his attention back to the telegraph pole. Crossing the narrow lane, he found what he'd expected.

'What is it?' Anna shouted. She could see Eddie reaching out to touch the tar impregnated wooden pole.

'Come over here and tell me what you think.'

It took Anna a matter of seconds to join him. She could see a crisp, narrow cut, stretching around the telegraph pole. Instinctively, she looked across to the tree to see if the two had any relation to each other.

'See, it's roughly the same distance from ground level as the mark in the tree over there. Your postman didn't have the bad luck to fall off his bike and cut his neck open on a tangle of barbed wire. He was thrown backwards off his bike and virtually garrotted. Someone stretched a steel wire across this lane. They knew exactly what would happen to anyone riding into it.'

Chapter 3: What's it to be?

Anna's ankle continued to cause considerable pain as she hobbled along the village high street the next day, towards the thrift shop her mother had established in 1940. It was something Anna was proud of, not least because it allowed her to contribute directly to the war effort.

'Good morning, Mr Blackburn, was it quiet last night?'

Her cheery greeting to the ARP warden appeared to give the tired-looking villager a lift. 'If you says so, Miss Grix. Does you know, if I shouted "Put yer ruddy lights out" once last night, I did it two dozen times. It gets my goat they hears enemy bombers overhead most nights, yet they can't be bothered to fix their blackout curtains proper like.'

Anna sympathised with a pronounced nod and supportive look. 'Well, Mr Blackburn, heaven forbid one of these nights a squadron of those infernal bombers sees lights twinkling below and we all pay for it. So, I'm with you. In fact, I say we should name and shame the offenders.'

Blackburn smiled as if Anna's words were music to his ears. 'That's a good idea, is that. I'll suggest we makes a list at the next warden's meeting. Now, if you don't mind, I haves my bed waiting for me.'

I think my idea might come back to bite me.

Limping a further ten yards along High Street brought Anna to the door of the thrift shop. She took two steps back to view the window display.

Same old stock.

As she stepped forward to open the shop door, the sound of a small bell rang, much the same as it had done to alert shopkeepers down the centuries to customers entering the premises.

'There you are, Anna. I thought you'd got lost. Come along, now, we have lots to do.'

She knew there was little point in protesting. 'Sorry, Mum, I got talking to Mr Blackburn. He was not a happy chappy.'

Anna's mother raised an eyebrow. 'Joe Blackburn has been the same since I was at school with him. He's not known for looking on the bright side of life.

'I swear he puts his tin hat on and checks his whistle in the belief that this'll be the night he saves the village by leading us to safety like the Pied Piper as the bombs rain down.'

Two women at the entrance to a storeroom giggled.

'Morning, Alice. Morning, Flo.'

'Morning,' replied the volunteers.

Anna looked around the shelves of the old leather shop and sighed. 'Some of this stuff has been hanging around an awfully long time, Mum.'

Helen mirrored her daughter's glance around the establishment. 'It's a worry, I'll give you that. I suppose with things getting tighter, people want to hang on to everything. All we've had over the last few days is that lot.' Helen pointed to a heap of assorted clothes resting on an oak countertop.

Anna crossed the shop in five strides and began sifting through the pile of mixed materials.

'Shall we play "Guess the doner"?' said Alice in a cheery tone.

'That's very naughty of you, Alice, but I suppose it's quiet this morning. OK, you sort whatever it is you want us to guess at.' Helen's voice contained an element of mischief.

'Right, everyone, stand in a row with your back to the counter.' The shop team complied with Alice's command instantly, causing a surprising amount of hubbub for three people.

'This item is a dark green ladies' cardigan with large pearled buttons. The left cuff looks bigger than the right, caused, I think, by the owner always having a handkerchief tucked inside. Whose is it?'

The three women giggled as they suggested who the item might have originally belonged to.

'Ethel Brown donated that. Green is her favourite colour, and she's had a blocked nose for as long as I can remember,' said Flo.

Alice looked at the tag in the collar of the garment and read out the initials. 'E.B. Spot on, Flo.'

A brief round of applause followed to acknowledge the successful guess. This set the scene for the next twenty minutes, as each garment was described and its owner more often than not identified.

'Now, Anna, tell us all about the tall, handsome American you're seeing.' Flo's penetrating question threw Anna off guard.

'I'm not "seeing" anyone. If you mean the gentleman who is chauffeuring me around because he crashed into my bike while I happened to still be on it, then yes, he seems a perfectly pleasant sort.'

Anna hoped her response might shut the conversation down. The furtive laughter bouncing between the two volunteers told her otherwise. She was saved further interrogation, courtesy of the doorbell announcing someone's entry.

'Thank you so much.' Anna smiled as she took a roll of glossy paper from the uniformed dispatch rider. 'These are great, Mum.' Helen, Flo and Alice huddled over the countertop as Anna laid out a series of new posters issued by the War Office.

'We need to put these in the windows as soon as we can. They'll do a great job in encouraging villagers to contribute to our Spitfire Fighter Fund.' Helen pointed to the positions that she required the posters to be placed.

'Look at this, they've issued a price list covering everything from a complete Spitfire for £5,000 down to rivets at sixpence each. Why don't we get the children involved by suggesting they can buy their own rivet? They'll love it.'

Her mother took another look at the posters showing a Spitfire racing through a clear blue sky as it chased down its adversary. 'Do you know, Anna. That's not a bad idea. We'll have to make sure that the families with several children, who are struggling at the moment, don't feel pressured into giving money they don't have. I'll have a word with your father and see what we can do.'

Closing the shop door behind her, Anna began the painful journey home as she limped to offset the pain in her aching ankle which had not been helped by being on her feet all morning.

'Now, Miss Grix, what have you been up to?'

The firm voice brought Anna to a halt. Looking over her shoulder, she saw Police Constable Tom Bradshaw.

'Oh, it's you. I nearly jumped out of my skin. As for this, let's say I've been doing my bit for Anglo American relations.'

Tom wagged a finger at his long-time friend. 'It serves you right for riding a bicycle in the dark and getting in the way of an American, who, I assume, is more comfortable driving along wide highways on the wrong side of the road.'

Anna could feel her cheeks flushing. 'Never mind the American, there's something I wanted to ask you.'

Tom's eyes lit up. 'If you mean have I got anyone to go with to the barn dance, the answer is no. Are you up for it?'

Oops, how do I get out of this one?

'Thanks for offering, Tom, but I doubt I'll be going, what with this stupid ankle and everything.' She could see how disappointed he was but thought it the gentlest way to let him down. 'But I tell you what I'd like you to do, I—'

'Anything at all, Anna. What is it?'

I'd better get this right.

'The thing is, Tom, Peggy is falling to bits trying to understand what happened to her husband. She's in no fit state to suggest it, so I need your help. I'm not asking you to betray any confidences, mind, but you're the only one I can trust.' Anna noted a hint of cynicism in Tom's expression. 'No, honestly, we've known each other since we were children. If I walk into your police station and start barking questions at the inspector, you know what will happen. What do you think?'

Tom's tenseness eased. 'I told you the other day, Anna. You probably know as much about Ted's death as I do, so what is it you want?'

Seizing her opportunity, Anna pressed on. 'All I want to know is whether anything else was found near Tom's body. You know, metal that could have been used to bash him with, or bits of thin wire, anything?'

Tom frowned. 'That's a strange question to ask. Are you thinking of becoming a detective? Anyway, the answer to your question is no.'

'Anna, do come in.'

She could see Peggy Fleming had been crying and knew she'd need to be mindful of the woman's fragile state. 'Good to see you again, Peggy. I thought I'd pop back to give you an update.'

Anna was relieved Peggy appeared to rally, even though the prospect of telling the truth meant Peggy would have to deal with her husband being murdered. 'I've just had a chat with Constable Bradshaw, who tells me the police are ready to close their investigation. I assume that also means they'll release Ted's body to you. Have you any thoughts about the funeral?'

Peggy shook her head as she glanced at the photograph of her husband on the mantelpiece. 'I doubt it will be for some weeks yet. I spoke to your father. He's ready to conduct the service whenever I'm ready. Unfortunately, the undertakers tell me there's a shortage of material to line the coffin with. Something about parachutes. I've told them my Ted wouldn't care if they wrapped him in sacking. Anyway, until they can get a new supply of the good stuff, I'm stuck in limbo.'

Anna attempted to keep the conversation flowing, knowing silence might result in Peggy being overwhelmed by grief again. 'Have you any family nearby who might help?'

Peggy shook her head again. 'What relatives we have, and there aren't many, are scattered across the east of England. What with petrol rationing and all, it's hard for anyone to get over. I doubt they'll be able to make it for the funeral, never mind come and keep me company.'

What a cruel world we live in.

'What about the neighbours?' The widow smiled. Anna knew it wasn't born of levity.

'You know what small villages are like, and it's worse when your husband is the postman. For some ridiculous reason, everyone thinks they're entitled to know what's being delivered to their neighbour. Ted would never tell them, you know, but I knew when somebody had had a run-in with him because they took it out on me. Nothing was said of course. Over the years, I got used to it.'

Anna reached out to place a comforting hand on Peggy's shoulder. 'I wish I could help, Peggy. I suppose I'm lucky, I have my parents.'

The pair exchanged sad glances. 'You know, Anna. When we first married, we took the decision not to have children. Some folks might say that was a mistake, given what's happened to my Ted, but I'm still glad, because if we'd had a boy, he'd be away fighting now, or worse.'

Peggy's blistering honesty made Anna think about her own family. What if her mother and father had had sons? She knew it didn't bear thinking about.

'Anyway, listen to me, I'm a right misery guts. Now, you said you wanted to tell me something. Apart from talking to the young bobby, what else have you been doing?'

What a brave woman.

Anna took her time to correctly phrase her next few words. 'You said when we last spoke, you want me to tell you the truth.' She watched as the widow responded with a pensive glance. 'I don't think Ted's death was an accident. It would be wrong of me to go into too much detail now because I don't have all the facts yet, and the last thing I want to do is make guesses you might take as facts. But I'll say this: it's my belief somebody arranged your husband's death. You mentioned skeletons in cupboards, Peggy. Now is the time to open that cupboard door for me. Can you do that?'

I hope I've done the right thing.

Peggy leaned back into her beech-framed chair and concentrated her attention on the cottage's stone floor, worn smooth by centuries of use. 'Usually, my Ted didn't drink, in fact, it didn't seem to bother him if he went months without a pint. But sometimes something got into him. He was a sapper in the last war, you know, digging tunnels and that, but he never said a word about what he went through. I always thought it caught up with him from time to time.

'Anyway, if he got into a mood, some were happy to ply him with alcohol. Then the cards would come out. They knew he was an easy touch when he was drunk. Once or twice over the last couple of years, he ended up in trouble with some bad people because he couldn't pay his gambling debts. It took us quite a time to get straight again. I warned him if he gambled one more time, that was it.'

Anna worked hard to make sure her facial expression didn't betray her utter surprise. 'But it did happen again, didn't it?'

Peggy rose from her chair and made for a photograph showing them both smiling.

33

'A few weeks ago, he got drunk again. Then, the other day, I saw him having words with a man in the street. They didn't seem to be arguing, but I could see my Ted was frightened of him. When the man left, he didn't even lift his hat, which I thought a little rude. When I asked Ted about it, he brushed me off. I'd been married to him for long enough to know when not to push.'

Anna purposely allowed a short silence to develop before asking what was, to her, the obvious question. 'Can you describe the man, Peggy?'

At first, the widow shook her head. 'Not really, I was more concerned with keeping an eye on Ted.' A second or two later, she appeared to have second thoughts. 'One thing, though. I remember thinking he was too posh to be from around here. After all, who wears black patent leather shoes to walk over cobbled streets?'

Tuesday lunch was always somewhat different at the vicarage because it was Anna's turn to cook, while her mother continued her work in the thrift shop.

'I heard about your run-in with Walter Plowright yesterday. How are you feeling, my darling?'

Anna smiled as she carefully placed a large bowl of mixed vegetables on the kitchen table. 'It was quite funny, really. You should have seen how Eddie towered over the little squirt. It didn't take him long to see Walter off.'

Her father raised an eyebrow. 'So, it's Eddie now, is it?'

Anna shrugged her shoulders and gave her father a well-practised little-girl-lost look. 'I have to call him something.'

The vicar laughed. 'How about Lieutenant?'

She ladled a portion of steaming carrots onto her father's plate and offered him a piece of freshly baked bread, which he declined. 'Don't be so old fashioned, Dad. The war is changing everything, so who cares about that formal stuff anymore?'

About to take a mouthful of lunch, her father hesitated, his fork halfway between plate and mouth. 'Stuff? What is "stuff"? I heard the same sentiments after the last war, which led to the Roaring Twenties for the few and unemployment for most, so yes, things change, yet somehow they always remain the same.'

Anna looked at her father, then his plate. 'Spuds OK?'

Her father offered a friendly smile again. 'My darling, if you mean the boiled potatoes, then yes, they're remarkably good.'

She frowned. 'Don't say it in such a surprised tone just because I cooked them instead of Mum.'

The vicar held his hands up in mock surrender. 'Do I still get my bread pudding?'

Ten minutes passed as the pair ate their meal in comfortable silence. The back door creaking open and the head of a tall man peering around its weather-beaten edge put an end to that.

'I've been waiting for you, you're late. In fact, you've only just made it in time for the bread pudding.'

Eddie crossed to the pine dining table and looked at the vicar. 'Bread pudding?'

'A British delicacy, you might say, Lieutenant Elsner, but delicious for all that. Now, sit down and tuck in. I ask that you suspend your natural instincts and simply enjoy both its texture and taste. By the way, you might like to know my wonderful daughter made it.' The vicar winked.

'In that case, I'm not brave enough to refuse your kind hospitality.'

Anna presided over proceedings with the look of a matron hunting down misbehaving patients plotting their escape. 'Eat it or leave it. I don't care. Your loss will be the Pig Club's gain.'

Having taken possession of his pudding, the vicar got up and turned towards the hallway. 'Well, I have Evensong to prepare for, so I shall leave you to do whatever it is young people do over a bread pudding these days. As you would say, Anna, doing stuff seems to be all the rage.' The vicar smiled, clinked a spoon on the edge of his pudding dish and made off towards his office.

'What was all that about?'

'You don't want to know, believe me. Anyway, how is your pudding?'

Eddie took a second large helping, spent some seconds chewing it, then gave Anna a severe look. 'Do you want the truth?'

Anna frowned but tried not to look too defensive.

'As a matter of fact, it's excellent. Strange, but tasty. You'll have to give me the recipe so I can send it to my Gran. She'll think I'm trying to poison her, but that's another story.'

Ten minutes passed as they exchanged light-hearted banter before Eddie changed direction.

'So, Anna, have you had any further thoughts about the case?'

I knew this was coming.

For the second time in three hours, she had to pick her words carefully. 'I saw Peggy again this morning, and we got into some pretty heavy stuff about her husband. To be honest, I don't know whether we're getting into something we won't be able to control. Worst of all, we might end up making Peggy feel even more wretched than she does now. There, I've said it.'

Eddie finished his bread pudding and pushed the dish forward a few inches. 'Are you saying we hand it back to the police?'

Anna tapped the table with the tips of her fingers. 'That's the problem. You see, I also spoke to Tom Bradshaw. He reckons the police will shortly close the case on the basis the coroner will rule it an accidental death, so unless new evidence comes to light, that's it.'

She shrugged her shoulders.

'You do that a lot.'

Anna rounded on her companion. 'I'm not a shop mannequin to be stared at.'

Lieutenant Elsner showed no reaction. 'Don't turn it into a fight. It's time for you to make a decision. You can tell Peggy you can't take your investigation any further, and you tell your constable friend everything we've discovered. Or, we can do what you promised the woman. Now, which is it to be? Because I need to know. I have a few days leave due, and I can either help you or spend my time in Norwich burning what candles I have left at both ends. What's it to be?'

Chapter 4: Out of the Sky

'Thanks for bringing me out here, I wanted to—'

'Apologise?'

'I was about to say, explain why I flew off the handle, but I guess saying sorry is in order, too.'

Eddie turned to his passenger and smiled. 'Apology accepted. As for the rest, that can wait until we've had the afternoon tea you Brits bang on about so much. Now, where did you say we're going?'

Don't think I'm off the hook yet, but that went better than I deserved.

'Sheringham. In old English it means "Place of the Sherr people", so be careful, you're in one of our tribal heartlands.'

Eddie crunched metal against metal as he changed gear, still not used to the army Jeep he had been lent. 'I'll keep that in mind, but I meant the place you're taking me to.'

Anna glanced at Eddie, raising an eyebrow. 'I see you're getting to grips with our sense of humour. Anyway, it's called The Teahouse.'

Eddie shrugged his shoulders. 'I'm disappointed, I thought it would be called something like Ye Olde Coffee Shopee.'

'So predictable, Lieutenant Elsner, so predictable.'

The café was a black and white timbered mediaeval building, complete with a thatched roof. Anna couldn't help feeling it would be easy to forget the chaos of war here.

'Welcome, madam, sir. Do come in, I have a table for you by the window. It has a lovely view across the fields and down to the sea.'

Anna glanced around the deserted establishment but thought better of commenting on the availability of space. After placing an order for two cream teas, she felt it was time to put Eddie under the spotlight.

'Tell me about southwest Colorado. What do you do for a living over there?'

Eddie fidgeted with the table salt and kept his eyes firmly on the crisp white linen tablecloth. 'There's not a lot to tell, really. We live on my grandpa's cattle ranch and do what farmers do. Farming is farming wherever you are in the world, isn't it?'

Anna studied her table companion; she detected a sadness in his voice. 'Missing them?'

Mention of his family caused Eddie to move his attention from the table salt to the precisely laid cutlery of his place setting. 'At least they're safe over there. If anything, I feel guilty.'

Anna replied with a single word, 'Why?' before letting the conversation lapse for a few seconds. 'I'm sorry, I didn't mean it to come out like that, but what have you got to feel guilty about?'

Before he could answer, a young waitress set two nickel-plated cake stands on their small square table. She poured tea into two delicate china cups before withdrawing into the kitchen.

'Two things: my father, and what's happening around the

world right now.' He turned his attention to one of the stands and lifted two delicate square-cut cucumber sandwiches onto his plate.

Anna went for the salmon paste before continuing to press him. '…And your country not being involved?'

Eddie nodded. 'Some of our politicians say we did enough last time and we should leave you all to it. Most of us know it's rubbish and believe the war will come to us sooner or later.'

'And your father?' Anna watched Eddie tense. 'I'm sorry if you don't want to talk about it, let's enjoy this wonderful treat, shall we.'

Eddie took a sip of tea, scrunched his nose and placed the bone china cup back into its elegant saucer. 'He was a pilot. Went over to France in 1917 and got himself killed on November 10th, 1918 during an observation flight over enemy trenches.'

His words hit Anna like a bolt of lightning. 'You mean he was killed one day before the Armistice came into effect, how awful.'

The lieutenant shook his head as he played with the sandwiches on his plate. 'There has to be a first and last soldier to cash in his chips in any conflict. As it happened, it was one of your guys who was first to go: John Henry Parr. My dad happened to be one of the last.'

A long silence followed. Anna thought about her father's experience, his friends who didn't make it, and the twenty or so names listed on the village war memorial. 'Is that why you're over here, for your father?' She could feel Eddie's eyes on her.

'I know it's a cliché, but I guess I want to do my bit. I want to make the father I didn't know proud of me, but more than that, we gotta put a stop to this once and for all. Twice in twenty years is too much. Does that sound crazy to you?'

Anna managed to stop her tears by distracting herself, fussing with the cotton napkin resting across her knees. 'I don't think it's crazy one bit. After all, what would become of us if we let them win?'

The solemn conversation was interrupted by the young waitress appearing once again to offer more tea. Eddie politely declined. Anna smiled and sat back, allowing the girl in the old-fashioned dress to refill her cup. The youngster vanished as quickly as she had appeared without saying another word.

'Anyway, let's stop depressing each other and talk about your murder investigation instead.'

Surprised by the sudden change in direction, Anna let out a short burst of laughter. 'Well, from war to murder in one short sentence. I'm impressed.'

Eddie lifted his delicate teacup. 'I propose a toast: To amateur sleuths everywhere.'

The lieutenant's table companion mirrored his actions. 'Amateur sleuths.'

For the first time since they'd met, Anna felt at ease with what she was doing – and her choice of companion. 'Have you done this sort of thing before?'

He laughed. 'If you mean investigate a murder, no. But I'm good at puzzles.'

'What, like crosswords?'

Eddie smiled as he grabbed a tiny sponge cake from the delicate stand. 'As a matter of fact, I am, but I didn't mean that. The hotshots in white coats say I process things differently to most people, which, they reckon, makes me good at making decisions to solve difficult problems. My mom would probably disagree with that.'

Anna finished her cake by licking the last of the cream from her fingers. 'Well, brains of America, tell me what we should do next.'

Eddie reached over for the teapot left by the waitress. 'I'm going to be brave and try another drink of this stuff. Do you want any?'

Anna frowned. 'Is that what passes for Colorado satire?'

He smiled and began topping up her cup. 'I'm sorry, I guess we don't know each other well enough yet for me to tease you. That aside, your question tells me you've decided to carry on with the investigation instead of involving the police. What changed your mind?'

He's sharp, I'll give him that.

'If I said a lovely cream tea and good company, would you believe me?'

'Flattery will get you everywhere, Miss Grix. OK, I guess we need to make a list of the people Ted Fleming hung around with and see if they can tell us anything. Then there's the question of his injury. Can you get us into the mortuary, undertakers, or wherever his body is being kept?'

His sudden switch from light-hearted comment to incredible focus once again took Anna by surprise. 'What, view the body?'

Eddie looked her square in the eye. 'How else are we going to find out if the barbed wire or a steel rope killed your postie?'

The companions took in the incredible vista of field after golden field shimmering in the light breeze as each ear of wheat ebbed and flowed in perfect harmony with its neighbour. In the far distance, a blue ribbon sat between land and horizon as the

42

calmness of the North Sea belayed the sinister war machines plying their trade under its benign surface.

'Isn't it beautiful?'

'I have to admit, even though we have huge farms set against a backdrop of mountains, your countryside is quite breathtaking. Small, but breathtaking.'

Anna gave Eddie a look of reproval but softened its edge with a smile. 'You Americans, you're all the same.'

The lieutenant responded with a quizzical look. 'So, you admit it, I'm not the first American you've blackmailed.'

'That's for me to know and you to guess, Lieutenant Elsner.' She lifted a finger to the side of her nose in a conspiratorial fashion. The light-hearted exchange was interrupted by Eddie looking upwards.

'You've noticed what's so special about Norfolk; we call it the big sky.' She watched as Eddie shook his head.

'Can you hear that?'

Anna strained but couldn't detect anything.

'There, there it is and it's in trouble.' Eddie pointed into the distance.

Again, Anna strained to see and hear what her companion sounded so worried about. Then she heard it too. 'Is it one of ours, do you think?'

As the black dot came closer, it became easier to make out the fiery trail that followed the stricken plane.

'It's a fighter; he's not going to make it. Better watch out, Anna, it's heading straight for us.'

As the doomed aircraft continued to lose height, the repeated sound of its engine cutting in and stopping became more urgent. The fighter screamed low overhead and ploughed into a wheat field behind the teahouse. Stunned by the sudden violence of an otherwise peaceful afternoon, both stood motionless for a few seconds.

'We need to get him out, it's already on fire.' Eddie had started to sprint towards the plane wreck before finishing his sentence. Anna automatically followed. She wanted to help but somehow wished the horror would go away.

'We haven't got much time; once the petrol tank goes up, that's the end of it. Wait here.'

Anna did as she was instructed and watched as Eddie ran towards danger.

'Do you think he got out?' she shouted.

'Afraid not, his canopy is still intact.'

Seconds later, a massive explosion knocked Eddie backwards. Anna screamed and held her arms out as if trying to pull her companion back to safety. The commotion resulted in several locals appearing as if from nowhere until they were stood in a small arc around Anna.

'It's one of theirs, good riddance to him,' said one of the men, followed by a cheer from the others.

Anna ignored the new arrivals and moved forward, knowing it wouldn't be long before the whole field would be ablaze. As she neared where Eddie had fallen, a head popped up above the crop, followed seconds later by the rest of Lieutenant Elsner as he scrambled to his feet.

He implored Anna to move back. 'Come away, there's nothing more to be done here. Let's hope the poor man was dead before he crashed. Being burned to death is every pilot's worst nightmare.'

Anna took Eddie by the arm and helped him to a safe distance from the inferno.

'At least if he's dead it means one of our lads is still alive.'

She tried not to react to the local's sentiment. Although a part of her sympathised with the villager's logic, she couldn't help feeling sympathy for the young man. As they continued to put as much distance between them and the aircraft as possible, Anna turned to Eddie. 'Are you glad he's dead, too?'

Her companion remained silent for a few seconds. 'I know he'll have a mother, maybe a sweetheart or wife and, heaven forbid, children. Do you think he wanted to fight any more than we do?'

Anna stopped walking, forcing Eddie to look at her. 'Didn't you say you wanted to get your own back for your father's death?'

'Yes, I did. But it doesn't mean I wish for anyone's death. I just want to do my duty, like Dad did.'

The journey back to Lipton St Faith was a quiet affair. Anna felt deeply about what she had just witnessed.

'My father never mentions what he did in the first lot, you know. Do you think servicemen and women ever get over what they saw?'

Eddie took a few seconds to respond. 'Not only saw, Anna, but *did* in the service of their country. None of us want to admit what we're capable of when pushed to the limit. The military trains us to kill, then peace breaks out and we're all supposed to go back to our old jobs, you know; one month you're in a trench or blowing up a tank, the next you're filling some guy's car in the gas station you work at. How does that work? How does anyone get their head around that? I guess some guys never do and end up hurting themselves or those closest to them. Perhaps it's easier not to talk about it.'

Anna felt no need to respond. He seemed to feel the same way as she did.

She recognised a familiar landmark and realised they were about to travel through Three-Mile-Bottom, the place where Eddie mentioned he was staying.

'Since we're going through your village, why don't you introduce me to your hosts?'

She could tell the lieutenant was reluctant to stop. A reassuring smile did the trick as Eddie slowed the Jeep and pulled up outside a picture-perfect cottage complete with climbing roses clambering over the front porch.

'I still don't like using the key to let myself in, it feels sort of rude.' Eddie thumped twice on the front door.

'Any harder and you'll have it off its hinges.'

'That wasn't hard, but this is.' He thwacked the pine-panelled construction with such force that the borrowed light above the door rattled.

'Well, if that doesn't do the trick, they're either out or dead.' Anna took a step back to see if there was any movement upstairs. In that instant, the door began to open. Hilda Crossman's welcoming smile came into view.

'Ah, so it is you, Anna. I wasn't sure, but from the way this one described you, I guessed who he meant. He's very taken with you, mark my words.'

Anna turned to see Eddie blushing while doing his best not to look at her.

'Come you both in. I'll put the kettle on while Mr Crossman says his hellos.' The ever-smiling Hilda disappeared into the kitchen before re-emerging with a tin tray of tea and four pieces of cake. She also sported a clean apron in honour of her new guest.

'I do hope you're not using up your egg ration by letting us eat your wonderful cake, Mrs Crossman.'

'Please, call me Hilda, everybody does. It's not often we entertain a vicar's daughter. Anyway, we keep a few chickens, and Albert's brother owns Broadside Mill, so we get a bit of extra flour from time to time to top up our rations. Tuck in, there's plenty to go around.'

Anna took particular notice of Eddie as he lifted his cup. He had clearly learned the knack of appearing to take a sip without imbibing the merest hint of liquid. 'Well, thank you anyway, the cake is bliss, isn't it, Lieutenant?' Anna's question took Eddie by surprise as he concentrated on not drinking his tea.

'Lieutenant Elsner, never mind my cake, I told you before, you don't have to drink the tea, so don't think you're polite by faking it. There is only so much of the stuff my aspidistra can cope with.' Hilda pointed to a large-leafed plant to the left of Eddie's chair.

'But Hilda, it's—'

'Never mind "it's". Remember, you promised to send me some real coffee when you get back to your unit. The coffee essence stuff we have tastes of how I imagine engine oil might taste.'

Turning to Anna, Hilda's eyes widened. 'Did you know your father buried Albert's mum? He always says it was the finest funeral he'd ever been to.'

Mr Crossman gave a solemn nod to indicate agreement with his wife's assessment. 'Went off without a hitch. Even the rain held off till we got Mother safely in her grave. I'm convinced the vicar asked a special favour of him upstairs so that we didn't all get soaked.'

Anna smiled, Eddie's confused look making the moment all the more amusing. 'Well, if anyone is going to get a favour, it'll be Dad.'

'Mind you, it'll be Ted Fleming he'll be burying next. Awful do, was that. They say it was a terrible accident and there was blood everywhere. And to cap it all, a ghostly figure was seen in the trees looking down on him, I bet you didn't know that?'

Hilda rebuked her husband. 'Now don't start that again; we're having a nice cup of tea, so don't go putting a damper on things like you usually do.'

Albert was having none of it. 'I'm only telling the truth.'

Hilda wagged a finger at her husband. 'You know what Betty's like down at the telephone exchange; she listens in to every call and then spreads gossip by adding a bit of tittle-tattle.'

'Hilda Crossman. All I know is Ted Fleming will never deliver another letter, there's a war on, and strange stuff is happening all over the place. The world has gone mad… again.'

Like most other front gardens, the Crossmans' had been turned into a vegetable patch. The pair wandered through neat rows of lettuce, carrots and heaped lines of potatoes, talking about nothing in particular while enjoying the stillness and warm afternoon sun.

Anna and Eddie trailed along behind them, listening to their comforting chatter, when Anna suddenly came to a stop and turned to the lieutenant. 'I've made my mind up, Eddie. No more toing and froing. We have to catch Ted Fleming's killer, so you'll have to put your few days in Norwich off for another time.'

Chapter 5: Pig in a Poke

'Besides getting up at the crack of dawn, my guess is that the light now is as near to replicating Ted Fleming's experience on his way to work that morning as we can get.'

Anna tried to put herself in Ted's mind. What would he have been thinking about? Perhaps how long his round might take, how often nosy villages would ask what was being delivered to their neighbours.

'I thought back home could be scary in the dark, but Norfolk beats southwest Colorado anytime. I don't mean it as a criticism, but everything seems so—'

'You're not going to say everything is so small again, are you?'

'I was about to say *intimate*. You know, these narrow roads or tracks or whatever you call them. The high hedges and drainage ditches right next to the road. It's a recipe for disaster.'

The sound of owls calling out to mark their territory and pipistrelle bats scurrying about overhead added to the picture Eddie painted.

He has a point.

'Countryside or city, the surroundings don't seem to matter

when it comes to the blackout. So many people are being killed on the roads, you know; no streetlights, anything that moves having to use shielded lights… It doesn't take a genius to guess the result.'

Eddie nodded. 'You know, I'm beginning to appreciate what you guys are going through. We read the newspapers and listen to the radio. All we get is "the plucky Brits", but it doesn't go halfway to understanding what you guys have to deal with.'

Anna fixed her eyes on the American in the half-light and tried to put herself in his family's shoes, worrying as they must be about what Eddie had volunteered for.

The lieutenant walked along the narrow lane, turned and lined himself up with the tree and telegraph pole, between which he believed a wire had been stretched.

'Do you think he'd have seen anything?'

Her companion shook his head. 'Not a chance. Why should he? Ted made the same journey every day of his working life. As for the wire, in this light, in any light, he'd see nothing. With luck, Ted wouldn't have known what hit him. I want to believe as he was knocked backwards off his bike and rolled into the ditch, he was already unconscious.'

Anna froze. You know it means that—'

'That the killer hid somewhere nearby, watched his handiwork do its filthy business then calmly retrieved the wire? Yes, I guess that's how it happened.'

A stillness descended. Anna felt utter desolation as she pondered how anybody could be so cruel or hate someone enough to do that.

The quiet was shattered by the sound of an engine misfiring in the distance. Both looked up to the clear night sky.

'Not again?'

Eddie quickly regained his composure. 'Not a plane this time, Anna. It's a truck of some sort. Problem is I can't see which way it's coming.'

Without thinking, each looked in a different direction.

'It'll be on us in a few seconds.' Anna pointed to the same bend that Eddie had sped around a few nights earlier.

'Quick, get into the ditch. There's just time.'

Anna reacted instantly and launched herself into the deep, narrow depression, half a second ahead of her companion. Before she knew what had happened, Anna was enveloped in a stinking grey cloud of exhaust fumes. Fighting her instinct to climb out of the ditch, she lay flat into its floor to catch what fresh air remained. Within a few seconds, the thunderous noise of the vehicle began to diminish. The sulphurous cloud lingered much longer.

'I think that truck needs a new exhaust.'

Anna looked at her companion in admiration. 'You really are catching on to our British understatement, aren't you?' She tried to smile but caught another gulp of the noxious air and began to cough.

'I'll take that as a compliment, Miss Grix. Come on, let's get you out of here before you choke to death.'

Scrambling up the steep bank, both ended up on all fours in the middle of the lane. Anna, now able to catch her breath, sensed how ridiculous they both must look. She pondered what her father might think if he stumbled upon them in their current predicament.

'I thought you said nobody had petrol for driving around?'

Listening out to make sure nothing else was about to descend on them, Anna brushed herself down. 'I said the police were having trouble catching the spivs who have been stealing the stuff. That won't be a local lorry – that's a truck to you, by the way.'

'Thank you for interpreting. Anyway, I got the licence plate.'

'How did you manage that from the bottom of the ditch?'

'I caught it as he was disappearing. I told you, the hotshots said I was different, I don't know how it works, but it does.'

Anna tried to hide her scepticism. 'They'll be false plates anyway.'

Eddie nodded. 'You're probably right, but whatever it was using as fuel, it stank, so I guess they'd adulterated it. When times are hard back home, folks use all kinds of stuff to make gas go further.'

'Gas? You put gas in your cars?'

His laughter pierced their otherwise silent surroundings. 'It's short for gasoline. You need to learn to speak English, Miss Grix.'

They exchanged glances that spoke to an emerging friendship.

'Have you been to an English pub yet, Eddie?'

'Not had that pleasure.'

Anna's smile broadened. 'Time to put that right.'

Entering the narrow door of the King's Head, Anna's expectations were met in full as the hubbub of a dozen elderly local men ceased as soon as they saw the pair.

Eddie leaned into his companion. 'Is it because I'm an American?'

'No, it's because a local girl has walked in with a strange man. Don't worry, they'll go back to their dominoes and darts in a second or two.'

Her prediction held up as the men lost interest and fell back into their usual Wednesday night routine while sucking hard on pipes that frequently extinguished themselves.

'Now, what's the vicar's daughter doing in my pub with an American Army Air Force officer?' Betty, the owner of the village's only pub, barked her question, reinforced with the sternest of looks.

Anna sensed Eddie freeze as the substantial frame of their host leant into the bar, her arms folded and resting on the countertop.'

'Stop teasing, Betty. It's his first time in Norfolk, so go easy on him.'

Betty smiled before reverting to inquisitor again. 'He's not a German spy, is he? Because if he is, I'll have to charge him double.'

Eddie gave Anna a confused look before turning back to Betty. 'I assure you, ma'am, I—'

Betty stood bolt upright, placed a hand on each hip and roared with laughter.

'You'll get used to her,' said Anna as she wagged a finger at the landlady.

'You're welcome in my pub any time, son. No matter what some might say.'

Anna smiled to herself as she watched each of the old men break eye contact with the formidable Betty.

'Now, what'll it be? Mind, I've only got beer and half a bottle of rum I've had in the parlour for years.' Betty's welcoming smile melted the otherwise frosty atmosphere that had developed.

'Thank you for your, er, unusual welcome, ma'am. I'll try your British beer if I may – is it true that it's served warm?'

A chorus of coughs broke out as the locals tried not to attract Betty's ire.

The landlady let out a raucous laugh again. 'It's practically the summer, my lad. If you're still here in December, it'll be cold, and I can warm it up for you.' The woman winked at Anna as she poured a pint from a tall tin-glazed jug which rested on one end of the small bar top.

'Betty Simpson, you're a tease.'

'That's OK, Anna. If drinking warm beer is what you do here, that's all right with me.'

Another rumble of coughs ricocheted around the small space.

'Will you have one too?'

'You must be joking, Betty. My father would never get over it and spend every Sunday preaching about the evils of drink if I came home smelling of alcohol.'

Betty let out a third belly laugh. 'Then it's my homemade lemonade for you, young lady.'

'I hoped you'd have some made up.'

The landlady reached under the bar and whispered loud enough to be heard by everyone. 'This is the good stuff that I keep for special customers.' Betty then raised her voice. 'Not for the likes of these old fools.'

Several men muttered but lacked the courage to look at Betty.

The pair collected their drinks and made for a corner of the small room, taking particular care not to bump into any of the other tables as they completed the journey. Easing into a tall-backed settle, Anna pulled a small round table forward so that they could easily retrieve their drinks.

Peering through a blue haze of pipe tobacco, Anna noticed an old hand-painted sign above the enormous open fireplace in the centre of the wall opposite:

'No Spitting – Even in the Fire.
By Order of Betty.'

'You can see how civilised British pubs are,' said Anna as she drew Eddie's attention to the warning.

Her companion smiled as he read the instruction then reached out for his pewter tankard.

'Well, at least you know where you are, and I certainly wouldn't want to cross Betty.'

Anna smiled. 'Her bark is worse than her bite. She's run this place singlehanded since losing her husband in the last war. Betty is as tough as old boots with a heart of gold. What she doesn't know about what's going on around here isn't worth knowing.'

'Now that could come in handy,' said Eddie.

'My thoughts exactly,' replied Anna.

Minutes went by as they took in the scene and enjoyed their drinks. Anna became aware of an elderly gentleman on a nearby table looking at her companion.

'And will you leave it as late as the last time?'

Anna knew Eddie was aware of the old man's meaning. So was Betty.

'Clarence Woodman, if you don't shut your mouth, I'll shut it for you. Everyone knows if it wasn't for the Americans getting to France in 1917, we'd probably all be drinking Jägermeister by now instead of my wonderful beer.'

The old man bit on his pipe and scowled at Eddie rather than argue with Betty.

'You might want to know that his father—'

'It's OK, Anna. No need for that.' Eddie held out his right hand. 'A pleasure to meet you, sir. May I buy you some more beer?'

A voice from one of the other tables cut in. 'That's put you back into your box, Clay.' The old man continued to scowl at Eddie while holding out his tankard.

'You don't deserve it,' barked Betty, 'so mind your manners or I'll put you out – and your Pearl won't like you under her feet every night, will she?' Betty's threat caused the old man to bite down on his pipe again while mumbling something no one could catch.

Anna gave her friend a sideways glance. 'You OK? Sorry about that.'

He smiled. 'It's fine. I've had worse. Whether he likes it or not, if things go the wrong way in Europe, there will soon be a lot more of us over here, and it won't be to sample your warm beer.'

Anna gave him a long searching stare without needing further explanation. She watched as Eddie took another sip from his tankard.

'Get a proper mouthful down your gullet, boy. You're drinking that like a girl.'

Anna smiled at the local. 'Oi, be careful what you say, or it won't just be Betty you'll have to deal with.' She wagged a finger and watched the pub owner nodding while giving the man one of her looks. The short exchange resulted in a spontaneous bout of laughter from everybody in the pub except the grumpy man who'd let fly at Eddie.

After twenty minutes, the pair drank up and went to leave. Betty beckoned Anna with a curled finger. 'I've something I need you to take to your father for next Sunday. Nip into the back with me; it'll only take a second.'

Curious, Anna followed the landlady into a tiny living room situated directly behind the bar.

'Peggy tells me she's asked you to look into poor Ted's death.'

Anna wasn't quite sure how to respond. 'Yes, but—'

'I want you to be careful. Peggy doesn't know it, but Ted

rubbed one or two of the lads up the wrong way. He owed money all over the place. Liked the horses, did Ted.'

Peggy knew more than you think.

'Oh, I see. Thanks for that, Betty. As if Peggy hasn't got enough to worry about at the moment.'

The landlady leant towards Anna, lowering her voice. 'I mean what I say. I know you think I'm a tough lass, but there are people even I won't cross, so be careful which stones you turn over because you never know who you'll find underneath. That said, you might want to start with the grumpy one in there.'

Their conversation was interrupted by one of Betty's customers shouting to be served. 'I better get back before there's a riot. Here, take these.' She turned to her right, took hold of a bunch of flowers resting in a glass vase and wrapped newspaper around them.

'Flowers?'

Betty smiled. 'That lot heard me say I had something for your father. They'll be right suspicious if you appear without anything in your hands. The old fools will assume I've given you some blooms to decorate the church.'

Stepping back into the bar, the two women were surprised to see Eddie pouring a pint of beer for one of Betty's regulars from the tin jug.

Spotting a silver shilling resting on the bar top, Betty turned to the American. 'We'll make an Englishman out of you yet.' The landlady raised her voice to address all present. 'He's picked up more in half an hour than you dozy lot have in all the time you been boozing in my pub. No wonder your wives dump you here every night.'

* * *

Driving out of the village on a chilly Thursday morning, Eddie was keen to find out whether he had passed the pub test Anna had set him the previous evening. 'Well, how did I do?'

Anna repositioned her leg to take the weight off her still painful ankle as she tried to get comfortable on the hard seat of the military Jeep. 'You passed with flying colours. I thought the experience might put you off, but you rose to the occasion.'

She gave Eddie a sideways glance to see a broad smile spreading across his face.

'I suppose older people are set in their ways the world over. Change the accent and a British pub for an American bar, and I guess strangers will be treated the same. Now, remind me again why we're going to see the fella who got mad at me?'

Anna reminded him what Betty had said as Eddie navigated a narrow eighteenth-century stone bridge which spanned one of the Norfolk Broads. Nearing Woodman's pig farm, she could see Eddie taking in the lush landscape.

'We're what, about two miles outside Lipton St Faith, and we could be in the middle of nowhere. Combine that with you lot taking down the direction signs on all the road junctions, and invaders haven't a chance of finding their way across your fair county.'

She laughed. 'That's the idea. It also means we can tell who the outsiders are.'

The American shook his head. 'The only thing that makes any sense around here is that there is no point trying to make sense of anything.'

'You're learning.'

Five minutes later, the Jeep pulled into a cobblestoned farm-yard to see Pearl Woodman offering a welcoming wave. There was also the matter of a pig squealing at the top of its high-pitched voice.

'It's like back home; you hear and smell 'em before you see 'em.'

'Hello, you two. How're your parents, Anna? And this must be your fine American gentleman.'

Eddie lifted his cap. 'Just passing through, ma'am.'

'Well, the Crossmans speak very highly of you, so that's good enough for me.'

Anna gave her companion a knowing look. 'I told you news travels as fast as a marsh harrier going after a frog.'

'You're right there, girl. Now, what can I do you for?' said Pearl.

'It's great to see you, but is Clarence about? We need a word with him if that's OK.'

'More fool you because the man talks rubbish half the time. He'll be in when he hears the sound of the kettle whistling its head off. Is it anything I can help with?'

Anna thought hard before framing her response. 'The thing is, Pearl, Ted's wife has asked us to do a bit of digging to see if her husband was in trouble with anyone.'

'You mean the bookies?'

'So you know?'

'Not much passes me by. My old man will tell you more, but promise me this, you be careful what you get yourself tangled up in. There's some bad'uns around here.'

The protestations of the pig intensified. 'Something tells me that pig is about to have a terrible day. How many is Mr Woodman seeing to today, ma'am?'

Pearl came closer to the Jeep and placed a hand on the driver's door. 'I'm impressed. You're from farming stock yourself?'

'We keep a few animals.'

Pearl nodded in acknowledgement of a kindred farmer. 'The ministry is so strict with what we can and can't do. We have to keep a record of everything.'

Presently, the sound of the squealing pig stopped. All eyes turned to the piggery to see a young woman with a bloodied apron shielding her eyes as she walked into the brightening day.

'You managed all right then. Clarence was a big fella, that's for sure,' said Pearl.

Anna could see Eddie looked horrified and she started to laugh, quickly joined by the other two women.

'You daft lummox. Mabel here is one of our Land Army girls, and Clarence is, or *was*, a pig.'

Anna could hardly contain herself. 'It doesn't take much to catch him out.'

Eddie protested. 'I thought you said your husband saw to the pig?'

'No, *you* said Clarence was seeing to the pig. My Clarence, or Clay, as we all call him, is where you'll always find him at this time of the day: on his throne.'

Eddie gave one of his confused looks.

'Don't worry, Pearl, I'll translate for you. She means he's on the outside loo, or John, as I think you call it.'

The three women broke into the second round of giggles. The American settled for scratching his forehead.

'I'll get the kettle on for a cuppa and you watch my lump of a husband come running, or should I say, a-waddling.'

Sure enough, as the kettle whistle announced it had boiled, Clay wandered into the untidy living room of the farmhouse.

Pearl returned from the kitchen carrying four chipped mugs

of tea. 'Listen up, you, Anna and her young man have come to see you, special like, so get yourself sat down and behave. No swearing or belching or you'll be cooking your own tea. Mark my words, now.'

As Eddie settled himself into a leather armchair with bits of material hanging off, Anna realised Clay was biting down on his pipe again. She guessed her companion had seated himself in the man of the house's favourite chair.

'You sit there, Clay, and stop your fussing and mind what I said.'

The husband, having done as instructed while muttering beneath his breath, continuously lit his pipe with a Ronson lighter. Occasionally he scowled at Eddie while eyeing up his favourite chair.

Soon, Pearl was on her feet again. 'Well, Mabel, Clarence won't cut himself up, so let's get to it.'

The two women clasped their mugs and left. The resulting silence was deafening. Clay and his guests variously stared at wallpaper peeling from the damp walls down to the carpet that seemed to contain more holes than woven fabric.

Anna took control. 'Clay, we're here to ask for your help. Do you know if poor Ted was in trouble before he died? Word has it he was in hock to a bookie.' She noticed he tensed at the mention of a bookie.

Tapping his pipe into a glazed earthenware ashtray, he watched a pyramid of burned tobacco collect in the receptacle. Taking a small penknife from the breast pocket of his threadbare suit jacket, he scraped the inside of the pipe bowl, filled it with fresh tobacco and lit it. 'Who says that, then? People who poke their nose in places they shouldn't, sometimes get them bitten off.'

Unimpressed, Anna pressed on. 'Perhaps Pearl might know something. I won't be long, Eddie. Back in a minute.' She stood and began to make her way to the doorway.

'Sit you down, girl. For a vicar's daughter, you're a bit sharp, aren't you?'

'So, you're a betting man too, Clay? Look, all we want is a name. We want to find out why Ted was killed.'

Clay drained of colour. 'Killed? I thought it was an accident?'

Eddie joined the fray. 'That's what the police think, too, but we're not so sure. We know Ted was involved in illegal gambling and we need to know where he placed his bets. The alternative is that we share what we know with the police and let them have a chat with you.'

The old man raised his pipe. 'Now, don't be too hasty. No need for the police. I can't give you a name, you understand, but you never know what you might see if you call in at the Cock and Sparrow in Three-Mile-Bottom just after lunchtime opening. I've noticed how funny it is so many men need to use the lavatory as when they arrive. Remember, you didn't get that from me.'

Anna leant forward to touch the old man's knee. 'Your secret is safe with us, and from Pearl.'

Clay smiled for the first time. 'Pearl? She likes the odd sixpence each way now and again.' He winked.

As the pair went to leave, Clay looked at Eddie. 'Sorry about last night, son. It was the beer talking. I know full well what our two countries owe each other.' He pointed with his pipe. 'By the way, if you ever come back to this house, that's my chair.'

Eddie smiled and gave a smart two-fingered salute to his right temple. 'Got you, sir.'

Chapter 6: A Betting Man

Three-Mile-Bottom went about its business in the same quiet way it had done for hundreds of years. The only clues of war included women queueing outside the butchers clutching their ration books and the masking tape crisscrossing every pane of glass in the tiny hamlet.

'Does it feel strange to be wearing civilian clothes, Eddie?'

'I do feel uncomfortable out of uniform; the last thing I want anyone to think is that I'm a shirker, but you were right to suggest the idea.' He pointed to a crooked old wooden door that served as the entrance to the Cock and Sparrow pub.

'There goes that understatement thing again. Anyway, civilian clothes or not, prepare yourself to be gawked at again the second we step inside.'

To Anna's surprise, the two locals already in the pub took no notice of the new arrivals. The pair exchanged glances before Eddie stepped towards the bar.

'Good afternoon, sir. May I have a pint of your best and a lemonade for the lady?'

The barman's eyes widened as he let out a short burst of

laughter. 'You're that American what lodges with the Crossmans, aren't you? As for lemonade, we're not a seaside café, you know.'

Anna felt for her companion as he turned to give her one of his now-familiar confused looks.

'I'll have half a shandy,' she whispered.

Eddie turned his attention back to the barman and confidently announced Anna's choice without knowing what it meant.

'Right then, you want a pint of best bitter and a half-pint of bitter with lemonade. Is that right?'

Anna knew the unshaven bald barman was making fun of Eddie.

'I thought you said you didn't serve lemonade?'

His question increased the barman's amusement. 'I said we weren't a seaside café. You can't get alcohol in a café, now, can you?'

Anna had seen enough. 'Give us our drinks and don't be such a smart Alec. If he charges you more than one-and-seven, he's cheating you, Eddie.'

The American looked at the unkempt barman, waiting for a reaction. Instead, all the man did was hold his hand out, palm up. Eddie retrieved a two-shilling piece from his trouser pocket. 'So, what's the current exchange rate, about four US dollars to one of your British pounds? I think you can keep the change.'

Eddie turned to see Anna smiling at him.

'I'll bring your drinks over to you,' growled the barman as he snatched the coin from between Eddie's fingers without a word of thanks.

Settling themselves down onto a pair of three-legged stools, they watched as man after man entered the almost empty hostelry. Each headed for the men's lavatory, only to emerge within a minute and disappear from the pub without the barman having acknowledged their brief visit.

Shortly after, Clarence Woodman entered the establishment. As before, the disinterested barman ignored his visitor.

Anna whispered to Eddie, 'Don't look at Clarence. If that barman cottons on we know him, we'll all be in trouble.'

The American took Anna's advice and busied himself with attempting to decipher an engraving on his pewter tankard, which had arrived at their table along with Anna's shandy.

A further ten minutes passed as the procession of individuals in and out of the bar continued. Anna could see Eddie itching to make his move. 'If you're going, be careful. Don't take anything for granted and don't be too cocky. We hate that.'

Her companion downed the last of his pint while simultaneously giving Anna a curious look. 'And cocky means what, precisely?' He raised an eyebrow to reinforce his question.

'I could be sarcastic and say it means being an American, but let's not cause a diplomatic incident. Look nervous, they'll know it's your first time. Don't be a Jack-the-lad, and no, I won't explain that as well. Just behave yourself.'

Eddie shook his head, turned to see the barman leaning lazily on the bar top reading a newspaper. He took his opportunity and quietly made his way to the men's room. Anna noticed the barman turn his head the merest fraction as Eddie exited the bar.

Not as stupid as you look, are you?

As the seconds dragged on, Anna began to get anxious, knowing he'd been in there too long. Her fears proved unfounded as Eddie re-emerged, stone-faced.

'Well?' asked Anna after what seemed like an age.

Eddie looked into his empty tankard, moving it around in a small circular motion on the beer-stained surface of the wooden table. 'The ugliest man I have ever seen in my life stands on the other side of that door. You're hard enough to understand, but I think he's Scottish.

'He growled something about me being a stranger, or at least, I think that's what he said. It was only when I pulled a pound note out of my wallet and said that Clarence could vouch for me that he stopped jibber jabbering. He pointed one of his filthy fingers at another man standing next to a chalkboard and easel, you know, like the ones at school? Anyway, I picked a horse called Wing and a Prayer then handed over the money. The man gave me a ticket and handed my money to a bloke sitting at a small table recording the bets.'

Anna's smile disappeared. 'You shouldn't have mentioned Clarence. They'll already have been suspicious of you. All you've done is to implicate Clarence Woodman in what they think you're up to.'

'I'm sorry, I wasn't thinking. I guess a situation like this brings home I'm a stranger here. Sorry, do you think we should tell Clarence?'

'No, the last thing we need is the man worrying himself to death. Let's hope all they were interested in was your money, which, by the way, was around twenty times the size of bet they'd be used to around here. With luck, they'll assume you're a naïve foreigner with too much money to spend, which they'll have been only too happy to take from you.'

Standing outside the Cock and Sparrow, the two companions continued to discuss what had happened and what to do next.

'The thing is, Anna, I've got a few things I need to do, so let me drop you off at home, and I'll see you tonight at that bingo thing you told me about.'

'The top of High Street will do; I've a bit of shopping to do.

Anyway, I thought you said you were on leave. Don't forget you still owe me.'

Eddie smiled. 'As if you were going to let me do that.'

Anna's progress as she hobbled into the village was slow, courtesy of her ankle, which she considered was healing much slower than she'd expected. As she neared Butchers Row, a narrow passageway between the milliners and ironmongers, Anna was brought to an abrupt stop by a man jumping out in front of her. Without thinking, she struck out, sending the man sprawling onto his back.

'What did you do that for?' moaned Walter Plowright as he scrambled to sit up while rubbing an elbow, sore from his hard landing, and looking around to check if anyone had seen him fall.

'Is that gentleman bothering you, Miss Grix?'

Anna and her ex-boyfriend simultaneously looked to the opposite side of the road to see Sergeant Ilford looking back at them, open notebook and short pencil in hand.

'She attacked me,' shouted Walter, still rubbing his elbow.

'That's not the way it looked to me, sir. Would you like my assistance, miss?'

Anna looked down at Walter, then across to the constable. 'With him? Not at all.'

The policeman folded his notebook, slipped the stubby pencil into its spine and placed it into his breast pocket, taking particular care to button it closed. 'I thought not. I'll leave him to you, shall I?'

Anna grinned. 'Thanks, Dick.'

Sergeant Ilford touched the rim of his police helmet, gave a slight nod, then continued his beat up High Street after placing both hands behind his back in regulation fashion.

'I suppose you think that was funny?' mumbled Walter as he got to his feet.

Anna's smile had vanished to be replaced by a look of pure contempt. 'What did you expect? We're not children anymore. I've told you once, I've told you a dozen times, leave me alone because if there's a next time, I'll lay you out flat and it'll be more than your elbow you're rubbing. You'll be lucky if you're able to father any children after I've finished with you. Do you understand?'

Walter scowled at his ex-girlfriend. 'I'm warning you, Anna, I'll—'

'You'll what, Walter? Don't be so pathetic. Why don't you crawl back to wherever you came from before those ladies ask for an encore.'

Her ex looked around to see the church knitting circle sat on the village green, laughing as they kept a close eye on developments.

Walter adopted his familiar scowl and scurried into the narrow passageway. 'I know that Miss goody-two-shoes thing is just an act. We had a good thing going and then you got shot of me, just like that. How am I supposed to feel?'

Afternoon tea was something of a tradition at the vicarage, and today was no exception. The topic of conversation between the vicar, his wife and Anna varied depending on the news of the day, whether received via official channels or village gossip. Uppermost in their minds today was Peggy Fleming as she grieved for her husband.

'So much loss, both at the Front and at home. Who would've thought this could happen a second time in one generation. It makes me so sad. Does it ever test your faith, Dad?'

Anna glanced at her father, unsure how he might react to her pointed question. At first, he seemed tense but soon relaxed.

'You know, when I was a medical officer in the last war, I saw such terrible things. Nevertheless, I came out of it with a clear conviction that what I experienced was what man could do to man. We have the free choice to decide: do I steal, or not steal? Do I fight or try to talk the other side down?'

She could see how sad the conversation had made her father and realised why he rarely talked about his war service. 'But Dad, it's the politicians who are the ones who start and stop wars, not us ordinary people. What are we supposed to do?'

The vicar reached out to take her hand. 'Anna, my darling, all we can do is pray that politicians the world over make the right decisions. As Mr Churchill said in his recent radio broadcast to our American friends, "Give us the tools and we will finish the job".'

Anna's mother, who, until now, had sat quietly listening to her husband and daughter, offered her insight. 'I agree with Mr Churchill. As we've found to our cost twice in a little over twenty years, there comes a time when the talking must stop.'

'I thought you were a pacifist, Mum?'

Her mother nodded. 'I am, my darling, but I'm also a mother. When it becomes clear that another country is intent on hurting us, we must protect family and friends. Of course, there is also the important principle of maintaining our own way of life, instead of allowing an aggressor to impose their regime on us. That's what Mr Churchill is doing, so we shall play our part in raising a few shillings at tonight's event for the Spitfire we hope to buy for our boys.'

Anna took a deep breath before standing and placing a

daughter's gentle kiss on the cheeks of her mother and father. Leaving the kitchen for her bedroom, she turned to look at her parents. 'I love you both dearly and respect each of your views. I guess I'm with you, Mum, but would go further. Threaten me and mine, and I shall come for you; that's what I say to Mr Hitler.'

'I didn't realise so many folks lived around here.'

'All it takes is the chance to win something and people from miles around will turn up,' replied Anna, holding on to Eddie for support as they approached the small village hall.

'What, you mean folks have walked and cycled on your crazy roads for the chance to win a few pennies?'

Anna laughed as they passed through the open entrance doors and into the packed space. 'It might have been money before the war, but now it's just for a few extra eggs or a lamb joint, in fact, anything anybody donates.'

'It sure is a cosy place,' remarked Eddie is he slid through a crowd of people, all attempting to buy bingo tickets from a harassed-looking elderly lady wearing a green tweed jacket and matching beret. 'Seems to me like this place is held together with a few nails and a lot of prayers.'

Anna was having difficulty hearing her companion above the noise but caught his drift. 'It was paid for by public subscription. You've seen the war memorial on the edge of the green? Well, the villagers concluded they wanted to do more, so got together and paid for this. Its proper name is the Memorial Hall, for obvious reasons. I wonder what those for whom the hall was built in remembrance would say if they could see us now.'

Eddie leant into Anna to catch her words. 'I'm certain they're looking down and smiling.'

Anna turned to her companion with a warm smile. 'What a nice thing to say. Do you—'

'Are you feeling lucky tonight, Anna? Look, I've got loads of tickets.' Young Timothy Brownlow grinned happily as he spread his tickets out to look like a fan.

'And what will you do with your winnings; treat your young lady to a nice bit of lamb?'

'Don't think so. I think I'll donate the prizes back so we can raise more money for the Spitfire.'

Anna leant forward and placed a friendly kiss on the young man's forehead. She watched as he began to blush. 'Don't worry, Tim, I'm only teasing.'

The young man soon recovered and turned his attention to Eddie.

'You're that American, aren't you? And a pilot, too. That's what I want to be.'

Eddie towered over Timothy. 'I think my uniform is a giveaway for me being from the other side of the pond, and you're right, I'm Army Air Force, but don't rush to get up there, kid, it's no picnic.'

The young man continued undaunted. 'I can't wait. I should get my call-up papers any time, so—'

'Come on, Tim, we're going to lose our place if you don't come now and you haven't even got me a bottle of pop yet.'

The pair gave Tim a broad smile as the teenager's young lady pulled him by the arm into a throng of people.

'Does he remind you of anyone?'

Eddie turned to Anna, his smile almost gone. 'The difference is, I'm twenty-seven years old. He's what, seventeen?'

Anna sighed. 'Seventeen years and ten months precisely. Come the end of August, he will be in uniform.'

Their moment of quiet reflection in the bustling space was brought to an end by a familiar voice straining to be heard on the hall's tiny stage. Resorting to the use of a handbell, the vicar succeeded in his quest for silence. After saying a few words of welcome, he handed over to his wife.

'Remember, everyone, tonight is about raising funds for perhaps the most important cause we have ever raised money for. I know it's a huge task to raise the £5,000 we need to buy our Spitfire. However, I have some splendid news to share with you. Sir Reginald Fischer has sent me another cheque for £25. Isn't that wonderful? That said, one or two of you have suggested we join with other villages to combine our efforts, and that's something I'll be taking up over the coming weeks. But for now, let's enjoy the evening and try to forget the fighting for an hour or two.'

Following a minute or so of hurried conversations, the crowd hushed into silence as the first game began.

'So, what are you supposed to do?' enquired Eddie.

'When he calls a number, check whether you have it on your ticket. If you have it, put a pencil line across it. When someone has marked all their numbers, they'll shout out to tell the caller they think they've won.'

'Is that all there is to it?'

'Will you be quiet, please, we've already missed three numbers. It's all right for you with the special gifts, us mere mortals have already forgotten—oh, for heaven's sake, that makes four.'

'He said six, nineteen, forty-one and then he said two little ducks. This is one crazy game.'

Anna tutted. 'That means twenty-two, now be quiet.'

Forty minutes later saw the last game in the first half of the evening completed, and as Anna and Eddie pushed their way to the refreshments table, she felt a tap on her shoulder.

'My fool of a husband tells me you were in the Cock and Sparrow earlier today. You didn't waste much time, did you?'

Anna turned to see Pearl Woodman frowning.

'It turns out my American friend has plenty of experience of illegal betting in Colorado, so he felt quite at home in the pub's lavatory.'

Eddie returned Anna's smile. Pearl remained straight-faced.

'The word is, you two turning up has been noticed. Remember what I said about being careful? Take care who's keeping tabs on you two.'

Chapter 7: Shopping Day

Friday morning breakfast came to an abrupt halt as the vicarage telephone rang. Helen Grix went to answer the call. As usual, she'd decide whether it needed her husband's attention immediately or if it could be dealt with later. Instead, the call was for her daughter.

'It's for you.'

Surprised, Anna reluctantly put down the last of her honey covered toast and sauntered into the red-tiled hallway to take the phone receiver from her mother's outstretched arm.

'She's in a public telephone box, so you better hurry.'

'Hello?'

'Anna, it's me, Beattie. Fancy catching a bus into Walsingham for a bit of shopping? There's a new hat I want to buy.'

Anna hesitated, knowing there were several things about Ted Fleming's death she wanted to follow up.

'Anna, are you there? Do make your mind up one way or the other, the pips are about to go, and I haven't got any more change.'

'Er, yes, I'd love to, Beattie. The thing is, I've hurt my ankle, so don't go thinking we can walk around every shop in Walsingham.

OK, I'll get the ten o'clock bus. Make sure you're at your bus stop for twenty past or you'll miss me.'

She could hear the pips sounding at the other end of the line and wasn't sure whether Beattie had heard her.

I bet she misses the bus like last time.

Anna hobbled to the village crossroads in plenty of time to catch her bus. To her dismay, old Miss Flowers was sitting bolt upright on the only seat to survive Jack Lincoln's pony trap after a heavy night drinking in the King's Head.

It's beyond me why he gives his horse beer.

'Good morning, Miss Flowers, how are you?'

The elderly lady peered over her half-rimmed spectacles. 'In truth, Miss Grix, I have a slight pain in my chest, and my knees aren't getting any better. However, I mustn't complain, especially when I see you dressed like that. I think the saying that youth truly is wasted on the young has a great deal of meaning.'

Silly old bat.

Anna refused to be intimidated by the villager's acid tongue. Instead, she held tightly on to the rusted metal pole of the bus stop sign and smiled at her tormentor. 'I'm sorry you're not feeling too well. Perhaps a spell of quiet reflection and rubbing your knees with nettle leaves might at least take your mind off the problem.'

Before the old lady could respond, both turned their heads in the direction of a spluttering noise. A few seconds later an ancient single deck coach shunted into sight.

That thing will never get me to Walsingham.

'Are you going to north Norfolk, Miss Flowers?'

The old woman smiled mischievously. 'Fortunately, no. If you intend to get on that monstrosity, you're more of a fool than I thought you to be.'

Seconds later, the cream and brown-painted coach stuttered to a halt, feet from where Anna was still clutching on to the metal pole. The driver pushed a lever, which caused the coach door to open.

'Hop on as quick as you can; I'm running behind schedule.'

Anna didn't feel capable of hopping anywhere; nevertheless, she made a valiant effort to hurry herself up. 'Walsingham, please.'

Having handed over a few pennies to the conductor, Anna grabbed at a seat corner for support and lowered herself into surprisingly comfortable upholstery.

Ten minutes after the coach crawled into life, a sign for Kirkby Magna came into sight. At the bus stop stood Beattie Longman, excitedly waving at Anna.

You never change, thankfully.

She bounded onto the coach, thrust a thrupenny bit into the conductor's hand and almost toppled onto Anna as the driver pulled away too quickly for Beattie's liking. 'How's the ankle? How did you say you hurt it?'

Anna rubbed her lower leg. 'It's a long story and yes, it's still hurting, I'm afraid, so remember, don't be doing your usual stunt of rushing around everywhere or we'll lose each other once we get to town.'

Beattie offered a sympathetic smile before lowering her petite frame next to her friend.

'What's this about a new hat? I thought you hated them because they ruined that long hair of yours.'

Beattie giggled. 'You're right, but I saw this new design advertised in the papers and thought, I must have it. You know I'm not normally bothered about clothes and suchlike, so the ration coupons aren't a problem.'

Anna gave her companion a searching look. 'You're after a fella, aren't you? Come on, Beattie Longman, spill the beans.'

Her friend began to giggle again. 'Not really, except there is this chap who works on my uncle's farm. He's a real dish.'

Anna frowned. 'What do you mean, works on your uncle's farm? If he's our age, he'd have had his call-up papers by now?'

Beattie's smile morphed to indicate nervousness. 'Well, to be honest, he's—'

'Let me guess, an Italian prisoner of war?'

Beattie lifted a finger to her lips. 'Shush, people will hear.'

Anna clasped her friend's hand. 'Be careful, Beattie. You know what people will say when they find out – and they will find out. And what happens when he goes home after the war?'

Beattie gave her friend a wistful stare. 'By the looks of things, that's a long way away. Who knows what will happen in the meantime? My grandpa says live for today, so that's what I'm doing; I don't give a stuff about what people think.'

This won't end well.

The friends fell into a reflective silence for the remainder of the short trip into Walsingham. Within minutes, they stood in the ancient town's market square.

'Listen, Beattie, Dad asked me to call in at The Shrine of Our Lady of Walsingham and say a prayer for those who have suffered a loss recently.'

Anna noticed her friend was less than impressed.

'You mean to tell me that with all that's going on, you still believe?'

'Look, I'm a vicar's daughter and around it all day, every day. But I do have to say that recently I've started to think about things differently.'

The friends' tense exchange was briefly interrupted as a young man in army uniform walked between them in the bustling square. He gave each a cheeky grin before disappearing back into the crowd.

'After our John was killed at Dunkirk, I thought all that religious stuff could take a running jump. Mum thinks I'm terrible, but I don't care; no matter what happens, my brother isn't coming home.'

How must that feel?

Anna was spared the need to think of a rational response due to the sound of a local Church Boys Brigade bugle and drums band, closely followed by a detachment of the local home guard marching more or less in step.

'Look at that daft lot,' laughed Beattie as she drew Anna's attention to the mixed bag of old men and young lads turned down for active service for any number of reasons. 'They still haven't got their uniforms, and look at those wooden toy rifles, I ask you.'

Anna worked hard not to laugh. 'They're only trying to do their bit, Beattie; it's not their fault they haven't got the equipment needed for the job.'

Beattie was having none of it. 'My dad has joined, and you know he's as daft as a brush. Believe it or not, he's been made a sergeant because he still has his service revolver which, by the way, he shouldn't have. He says a lot of the men kept what he calls "souvenirs" from the fourteen-eighteen war.'

Anna gave up trying to instil a measure of gravitas into the conversation. 'Well, I'm off to—'

'There it is.' Beattie pointed to a shop on the far side of the market square. 'Les Chapeau Femmes. Look at all those beautiful hats.' She began to make off before finishing the sentence.

'I'll meet you in half an hour at Little Walsingham Cross, OK?' Anna wasn't at all sure Beattie had heard in her eagerness to reach the milliners.

Anna exchanged worlds as she passed from the hustle and bustle of the town centre through a wide gate into the peaceful gardens of the shrine grounds. She then entered the newly enlarged church in which the shrine was situated.

She joined several worshippers as they prayed in total silence. Anna fixed her gaze on the shrine as she fulfilled her father's request.

I so want to keep believing.

After a short period, Anna rose from her pew and walked over to a wrought iron stand, which held several tiers of candles. Dropping a coin into the collection box, she lit one and said a further short prayer.

She attempted to disguise her limp as she left the church so as not to draw attention to herself. Anna took her time to walk around a pristine lawn which sat in the centre of the holy complex. Now at the exit, she was propelled back into the noisy realities of everyday life.

Crossing the marketplace, which necessitated navigating between a throng of civilians and uniformed personnel going about their business, Anna eventually reached Les Chapeau Femmes. Peering through the small panes of glass of the Georgian window, she could see Beattie was in a world of her own, trying on a variety of hats. About to enter the shop, Anna's attention was drawn to a group of people twenty feet away, gathered around a man with an open suitcase at his feet. Intrigued, she hobbled over to the small crowd.

A man in a loud chequered suit and trilby hat spoke animatedly to his audience. She was excited to see that amongst the several children's toys that the battered suitcase contained were a selection of balloons.

They're just what Mum's been looking for.

She tried not to show too much interest in the American nylon stockings which she also caught sight of, to say nothing of the lace and lipstick he had on offer.

'Come on, ladies, plenty to go around. Stockings for that special date, toys for the kiddies and balloons for, well, that's up to you – no laughing madam, that's rude.'

Anna joined in with the general hilarity caused by the spiv's cheeky sales patter. Before she could make a beeline for the balloons, a sharp whistle caused the man in the loud suit to slam shut his suitcase, collect it under his arm and make for an alleyway a few feet to his left.

The crowd quickly melted into thin air as Anna sighted a second man wearing a loud suit in the far corner of the market square making off at speed.

He must've been on the lookout for the police.

Seconds later, two police constables entered the square to be met with hundreds of people going about their lawful business.

I've got to find him.

Anna disappeared into the same alleyway into which the spiv had fled and hobbled as quickly as she felt able without damaging her ankle further. As she got deeper into the narrow passage, the hubbub of the market square receded. An eerie silence and dark shadows from overhanging buildings prevailed, even though it was approaching noon on a bright summer's day.

She felt no concern as she rounded a tight corner of her claustrophobic surroundings. As soon as she turned the corner, Anna was faced with a flick-knife pointed towards her head.

'What's a nice girl like you doing chasing the likes of me? Take one step nearer, and I'll spoil your pretty little face.' The spiv jabbed the air with his knife to reinforce his point.

What have I got myself into?

Deciding she had two choices, to run or face the man down, she chose the latter.

'Please put that thing down; you'll cut yourself with it. I'm after your balloons, not ill-gotten gains.'

The spiv began to smile as he retracted the flick-knife blade. 'You're a plucky one, I'll give you that, young lady.'

Anna scowled at the pencil-moustached man. 'Call me that again, and you'll need more than a little knife to protect you. Now, open that suitcase and show me your balloons. I'm a vicar's daughter, so don't even think of cheating me or I'll tell God.'

Did I really say that?

Her opponent roared with laughter as he set his battered fake crocodile skin suitcase on the paved floor, flicked open the catches and threw the lid back. 'Here, take the lot for your cheek, and don't forget to tell God that I was kind to you.'

Anna knelt down, despite the pain in her ankle, and retrieved all the balloons she could find. As soon as her hands were clear of the suitcase, the spiv kicked its lid shut, retrieved the case and winked at Anna before turning to make his getaway.

'Wait,' whispered Anna.

The man turned towards his pursuer. 'No more free gifts, lady.' He winked a second time.

'No, you've been very kind. I want some information.'

His smile disappeared. 'What's your game then?'

Anna watched as the man placed a hand in his jacket pocket. She knew it contained the flick-knife. 'Don't be silly, and take your hand out of that pocket. What I mean is, I need your help.'

The spiv began to relax. 'Help? From the likes of me? Are you drunk or something?'

Anna tried to calm the man with a warm smile. 'I told you, I'm a vicar's daughter, so I don't drink. I only want to know where you get your stuff from?'

He let out a throaty laugh, before swivelling his head to check no one had heard him. 'Are you joking? If I told you, which I won't, vicar's daughter or not, you might start selling stuff yourself, or get us both killed.'

Anna gave the spiv a second smile. 'I'm not interested in the former and should most certainly wish to avoid the latter.'

Removing his hat, he scratched his forehead in bemusement. 'Look, I like you, you're different. Mad, but different in a nice way, and very different to the people I have to deal with to make a few shillings. Take my advice and leave it alone. I'll do you a deal, right?'

'A deal?'

The spiv nodded. 'If ever you need anything special, you know where to find me, and I'll see what I can do – deal?'

'Deal.'

He smiled. 'Now, turn around and don't look back.'

For the first time, Anna became anxious. 'Are you going to stab me in the back?' She waited for an answer. None came. Eventually, she turned around. The spiv had vanished.

Limping to their agreed meeting place, she saw Beattie furiously waving.

'Where have you been all this time? You must have said lots of prayers.'

Anna smiled. 'You wouldn't believe me in a thousand years.'

Taking the seat next to Beattie on the bus, Anna reached down to her ankle and began to massage it. 'I didn't expect to walk so much; it really hurts.'

Her friend offered a supportive smile. However, she quickly returned her attention to a pretty circular box she was holding. Beattie untied the ribbon and lifted the box lid to reveal its contents. Carefully retrieving the creation from its protective container, Beattie placed the precious object on her head. 'What do you think, do you like it?'

Before Anna had a chance to offer her verdict, a middle-aged woman sat opposite made her opinions known. 'That's a smart hat.'

'Thank you, that's nice of you to say so,' replied Beattie.

'It must have used a lot of coupons. Isn't it funny how some people seem to have plenty, while others struggle?'

Beattie wasn't smiling now. 'And what is that supposed to mean?'

Anna thought better of intervening but could see the exchanges had garnered the interest of everyone on the bus.

'Well, I suppose you young ladies have the means to attract that little bit of extra. I'm not one to judge, mind, but buying fancy hats seems a bit frivolous when the country is fighting for its very existence.'

Neither friend was sure how to react since the stranger had set the purchase of a relative luxury against the danger the country faced.

A voice from the back of the bus called out, 'Then you won't mind sharing all that extra meat you always seem able to lay your hands on, will you, Mavis Watkins?'

The bus erupted into laughter, before it came to a shuddering halt, steam billowing from the radiator.

'She's overheated again, I'm afraid, ladies,' said the driver.

'Just like Mavis Watkins,' shouted an anonymous man from the rear of the bus. The passengers erupted into another round of raucous laughter. At the same time, Mavis Watkins fixed her gaze on a magazine, with which she tried to avoid attention.

Ignoring the general hilarity, the driver decamped the bus with the ticket collector. Together they peered into the engine space and disappeared in a cloud of steam.

Thirty minutes passed as the driver waited for the radiator to cool down sufficiently for him to refill it with the supply of water he carried for just such occasions. Once topped up, the bus set off to an accompanying cheer from all on board.

As the vehicle meandered through the sedate Norfolk landscape, Anna caught sight of a uniformed American holding his palms outward towards a clearly unhappy man.

What's Eddie up to?

Anna arrived home late but in time for lunch. She opened the kitchen door to see her parents seated at the large pine table listening to the one o'clock news headlines on the wireless.

'The government has made an announcement concerning the capture of Rudolf Hess. 'Do let's turn the wireless off, Charles, I'm sure it's fascinating but can we forget the war while we eat?'

The vicar gave his wife an affectionate smile before turning to Anna. 'Would you switch the wireless off before you join us for lunch?'

Anna smiled, doing as she was asked, before flourishing a supply of balloons the spiv had gifted her. Helen squealed with delight.

'How on earth did you find them? As you know, I've been looking all over without success. Well done you.'

Anna gave her parents the edited highlights of her time in Walsingham, making sure to omit the danger she had been in.

'I cannot condone you dealing with those types of people. You're not a child anymore and are well aware of the harm those awful men cause.'

Anna tried hard not to show irritation at her father's comment. 'Then should I throw them away?'

Her mother gave the vicar a stern look. 'Well?'

He hesitated before responding. 'I suppose God loves all his children, so let some good come of this minor error of judgement on your part, Anna. We shall donate them to the village school once your mother has finished with them at the thrift shop.'

Before either woman could respond, the back door opened. Eddie stepped in hesitantly and removed his military cap. Expecting a warm welcome from Anna, he was met with a cold stare.

'What were you doing talking to that chap by the field gate?'

Anna's parents exchanged amused glances before taking their leave.

'I was doing my job.'

Anna shot back. 'And what is your job, Lieutenant?'

Eddie hesitated. 'I can't tell you, at least, not yet. Don't you trust me? What you don't know can't hurt you.'

'It's not about trust, it's—'

'It's about trust, Anna. Perhaps I should leave before one of us says something we may regret later.'

Eddie stepped back into the doorway and, after giving Anna a final glance, closed the kitchen door quietly behind him.

Who does he think he is? I can find Ted Fleming's killer on my own. I don't need anyone.

Anna's mother returned to the kitchen as her daughter sped out, making for her room. She sat on the bed and mulled over what had just happened. Still angry with Eddie, she threw a pillow at the window, before immediately regretting her action. As she retrieved it from the window seat, Anna saw Eddie sitting on a stone step at the gate. She knew she'd have to make the first move.

Opening the window, she leant out. 'You're still in debt for nearly killing me. Wait there while I come down and tell you what your further punishment will be.'

Anna limped downstairs and through the kitchen as quickly as she could, leaving her mother, who was sat at the kitchen table, to wonder what was going on.

Eddie was halfway up the path by the time Anna got to him. 'You said we didn't know each other, and you're right. So, you're taking me to The Regent cinema in Norwich tonight, then we shall have fish and chips and a stroll by the River Wensum. If we are going to work together, we need to know much more about each other. Pick me up at five-thirty sharp; I don't want to miss the start of the film.'

Eddie tried to speak without success.

'Five-thirty, remember.'

Chapter 8: At the Flicks

'Hurry, or we'll be late for the film trailers. You can park at the station.' Anna's impatience intensified as she kept a close eye on the station clock while directing the lieutenant to their destination.

'My grandma has a saying: you can holler all you like but it ain't gonna get done any quicker.' Eddie continued to fight with the Jeep's gears as he dodged pedestrians rushing to get their business done before blackout.

Eventually, Anna succeeded in getting Eddie to the train station, where they managed to bag one of the last remaining parking spaces.

'I'm surprised how busy it is – the car park, I mean.'

Anna gazed around the small area in front of the main entrance to the Victorian station. 'Yes, but very few will be civilian vehicles. Most of these drivers will be waiting for the next London train to pick up whoever it is they're ferrying around.'

Eddie smiled. 'What, you mean like me?'

'Watch it, airman; if you don't behave, I'll leave you here and watch the film on my own.'

'I can see why so many men have the hots for you, Anna,' he replied sardonically. 'What are we going to see, anyway?'

'It's a comedy called *Crook's Tour*. It's supposed to be quite good, but I don't see much of a queue, which is unusual.'

She soon realised the reason for the cinema's deserted entrance. The Pathe Newsreel and cartoons had started twenty-five minutes earlier.

'I thought you said we needed to be here for six-thirty.'

Anna scowled as she scanned the billboard showtimes. 'They must have brought it forward for some reason. Anyway, let's get in – that's assuming there are any seats left.'

The door commissionaire, a sprightly looking elderly gentleman dressed in an impressive scarlet uniform and matching peaked cap, smiled benignly. 'You'll find a seat easily enough; we've had quite a few air raid scares recently. My guess is people are staying away.'

Shown to their seats by a young woman holding a torch, they finally sat down. However, not before having endured several catcalls and jeers from customers unimpressed at having the film interrupted by the new arrivals.

'I think it's only just started so it shouldn't be too hard to catch up with the plot.' Anna coughed as she breathed the smoke from cigarettes that hung in the air like a London smog.

'I guess you're not a smoker?'

'Are you? I haven't seen you with a cigarette?'

'Nope, I saw what they did to my uncle back home and swore I'd never touch the things. Have you ever tried?'

A woman in the seat to their front turned around and asked them to be quiet. Anna wanted to tell the woman to mind her own business but thought better of causing a scene. Instead, she leant into Eddie and whispered, 'I tried rolling tea leaves into a cigarette paper when I was about eleven. Not something I would recommend; it tasted gruesome and put me off for life.'

The woman in front turned around for a second time.

'Yes, I know,' barked Anna, much to the disdain of the people sat nearby.

For the next forty minutes, all was relatively quiet, except for the peculiar sounds coming from the back row.

'What on earth do people get up to back there?' whispered Anna. She could feel Eddie's breath on her cheek.

'I know you're a vicar's daughter, but do you really need me to explain?'

Anna glared at her companion. 'I'm being rhetorical.'

Eddie shook his head. 'Whatever.'

Anna avoided further embarrassment as the house lights illuminated and ice cream girls took up their stations for the intermission. She looked behind to see several couples sitting bolt upright but looking as though they'd been pulled through a hedge backwards.

'What did you think of the film, then?' asked Anna as they waited in line at Joe's fish and chip shop just off the Prince of Wales Road.

'If you want my honest opinion, it was a bit wacky. Your British sense of humour takes some getting used to, but I think it would be popular back home.'

Anna smiled as they moved to the front of the queue. 'We'll make a Brit of you yet. Speaking of which, what's it to be? I highly recommend the cod and chips with mushy peas.'

Eddie fell back on one of his bemused looks and shrugged his shoulders. A portly man behind the stainless steel and green tiled counter looked at Anna as if she were her companion's interpreter.

'Two portions please, and may we have salt and vinegar?'

The portly man nodded without looking at either of them, while lifting a few chips out of the hot beef dripping fat with a stainless steel scoop. He pinched several between finger and thumb to check whether they were ready to be served. Within two minutes, the owner had wrapped both portions in newspaper, which soon began to discolour as beef dripping and vinegar began to soak through.

'There's something about eating fish and chips from a newspaper that gives them a smashing taste.' Anna unwrapped her food and made a paper tray as she began to eat while walking Eddie the short distance down to the River Wensum.

'I guess you mean the taste of newspaper ink?' The American followed his companion's lead in unwrapping his supper. He tentatively dipped a chip into the mushy peas.

'Are all Americans philistines?'

'You Brits may think you're smart, but we have Kentucky Fried Chicken. And, by the way, what you call chips are, in fact, French fries, and you call our chips, crisps. Who are the philistines now?'

Before Anna could respond to Eddie's linguistic challenge, the sounds of air raid warning sirens began to wail across the city. The few people on the streets reacted in precisely the same way as Anna and Eddie. All froze on the spot and looked skywards. A few seconds later, ARP wardens scurried around on their bicycles, blowing whistles and ordering everyone to take cover.

'I've no idea where the shelters are around here, and there's no time to search.' Anna pointed to a mediaeval covered archway spanning the narrow river ahead of them. 'That'll be better than nothing. Come on, hurry up, I think I can hear the bombers coming.'

Knowing that moving at speed would do little to help her ankle heal, she also knew they had no choice. She linked arms with Eddie as she guided him to relative safety.

'This is a pretty little place. I suppose if we're going to be blown to bits, it might as well be in nice surroundings. What's it called?'

Anna grabbed Eddie and pulled him tight against an ancient brick wall. 'It's not really time for a history lesson, but it's called Pull's Ferry.'

'Ferry? Even Americans know what ferries look like, and I don't see one around here.'

Anna began to feel anxious as the deep drone of the enemy bombers intensified. 'If you must know, the building we are sheltering under is named after John Pull. He ran a ferry crossing the river around a hundred years ago. Around eight hundred years ago, this bit of water used to be a canal that monks would bring stone along from France to finish the cathedral. Are you really that interested in history when we're about to be vaporised?'

Eddie took tight hold of his companion to shield her from harm. 'It's better than thinking about 500lb bombs raining down on us, don't you think?'

Anna failed to respond as she shielded her ears against the deafening chorus of aeroplane engines reaching a haunting crescendo.

Any second now.

She waited. No explosions, no screams. Slowly she loosened her hands.

Not our turn tonight.

'Look, they're heading north-west. I wonder if it'll be

Coventry or Liverpool that gets it again…' She felt guilty for being relieved the bombers had bypassed the city.

Eddie followed Anna's lead in poking his head out from under the archway. 'If they think your country can be beaten into submission, they're even more stupid than I thought them to be. But I know what you mean, I've seen what they've done to London.'

Soon, the all-clear siren filled the city air, and ARP wardens shouted that it was safe as they furiously peddled their bikes from street to street.

Strolling along the bank of the River Wensum, Anna fell into a reflective mood. 'Have you ever thought what crazy times we live in? Here we are, strolling along a riverbank as if we didn't have a care in the world and had known each other all our lives.'

Eddie gripped his companion a little tighter as he continued to help her walk. 'It's what war does. You said we needed to get to know each other better if we were to work effectively together. Do you not think what we've just experienced sort of does that?'

Anna slowed the pace, partly because her ankle was beginning to hurt again, partly because of what he'd said. 'I guess what's different from a film is that in the real world, people are exposed to genuine fear for their life. I suppose such an experience does tell you quite a lot about the other person.'

The journey back to Lipton St Faith took much longer than either expected as Eddie carefully navigated in almost total darkness. As the Jeep stopped at the vicarage, they both lowered their voices in an automatic response to the quiet stillness of the village. As Eddie helped Anna out of the vehicle, she stopped and looked around.

'Ever had the feeling you're being watched?'

Her companion briefly scanned their surroundings. 'I can't see anything. Are you worried it's your old boyfriend?'

She shook her head. 'I doubt it after the warning I gave him the last time. Perhaps I'm paranoid.'

Saturday morning saw the village busier than usual as Anna and Eddie made their way to the cottage hospital.

'Perhaps the weekend makes people feel different, whether there's a war on or not.'

'I'd never thought of it quite that way. There is a coffee morning going on at the church. Also, my mother has dressed the thrift shop with balloons and suchlike, ready for a big fundraising push, so perhaps that's why so many people are about.'

The Jeep proceeded sedately down High Street and onwards towards the edge of the village where the cottage hospital stood.

'How on earth did you persuade them to let you into the mortuary?'

Anna smiled mischievously. 'That's for me to know and you to find out.'

It didn't take long for him to understand what his companion meant. As he drove into the small hospital car park, he noticed constable Bradshaw beckoning them around the side of the red-bricked building.

'He's sweet on you, isn't he?'

'I've no idea what you're talking about.'

Tom Bradshaw signalled the Jeep to stop as if he were controlling the traffic on a busy intersection. 'Nice to see you again, Anna. We'd better be quick because if Ilford finds out what I've done, I'll be for the high jump.'

Eddie whispered to his passenger, 'I told you he was sweet on you, but you already knew that, didn't you?'

She gave Eddie a nonchalant look.

'You're a good egg, Tom, and I know how risky this is for you. I won't forget what you've done today. I suppose we should get inside?'

She knew her encouraging words would go down well with Tom, but she kept in mind she shouldn't encourage him enough to believe something beyond friendship existed between them.

Inside the compact morgue, 5'2" Irene Little, the duty technician, quietly welcomed her visitors. She had already pulled Ted Fleming's corpse from its storage locker. She folded back the crisp white linen cover to beyond Ted's shoulders, leaving his neck clearly visible.

'That injury is too neat and narrow for barbed wire to have caused it, wouldn't you agree, Irene?'

The technician shook her head at the American. 'That's not for me to say, nor to speculate.'

Anna intervened. 'Quite right too, Irene. You're doing us such a favour, the last thing we want to do is to compromise your position. Isn't that right, Lieutenant Elsner?' She knew from the look on Eddie's face that her point had been well made.

Irene nodded solemnly and turned to the corpse to explain to Ted she was about to cover his face and place him back into his locker.

What a dignified way to treat the dead.

Clambering back into the Jeep, Anna noticed a smartly dressed man wearing a collar and tie approaching.

'Anna, and I think I'm correct in saying you must be Lieutenant Eddie Elsner; good morning to you both. What brings you to the hospital, I wonder, or perhaps more precisely, the mortuary?'

Detective Inspector Edmund Spillers' question threw Anna for a split second.

Now what do we do?

'Good morning, Inspector Spillers. As a matter of fact, I wanted to catch up with my friend who works there. You know what it's like, what with the war and everything; everyone's like ships passing in the night, and I haven't seen her for so long.'

The inspector narrowed his eyes enough to make Anna feel uncomfortable. 'I do hope you didn't pop inside and come across any bodies because that wouldn't be ethical, would it, Miss Grix?'

Anna offered one of her hurt looks. 'Absolutely not, Inspector. No, as I say, it was a fleeting visit. I can assure you the very last thing I should want to do is look at a dead body. I'm sure the lieutenant feels the same.'

Both looked towards Eddie. 'I'm just passing through.'

Clever you.

Anna gave the inspector a sideways glance to gauge his reaction without making it obvious she was doing so.

'Good, I'm so glad we understand each other, Miss Grix. Now, I shall leave you to get on with the rest of your day, while I do the same.' Inspector Spillers raised his hat and turned on his heels.

'That was a close-run thing.'

'You're telling me. If you're not careful, you'll end up getting arrested, and I'll be on my way home. Now you wouldn't want that, would you?'

Anna frowned. 'There you go with that man thing again. I've no intention of ending up in a police cell, less still of being responsible for your early return to Colorado. Now, what do you suggest we do since we're certain barbed wire played no part in Ted Fleming's death?'

Eddie started the engine and drove the Jeep from the morgue entrance, out onto the main road. 'Do you have a hardware store nearby?'

Anna thought for a moment. 'No, but we have an ironmonger.'

'Isn't that the same thing? Never mind, tell me where to drive.'

She broke into a grin, knowing she'd succeeded in irritating him.

Within minutes they neared Umbolt Forge and Metal Supplies.

'This place looks like a scrapyard; are you sure it's a store… I mean, a shop?'

'Believe you me, if it's metal you want, be that raw materials or made into something new, Dicky Umbolt will have it.'

Eddie pulled into the untidy compound, carefully avoiding bits of metal which were strewn everywhere.

'Anna, good to see you, and this must be the American.'

She looked at Eddie, urging him not to rise to yet another comment about his country of origin.

'How's business, Dicky; doing well?'

The elderly man shrugged his shoulders. 'It's the War Office; they control absolutely everything, and it's the devil's job to get supplies. If I haven't got it, I can't sell it, can I? Then again, I suppose using iron and steel for guns and ships is more important at the moment. You know, instead of me making fancy metal gates for the gentry.'

'Is there much gentry around these parts?'

Anna detected that Dicky didn't entirely trust the American. 'It's OK, I checked, he's not a spy.'

Eddie raised an eyebrow at his companion as the ironmonger gave him another intense look.

'Don't be fooled by what you see around you, fella. There's plenty of money here; it's just not shared around that much. I call them The Norfolk Set. They're good people, mind, and do a lot for charity. But their roots go back hundreds of years, and they've got the land to prove it. Anyway, enough about that; I've got things to do, so how can I help?'

Anna pondered how to ask her question. 'Well, Dad needs some strong wire to hang one or two devotional paintings up in the church. They're a heck of a size, so he needs something quite strong without it looking too unsightly.'

Dicky scratched the side of his weather-beaten face. 'You know, I've had some stuff in stock for years, and nobody ever asks for it. Then, like buses that come all at once, I have two people asking for the same thing in just over a week. How strange is that?'

Anna and Eddie exchanged glances and tried not to look too excited.

'All I've got left is a few bits and pieces. Since it's for the church, tell your dad he can have them for nothing. Don't tell anyone, mind, or you'll ruin my reputation.' With that, the ironmonger left to begin the hunt for what wire he could find.

Soon the boiler-suited old gentleman returned with several short coils of steel wire held in his gnarled hands.

'Is this what you sold to the other villager?'

'He was no villager – he had a posh accent and he wore shiny black shoes, at least they were when he came into the yard; the state they were in when he left was something else.'

'Didn't it seem strange that a well-dressed man who spoke with a plumb in his mouth approached you to buy a load of old wire?'

Dicky failed to smile and gave the lieutenant another stern look. 'As long as they put money into my pocket, I don't care what they sound or look like. Now, I need to get on. Give my best to your parents, Anna.'

Chapter 9: An Unwilling Guest

Anna sat in the spacious lounge of the Victorian vicarage reading the latest edition of *Woman's Own* magazine. Back home from a busy morning visiting his sick parishioners, the Reverend Grix walked hesitantly into the room and perched himself on a seat arm opposite his daughter.

'What's up, Dad? I recognise that look.' She watched as her father toyed with his wedding ring. 'Come on, Dad, spit it out, I'm not a child.'

'An unfortunate phrase, my darling, but now you mention it, there is something I should like to discuss with you.'

What have I done now?

Intrigued, Anna lowered her magazine and rested it on her lap. 'I'm all ears. Let me guess, your parishioners are perturbed that I'm going around with an American serviceman? Or perhaps I was seen entering a public house to imbibe on the Devil's temptation? Maybe I—'

'Well, yes, something like that, Anna. One or two of my flock are concerned you're also developing a betting habit. They consider the good lieutenant is, perhaps, not the best role model you might look to. There, I've said it, so I shall leave you to your magazine.'

The vicar began to stand. Anna was in no mood to let the accusations rest.

'Father, is that it? You throw accusations purporting to come from that lot in church, then try to scarper?'

The reverend rested back onto the chair arm. 'Anna, there's no need for you to take that tone with me. I've faithfully passed on the comments I've received and have discharged my responsibility. I pass no judgement personally and am, in fact, quite fond of your new friend.'

Anna shifted position, making plain she was irritated. 'Dad, in the context of how you've just spoken to me, I think my response is justified.'

She knew her father detested confrontation, but it was important to her that she vented her anger. The only reason she'd kept it in check was out of respect for her parent.'

'Oh, bother, I told your mother it would've been best coming from her, but she wouldn't have it.'

Who's the child now?

'Well, they are, after all, your flock and not the responsibility of my mother.'

'Quite so, Anna, quite so. You see, what I think is one or two are—'

'Are ignorant, interfering and have nothing better to do than spread rumours. Is that what you were going to say?'

The vicar began to fidget with his wedding ring again. 'Well, not exactly, but you can, I'm sure, appreciate the position I've been placed in.'

Exasperated, Anna tried a different tack. 'Dad, I love you, but you always do this. You try to please everyone and end up satisfying nobody, then you make yourself ill worrying about it all. I apologise if I sound harsh, but I don't give a fig what people are saying. I gave Peggy Fleming my word that I'd try to find out what really happened to her husband. You've always taught me that a promise is a promise, haven't you?'

Anna saw her father beginning to get emotional but knew she was right to confront the allegations.

'Dear child, yes. I have taught you to keep promises whenever possible, just as I'm doing to my parishioners; you see the difficulties such responsibilities cause. I'm proud of your kindness in assisting Mrs Fleming. Is Lieutenant Elsner helping you?'

Anna nodded without speaking. Instead, she lowered her head and gazed at the magazine on her lap.

'You have my blessing, my darling, and I shall do my best to rebuke those amongst my flock who seek to disparage you. All I ask is that you're careful. You may have given your word to Mrs Fleming. Still, in the church's mind that does not necessitate either Lieutenant Elsner, or you, putting yourselves in harm's way. Wars make for strange bedfellows that would not be tolerated in peacetime. Promise me you'll be careful, child.'

Anna slowly lifted her gaze and hobbled over to her father to place an affectionate kiss on his forehead. 'And you promise me you won't make yourself ill again over this silliness.'

The vicar returned his daughter's affectionate embrace by holding her hand in his. 'It shall be so. Now, what are you doing with the remainder of your day?'

Having completed more fraught meetings with landowners about the possibility of future access to their land by American forces, Eddie was pleased to be back in the calming atmosphere of the vicarage. Making his way to the lounge, he opened the door.

'Ah, my intuition was correct. I shall leave you two to get on with your investigations.' The vicar shook Eddie by the hand and smiled as they passed each other.

Anna pre-empted Eddie's question by recounting what had taken place. 'He's a gentleman and hates conflict of any kind. The problem is, his faith drives him to take on so much that he makes himself ill trying to absorb other people's troubles. He's already had one nervous breakdown. Neither Mum nor I want that to happen again.'

The lieutenant listened patiently, but Anna sensed he was beginning to withdraw into his own thoughts. 'Listen to me babbling on, are you OK?'

It took Eddie several seconds to speak. 'I don't remember much about my father's death. I was too young, but I knew something had changed. My mom went from an outgoing and loving woman to someone who always seemed to be in a bad temper, which I could never understand. My grandparents did the best they could to compensate, but somehow, it wasn't the same.'

Silence fell for a short period before Anna took control of her emotions. 'Let's change the subject and talk about murder, shall we?'

Anna's complete change of direction made Eddie smile. 'I'll say something for you, Miss Grix; you certainly know how to make an impact. Tell you what, why don't we take a trip back to Three-Mile-Bottom and stake out the Cock and Sparrow.

Reaching out to open the passenger door of the Jeep for Anna, the lieutenant hesitated.

'What's the matter?'

After a few seconds, Eddie slowly turned around, holding a dead rat by its tail. 'Someone's left us a message.'

Anna scrunched her face on seeing the rodent. 'The Jeep hasn't got its roof on; that thing could have come from anywhere.'

Eddie held out a paper tag tied to the animal's tail. 'If that's the case, it's the only rat I've heard of that can write.'

She leant closer to read the label:

'People who rat get hurt.'

Eddie carefully removed the menacing note, then tossed the dead rodent into a patch of long grass several yards from the vicarage. 'I think someone is trying to tell us something.'

As they approached the lieutenant's home village, Eddie became animated. 'You see those three ugly morons standing by that old banger? They were the guys behind the lavatory door when we came here last time.'

Anna immediately latched onto the significance of her companion's words. 'They look as though they're talking to the smartly dressed guy in the car. Now, why would a man kitted out in expensive clothes be driving a clapped-out old Austin Seven and spend his time talking to thugs?'

Eddie pressed the brake pedal to slow their advance. 'My guess is he's their boss. What better cover than to drive around in an unassuming heap of junk? Looking at that carpetbag the tall man is putting in the trunk, I guess his goons are stowing the day's takings.'

Anna sighed. 'I assume by the trunk you mean boot? Remember what I said about learning to speak properly.' She smiled as Eddie raised his eyebrows.

'Whatever. Anyway, I have a plan. We need to take a look in that bag to confirm that it's full of cash, and you'll make it happen.'

'Are you mad? Oh, I know, I'll walk over to them and ask them to show me, shall I? Now that really does sound like a plan. Nothing ever changes, does it? Men, I despair.'

Eddie was quick to respond. 'Hang on a second, let me explain.'

A minute later, the Jeep was parked around a blind bend just outside the village. Anna stood in front of the vehicle with its bonnet open. Meanwhile, Eddie concealed himself behind a thicket of hedges a little way from where his companion was standing.

'What if he goes the other way out of the village or another vehicle comes?' asked Anna, raising her voice slightly to compensate for the distance between them.

Eddie popped up from behind the hedge. 'You were the one that said there was hardly any traffic on these roads. As for which way he will turn out of the pub, if he does go right, he'll end up in the middle of nowhere. Let's call it an educated guess. After all, remember what those top shots said about me?'

They didn't have to wait long for the lieutenant to be proved correct. Eddie quickly concealed himself again as he heard the sound of a car engine approaching from his right. 'Get ready, Anna, and remember to—'

'If you say one more word, you won't see straight for a week. Do I make myself clear?'

'Perfectly,' muttered Eddie as he crouched down.

Anna caught sight of the old Austin and settled into her role by leaning over the Jeep's engine with her back to the oncoming vehicle. Waiting for the car to stop, she turned and gave its occupant a friendly wave. A dapper gentleman exited the car, allowing Anna to see the quality of his outfit.

They've got to be made in London, and I bet he didn't need any clothing coupons.

The man's imposing appearance was completed by a perfectly trimmed pencil moustache and slicked-back hairstyle.

I'd say about 5'10" and forty-five.

'How come a pretty young girl like you is driving an army Jeep?' The suited man sauntered confidently over to the stricken vehicle.

'To tell you the truth, my stupid boyfriend has been working on it and he lent it to me. He's an army mechanic, you see, so he gets to drive all kinds of things when he repairs them. He told me he'd fixed this one, so wait till I see him, I'll give him what for.' Anna gave the man a doe-eyed smile as she curled her hair with a finger. She then played her masterstroke and started to cry.

'Now, don't you worry your pretty little head. Let's have a look and see what I can do.'

If you call me that again, I'll knock you into next week.

The man leant into the car's engine bay, giving no apparent thought to marking his expensive suit. Anna stood so close to the stranger that her hip and arm touched his as together, they inspected the oily tangle of rubber leads and engine parts.

'I've got just the thing for this in my boot. Hang on here while I get my tools.'

Anna watched as the man passed where Eddie was hiding, lifted his boot and seconds later, returned carrying a small metal toolbox.

'Now, let's see what we can find, shall we?'

Anna, feeling more confident in her acting role, gave the man a sweet smile and giggled.

Eddie couldn't believe his luck that the suited man had left the boot open. He quietly broke cover and crept up to the old Austin, all the time checking that Anna continued to keep her rescuer fully occupied. Peering into the interior of the boot, he immediately saw the canvas bag. Eddie slid the brass catch downwards, which released a leather strap holding the bag closed.

Anna took a risk by looking over her shoulder while her new companion continued to busy himself deep inside the Jeep's engine compartment. She caught sight of Eddie sneaking back to the thicket, giving her a thumbs-up signal as he ran.

'There you are, young lady, good as new. It was only a loose battery lead, but I know you girls haven't the first clue about these things. But then, why should you? What with your hair to do each day and getting those seamlines drawn on the back of your legs straight, I'm sure you're always fully occupied.'

Right, that's enough, I'm going to hit him.

It was only the sight of Eddie popping his head above the thicket that gave Anna second thoughts about assaulting the suited man. Brought back to her senses, she slipped back into the role. 'You're so clever. How on earth can I ever thank you?'

Anna could have sworn she heard a stifled cough coming from where Eddie was concealed as she realised what she said to the man.

Oh dear.

She watched as a sickly grin spread across the suited man's face, which confirmed her worst fears.

'Funny you should say that, young lady; might you have a little gift for me?'

Anna tried not to recoil as the man leant forward, his face only inches from hers.

Oh no you don't.

106

She took a half-step back, using the excuse to close the bonnet before more traffic might come along. 'Well, how would you like to take a young lady out for the night? There's a barn dance at Home Farm tonight. Do you fancy it?'

The man's eyes lit up, much to Anna's dismay.

'That sounds like an invitation, young lady. Perhaps you might tell me your name now we are to go on a date?

What have I just done?

'Er, yes, I suppose I should. It's Anna. What do I call you apart form my guardian angel?'

The man laughed. 'Anna, what a cute name. Me? Oh, just call me The Duke.'

'Are you?'

'Am I what?'

'You know, a real duke?'

His belly laugh filled the quiet space. 'Now that would be a turn up for the books. No, but everyone who knows me calls me The Duke. A sign of respect, you might say.'

Somehow, I don't think it's a sign of respect at all.

'Anyway, I need to be on my way, but first, we need to check this thing really is fixed.' He banged the bonnet with a clenched fist. 'Tell you what, jump in and reverse up to the crossroads. That way I can get to where I'm going and make sure the Jeep is in good order.'

Anna panicked.

I wish I'd learned to drive.

'Er… Yes, good idea.' She climbed into the driver's seat, relieved to see Eddie had left the key in the ignition. She watched as her rescuer sauntered to the rear of his car, hesitated for a few seconds before slamming shut the boot and getting into his vehicle. Relying on her wits and memory of watching how Eddie had driven the Jeep, she turned the key and pressed the accelerator. To her surprise, then alarm, the engine roared into life, spewing a cloud of blue-grey smoke into the air.

Please make this work.

Anna looked across to the gearstick and fixed her eyes on the tiny diagram etched into its top. Praying she'd interpreted the gear positions correctly, she jammed it into reverse. The sound of metal grinding on metal pierced her otherwise quiet surroundings as she realised something was wrong.

How does he do this?

Aware that the suited man was waiting for her to move off, she closed her eyes and tried to imagine Eddie's driving routine. She breathed a sigh as the solution came to her. Depressing the clutch, she tried again. The grinding noise came back but was nowhere near as loud as before. Cautiously, she eased the handbrake off, pressed the accelerator and looked over her shoulder so that she could see where she was going. To her colossal relief, she noticed a patch of clear ground next to the tarmac as she cleared the corner. Managing to pull the Jeep to one side, Anna reapplied the handbrake and turned off the engine, causing the vehicle to lurch backwards a few inches.

Forgot about putting the thing into neutral.

The suited man's car drew alongside. Anna watched as he leant over to wind down the passenger side window.

'Don't be late tonight, young lady, and put your best frock on; I want to be proud of you. See you at eight.'

Relieved the man didn't engage in any further conversation before pulling off, Anna slumped over the steering wheel as she reflected on what had just happened. By the time Eddie got to her, she was shaking uncontrollably.

'Take a minute. You did beautifully. Come on, deep breaths, it's fine now.'

Anna made no attempt to resist Eddie's calming presence as he placed an open palm on her shoulder.

'I didn't know you could drive.'

'I can't.'

It took a few seconds before Anna calmed down and gave a nervous laugh.

'Well, you can now. Even better, look what I got from his boot.' Eddie held up a business card.

'Emanuel Brownlove & Co. Ltd.
Shoemakers of Distinction
Patent Leather Footwear a Speciality
London W1'

Anna couldn't hide her excitement. 'Didn't Dicky Umbolt say a man with—'

'Yes, he did, which means we have a very dangerous man, possibly a killer, on our hands. Thank heavens you managed to shake him off.'

She went quiet.

'What's the matter?'

'I did, but only until eight o'clock this evening. I told him we'd meet at the barn dance.

'You said what?'

Chapter 10: In for a Penny

Anna's trepidation at meeting The Duke increased by the hour as she prepared for the barn dance.

Something modest, I think.

She opened both doors of an old mahogany wardrobe and scanned the few dresses she possessed for one that would allow her to blend into the background. Settling on a white garment covered in a pattern of spring flowers, Anna looked into an art-deco mirror a favourite aunt had gifted her years earlier. Finishing her hair, she decided against make-up.

At least Eddie will be there to keep an eye out for any funny business.

She looked pensively at her wristwatch. Even with her injured ankle, Anna knew it would only take fifteen minutes to reach Home Farm.

I hope he remembers to wear civilian clothes.

Arriving early so she could get settled before The Duke arrived, Anna hoped to catch sight of Eddie in the crammed mediaeval barn. As she neared the colossal entrance doors to the ancient building, which had been tied back with rope, Anna tried to remain calm. Her stomach was another thing entirely as it tightened into knots.

Looking pensively at the young women dressed to the nines to impress their uniformed boyfriends, she was met with a multitude of smiling faces. It seemed all were known to each other. Lost in a sea of heads, Anna couldn't locate Eddie and began to panic.

What in heaven's name have I done?

Knowing it was too late to back out, she looked to the stage made from hay bales and timber boarding to see her father speaking.

'…Without further ado, I shall hand over to Joe Blackburn, our brave Air Raid Warden. He will instruct us on what to do, should those dreadful bombers dare appear this evening.'

What would we do without you, Father?

The crowd began a communal giggle before someone had the sense to cheer as a rotund gentleman wearing an oversized white tin helmet all but crawled onto the stage. By the time he stood to address his audience, the crowd were in raptures.

'All I says is that should those bad'uns turn up tonight in an attempt to ruin our barn dance, you listen out for my whistle.' Joe Blackburn retrieved his tool of the trade with one swift movement from his breast pocket and proceeded to blow it until his cheeks turned purple. 'If you hears it, you runs like hell into the fields. Make sure you spreads out now, so if they do drops their bombs, they'll only get one or two of us, which seems fair enough to me. Now, is that clear?'

Joe's liberal use of plurals whipped the crowd into a frenzy as one, then the rest began to cheer, causing flour dust to descend from the ancient roof beams.

Anna's father eventually restored calm by holding his arms out and imploring the crowd to settle. 'Two quick announcements before I ask Brian Jones, our village undertaker, to step onto the stage in his capacity this evening as dance caller. Firstly, may I remind you that soft drinks and homemade biscuits are available for purchase. And please, do only take two biscuits as flour is in short supply. I also wish to make clear that the drinking of alcohol is strictly forbidden. Any infraction of this rule will result in the perpetrators cleaning out the Home Farm piggeries for the next seven days.' The crowd laughed, not quite sure whether the vicar was serious. 'So, on that note of caution, please welcome to the stage Mr Brian Jones, and as you young ones say today, let's get ready to jitterbug.'

The vicar's attempt to use more modern language than was his custom was met with a supportive cheer.

Brian Jones' face dropped at the mention of the popular dance and his complexion drained of what little blood he possessed. He pulled his thin frame up to its full 5' 10". 'Now for the one you've all been waiting for, I want everyone on the dancefloor in five couple sets as we prepare for our first dance, *The Bottoms Up*.'

A collective groan filled the room as the undertaker signalled for the piano player to begin.

Making a dash for one side of the barn to avoid being grabbed by the nearest young man and pulled onto the dancefloor, Anna once again scanned the heaving space for signs of Eddie.

Where on earth are you?

Aware people were still arriving, she turned to the cavernous opening left by the open barn doors.

112

Here we go.

Anna flinched on seeing The Duke, flanked by two heavies, strolling confidently into the old barn. He flicked his finger, signalling his burly compatriots to take one side of the barn each to fulfil their quest. She knew who they were looking for. Meanwhile, their boss wore a sickly smile, which broadened into a disconcerting grin as Anna realised he'd spotted her.

Watching The Duke saunter across the hay-strewn compacted earth floor, those in his path moved aside.

Seconds later, the two heavies appeared as if out of nowhere and took up their positions, one each side of her.

'How wonderful it is to see you again, Anna. What a pretty dress,' said The Duke.

She watched as the immaculately turned out thug eyed her from head to toe. 'Well, I said I deserved a good night out after that stupid boyfriend of mine lied to me.' Anna worked hard to sound and look confident, knowing that he'd interpret any sign of nervousness with suspicion.

'His loss is my gain, and I like a person who keeps their word. Now, a drink?'

Anna looked at the two heavies, then back to The Duke, unable to see any sign of glass.

The Duke moved his head upwards the slightest fraction, at which one of the heavies produced two small crystal whisky glasses, and the other, a solid silver hipflask. 'A quick snifter?'

One of the heavies filled each exquisitely cut glass with a generous measure of double Scotch.

'I don't drink, at least, not whisky.' Anna kept her eyes firmly fixed on her unwanted companion.

The Duke gave another of his sickly grins. 'Then this is

a perfect time to start. You wouldn't want to make a man unhappy, would you?'

Anna sensed his two heavies flexing their shoulders as if making ready to encourage her into accepting their superior's hospitality.

'I suppose I'll try anything… once.'

He started to laugh. 'I like your style. Now, why don't we dance?'

The heavies retrieved the whisky glasses without invitation as The Duke took a firm hold of Anna's wrist. A few seconds later, he turned and held her close, their bodies touching. She tried to stifle her natural inclination to gag at his liberal use of cologne, while trying to stop him groping her without antagonising the thug.

'I respect that,' he said in a low, dominating voice as he allowed Anna to move his hands from her lower back. 'You're a classy lady, I can tell that. But nice ladies are sometimes naughty. Can you be naughty?'

'There you are, Anna, your father asked me to come and get you. Your Aunt Cissy has taken ill again. The doctor doesn't think she'll last the night this time and she's asking for you.'

Anna watched The Duke's eyes narrow as he fixed his cold stare on the intruder. She knew she had to act quickly as the two heavies closed in.

'But I can't, I'm with my friend. Anyway, Aunt Cissy is always at death's door, so why should it be any different this time?' She looked towards The Duke, who had begun to smile again. He flicked his head in Eddie's direction. Half a second later, each heavy had hold of one of the American's arms.

Hold your nerve, Eddie.

'Hey, what gives, fellas?'

'Now, what's an American doing in a tiny place like this, dressed in civilian clothes, going on about my girlfriend's sick relative?'

Anna detested his arrogance but knew she had to play along.

Eddie knew the score. 'Listen, I'm a distant family member who got stuck here when your Mr Chamberlain declared war on Germany. No mystery. As soon as I can get back, I'm going, believe me, pal.'

She thought he'd overplayed his hand and waited for The Duke to flick his head again, which Anna knew might not mean good news for either of them. Instead, she watched as the thug's eyes moved between Eddie and herself.

'Any pal of Anna's can call me The Duke, isn't that right, boys?'

The heavies made no attempt to respond.

'Ordinarily, I'd agree with you about Aunt Cissy, but I've been with her for the last hour, and she's barely breathing. The doc says there's no coming back this time.'

Anna looked at The Duke, knowing he was in control, not her.

'I think family is important. You should go to your sick auntie and give her my best wishes. Here, buy her something nice.' The Duke licked his fingers and, within a second, one of the heavies produced a fat role of £1 notes. He held five fingers up, signifying how many the heavy should release.

'That's so generous, I can't—'

Her benefactor resorted to one of his sickly smiles. 'Nobody says no to The Duke, Anna. I'll catch up with you later.'

Anna frowned. 'You don't know where I live.'

'Sure I do.'

'Come on, Anna, let's get around the side of the barn; he'll be out in a second to see where we've gone.'

Eddie led Anna into the shadows.

'Phew, Eddie, that was close. Thank heavens you made it.'

He smiled. 'I've been watching you since the second you arrived. You'd hardly expect me to make my presence known, would you? Anyway, it wasn't a lucky escape, it suited him not to make a scene. Don't think for a minute he didn't see through our little ruse. My guess is that he wants to let us run, watch, then decide if we are simply stupid or need dealing with.'

'You mean—'

Eddie's smile vanished. 'You saw what he did to Ted Fleming.'

Although Anna's faith was profound, she disliked the cliques which formed in small villages, particularly in church circles. She sat with her mother at the back of a consecrated building, its massive walls having welcomed the faithful for almost a thousand years. Anna could hear several groups of the congregation gossiping and straining to turn around without making it too obvious.

As her father began the service, Eddie entered the church in full uniform, settled himself into the pew and sat next to Anna. Heads turned at the new arrival and to watch her mother relocate to allow the two friends a measure of privacy. The commotion briefly caused the vicar to halt proceedings, before recommencing without comment.

Realising it was impossible to talk to each other without arousing more suspicion, Anna and Eddie quietly slipped from the pew with only the vicar noticing their exit.

They stood in the Sunday morning sunshine, watching butter-flies skipping between wildflowers that boarded a low flint wall. Eddie stood with his hands in his pockets while shuffling the short grass of the church pathway to no particular end. 'How are you feeling after last night?'

Anna leant against the church's ancient stones with her hands behind her back. Tilting her head to catch the warming sun, she shrugged her shoulders. 'After we left, I could feel myself getting angrier and angrier. What gives that spiv the right to frighten other people? Then I thought of Peggy Fleming. The deeper we dig into the death of Ted, the more we risk Peggy having to deal with the fallout. Who knows, perhaps The Duke may take his revenge on her. Do we have the right to allow that?'

Eddie shuffled the few feet to lean against the church wall next to Anna. 'Like it or not, you'll have to decide whether to drop it or go for broke. I know we've talked about this before, but after last night, things have got serious. It's OK for me; I can leave anytime I want, but you live here, everyone you care for is in this village.'

Anna pushed herself from the ancient stones and dusted herself down. 'I'll do what I think is right and no small-time thug is going to stop me. You can leave if you want. I'm going to get to the bottom of this mess.'

Eddie looked surprised and held out his open palms. 'Hey, I didn't say I intended to leave, just that I could if I wanted, which I don't. That all depends on if you want me to stay?'

She gave him a long hard stare. 'How else am I supposed to get around if you're not here to drive me?'

He shrugged his shoulders. 'But you've discovered you can drive?'

His companion offered a cheeky grin. 'That's true, but I'd prefer to use your petrol than buy my own, oh, and a car, of course. Anyway, they'd never give me ration coupons for petrol.'

Eddie shook his head. 'I'm glad I come in useful for something. So, what's next?'

Anna began to limp awkwardly towards the vicarage. 'A good old English Sunday roast, that's what.'

Chapter 11: An Unwilling Guest

Sunday lunch at the vicarage was a hectic affair as Helen Grix began to fill the dining table with large quantities of steamed vegetables. At least it made up for lack of sufficient meat.

The matter had been addressed to some extent by Brian Tidmarsh, the vicar's curate, Doctor Brabham and his receptionist, Lily Thwaite. All contributed their individual ration allowances for the week.

Anna and Eddie joined the somewhat subdued atmosphere as her father said grace.

'I see the Luftwaffe bombed London again last evening. I suppose it was the docks they were after. The papers say we suffered only a few casualties, though I'm not sure I believe much that we are told anymore.' Doctor Brabham's downbeat assessment set the tone.

Lily added her downbeat contribution. 'And I heard on the nine o'clock news this morning that one of your ships, the SS Robin Moor, was sunk by a U-boat. How do you think the American people will take that, Lieutenant?'

All eyes fell on Eddie as he pondered how to phrase his

response to ensure he sounded neither angry nor dismissive, given what was happening all around him. 'To be truthful, ma'am, I'm not sure. There will be Americans whose anger will try to push the president to hit back. There are also many people, and please don't take offence, who remember the last time and are frightened. That fear shows itself in their trying to isolate the USA from the rest of the world.'

'Do you think your government will let the attack pass by without retaliation?' asked Lily.

Eddie frowned as he once again considered his response. 'Without saying too much, I think my presence in your fine country may give you at least a partial answer.'

Anna's mother busied herself, making sure each of her guests had enough to eat. Catching her husband's eye, she urged him to move the conversation to something more positive.

'Whether the tragedy takes place in the middle of the Atlantic Ocean or strikes down Ted Fleming here in the village, the effect on the loved ones of those affected is the same the world over.'

Helen glared at her husband, before he added, 'Dreadful though these things are, we must, and shall, overcome all adversity. Now, on to more positive things. What are you two up to for the rest of the day?'

Anna immediately caught on. 'Believe it or not, Eddie has persuaded – or should I say bribed – me to go fishing. My price was a slap-up meal in Aylsham.'

The vicar almost choked on his carrots. 'But you can't bring yourself to handle anything from the fishmongers; how will you manage to catch live specimens?'

She laughed. 'I've no intention of going anywhere near a fish. However, I still get the meal in a posh restaurant, don't I, Eddie?'

By one-thirty, they were parked up at Narborough Waters, which she'd promised her companion was famed for its large trout.

'I see someone has beaten us to it.' Eddie pointed to an extensive range of fishing equipment resting by the water's edge. A few feet back stood a small canvas tent. 'I guess he's been night fishing, so he must have a real love of the hobby to still be here.'

Anna glanced around the open water surrounded by a thick stand of trees. 'I assume he's answering the call of nature. Well, shall we set up next to him?'

The American gave Anna an astonished look. 'Of course not. If we do, we'll be in each other's way and scare the fish off. They can hear as well as see us, you know.'

'Don't say it as if I should know these things. This is the first time I've been anywhere near a fishing rod, so – now how do you Americans put it – suck it up, pal.'

She could hear Eddie chuckling to himself as he selected a spot fifty feet from their absent neighbour.

The next ten minutes passed as Anna watched in fascination as Eddie unpacked then assembled his rod and line, hooks and bait. 'Are you quite ready now? Otherwise, it'll be dark before you get that thing into the water.' She pointed to a brightly coloured, artificial feathered fly attached to a fearsome-looking hook.

Eddie took up position for his first cast. 'I make my own flies. Attractive, don't you—'

'Are you mad, why are you getting into the water?'

'It's fine; I've got my waders on, and the water's not too deep. By going in a few feet, I get my line exactly where I want.'

Satisfied of his sanity, Anna rolled out a waxed canvas ground-sheet and sat down as she listened to Eddie explain the intricacies of trout fishing and what sort of beast he was up against.

'From what you say about the size of the teeth, I'd be surprised if they're frightened of anything.' She caught a glimpse of the water's surface rippling where their absent companion had been fishing. 'Look, I think he's caught something.'

Eddie gave Anna a quick glance as he began to feel something pulling on his line. 'That doesn't make any sense because he's taken his rod with him.'

Realising her companion wasn't paying her any attention, Anna got to her feet and strolled towards the night fishermen's tiny tent. She moved towards the water's edge and froze. 'Eddie, there's something below the surface. I can't quite make it out, but—'

The American's irritation became apparent as he pulled his rod, only for his catch to slip away. 'But what, Anna?'

Picking up a broken branch, she poked the object. To her horror, it rolled over and surfaced. She screamed.

In seconds, Eddie managed to get out of the water and run to Anna's side, despite the restrictions imposed by his rubber waders. 'Dear Lord, poor man. We need to get him out. Are you OK?'

Anna quickly recovered her composure and took hold of the man's legs. At the same time, Eddie slid back into the water and lifted the corpse up by placing his hands under its shoulders.

For a few seconds, both stood looking down at the sad scene.

'I know him. It's Cyril Trubshaw. He's the village baker. Do you think he's the absent angler?'

Eddie bent down to take a closer look at the cold, pale figure, his wet hair continuing to shed droplets of water onto the short grass. 'It's hard to say, but it's too much of a coincidence that an angler disappears, then a body turns up, right by all this gear.' He went through the man's pockets to identify the corpse. 'Wait a minute, look at this.'

Anna watched as her companion unbuttoned the man's shirt to reveal more of his neck. 'Is that what I think it is? Perhaps he got caught in the line, fell in and drowned?'

Eddie shook his head as he diligently inspected a piece of wire around the baker's neck. 'This is no fishing line, at least, not for trout fishing. He'd have to have been fishing for tuna to get anywhere near using such a heavy gauge.'

'Perhaps that's all he had, what with rationing and everything?'

The American rubbed a finger along the steel cord. 'Judging by the quality of what he's wearing and the gear on the bank, this man was a serious angler and would never have attempted to use this stuff.'

Eddie realised Anna had fallen silent. 'What's the matter?'

She leant closer to the body, brushing wet hair from his forehead. 'Ted Fleming and this man were best mates.' Anna looked at Eddie with foreboding.

'And seemingly both died from being garrotted, Anna.'

Finding a public telephone box to inform the police took some time. It took even longer for the police to arrive, by which time, daylight was beginning to fade.

'You say you found him around four-thirty?' Detective Inspector Spillers listened carefully as Eddie recounted the afternoon's events.

Meanwhile, Constable Bradshaw busied himself donning his waders and slipping into the ice-cold water, which amounted to an attempt to impress his superior by finding any evidence he could lay his hands on. It didn't take long for his efforts to be rewarded. 'I found the rod, at least, what's left of it.' All eyes fell on the beaming policeman as he held the broken artefact above his head, its reel still attached just beyond the handgrip.

Inspector Spillers took a close interest in what was left of the fishing line, comparing it to the material wrapped tightly around Cyril Trubshaw's neck. 'It's a match. I've asked Doctor Brabham to join us so he can certify death. He should be here soon, but I don't think there's much doubt concerning cause.'

On cue, a cream Austin Windsor saloon pulled up next to the detective's car. 'Sad sight, Inspector. Anna, what are you doing here?'

She quickly briefed him as he knelt beside the body.

'It's clear to me what killed this man. What is less clear is how it came to be. How does an experienced angler end up with that lot around his neck? I can tell you that Cyril had a heart condition. It's possible that he suffered another angina attack, panicked and got himself tied up in his line. However, we won't know for sure until an autopsy is completed.'

Having documented an approximate time of death, the doctor departed as an ambulance arrived. Within twenty minutes, the body had been removed. Inspector Spillers had also left with clear instructions to his constable that nothing should be disturbed.

Anna noticed Tom Bradshaw looking at her, his chest puffed out as he guarded the death scene. She gave him a broad smile in recognition of their long friendship.

Walking back to collect the rest of his gear, Eddie turned to Anna. 'This wasn't an accident. No angler I know would allow himself to get tangled up in his line, which, by the way, does not match the remnants left on his reel, despite what the good inspector says.'

Helping her companion to pack his fishing tackle away, Anna nodded. 'I agree. The worrying thing is, it means two villagers, both known to the other, died in broadly the same way within eight days of each other. Common sense tells me this is more than a coincidence.'

'I don't believe in coincidences,' replied Eddie.

Monday morning was an important one for Lieutenant Elsner. He had been summoned by his superior, Colonel Bob Murphy, to a meeting in their London Headquarters.

After disembarking his train at Liverpool Street Station, Eddie walked the half-mile instead of hailing a taxi.

He was appalled at the amount of damage that enemy bombers had caused in only a few weeks. A bus lay upended against a derelict row of houses, its paintwork blackened from the intense heat of the explosion.

Further along the busy thoroughfare, emergency vehicles meandered their way around bomb craters in the road. Then Eddie came upon a scene that astonished him. In what remained of the shopfront of a men's apparel shop, its employees busied themselves brushing shards of glass from the pavement. In another, staff completed a new window display out of the wreckage. In a prominent position, leaning against one of the mannequins, rested a sizeable handwritten sign:

'Open for business as usual.'

Eddie marvelled at the tenacity and bravery of the locals as they got on with everyday life in what they appeared to regard as their new normal.

As he entered the heavily sandbagged entrance of his headquarters, two American servicemen snapped to attention and saluted the lieutenant. Returning the salute without looking at either man, Eddie passed into the ornate entrance lobby of what he judged must have been one of London's grander residences before the war.

'Good morning, Colonel.' It was Eddie's turn to snap to attention and offer a salute. Formalities over, Colonel Murphy gestured for his subordinate to join him at a large mahogany table, where a detailed map of Norfolk was spread on its pristine surface.

The lieutenant spent several minutes briefing the colonel on potential sites for airfield installations, along with his recommendations.

Colonel Murphy thanked Eddie for his detailed report before commenting. 'You've done what I asked you to do, and there's no doubt we'll accept many of your recommendations. However, things have become more urgent. You have seen, I'm sure, the devastation that's taking place in London. Our assessment is that the rate of attrition will intensify, not only here, but in all of England's major cities and ports. We need to be able to intercept enemy bombers hard and quick. We must also get Allied assets over enemy targets quickly when it's time to go on the offensive. That's why I want you to look at potential airfield sites much closer to the East coast—'

'But Colonel, they'll be—'

'I know the dangers, Lieutenant. Yes, they will be more

vulnerable to enemy attack than inland airfields, but the prize of shorter flight times to get our boys back home safe outweighs the risks. Do I make myself clear?'

'Yes, sir.'

The colonel turned his back on Eddie as he made his way to a rich wine-coloured leather chair. 'I want your report on my desk within two weeks, Lieutenant, so I suggest you hightail it back to Norfolk.'

Eddie's head spun as he left the grand building. He knew there was no time to be lost, and his superior would not accept failure. As he walked back to the train station, his progress was halted by an exhausted-looking fireman shouting for silence. In a well-practised drill, all those in hearing distance fell quiet. As he neared the dreadful scene, he watched as a second fireman delicately removed various bricks and roof tiles which had collapsed in on themselves.

'I can hear someone. It's a woman. Hey, you, get up here and help me.'

Eddie realised the exhausted man was speaking to him. Without thinking, he did as he was ordered. Carefully climbing the grotesque mound of debris, he lay on his side opposite the fireman.

'Gently as you can, now, throw this stuff down. We need to be quick; her voice is getting weaker.'

Minutes passed, which felt like hours to Eddie as they began to reveal the ashen face of a woman. Her hair felt rough to his touch from brick dust as he tried to comfort her.

'Can you manage here, my friend? I'm being called to investigate another possible survivor. Give me a shout when you need a hand to get her out, OK?'

Eddie acknowledged the man without speaking as he focused his efforts on trying to release the strangely calm woman from her obliterated home. He worked quickly until the whole of her upper body and both arms were free, yet she made little movement. Eddie watched as her eyes began to close.

'Stay with me. What's your name? Keep your eyes open, come on, lady, stay with me.'

He quickly realised her injuries were so severe there was no way she'd survive. Nevertheless, he continued to peel away layer after layer of plaster, wood and brick. For a few seconds, she regained consciousness. Eddie became aware of a hand movement. He looked to see what she was holding between a grime-covered finger and thumb. 'Family?'

The woman managed to blink her eyes in acknowledgement.

Eddie delicately removed a three-inch square faded photo-graph of a young girl and adult with their arms around each other. 'Your daughter?'

He watched as, for the first and last time, the woman managed the tiniest of smiles to break across her cracked, dry lips and sunken cheeks.

Suddenly she seemed energised. 'Find… tell Mum loves…' Her energy leeched away. Eddie held her hand as she closed her eyes for the final time.

No more pain. Rest in peace, lady.

Meanwhile, Anna busied herself hobbling to see Doctor Brabham, concerned that her ankle was taking much longer to heal than expected and keen to get the matter sorted. She became aware of somebody watching her as she made her way down High Street.

'Miss Grix, I work for The Duke and—'

'I know who you are. What do you want?'

The burly man smiled. 'Me? I don't want anything. The Duke, on the other hand, well; let's say he enjoys your company and would like to see you again.'

Anna tried to dodge the colossal frame of her interrogator. 'I should love to meet your boss again after our date was cut short on Saturday; however, I have an appointment with my doctor.' She tried to sidestep the heavy once again.

'Perhaps I have not made myself clear. You'll be driven to see The Duke now.' He pointed to something behind Anna.

She turned to see a glimmering black Bentley parked a few yards up the road, its engine hardly audible, save for a faint rumble from its powerful engine.

Anna knew it was pointless offering further resistance and settled into the back of the luxurious car.

No one spoke for the next twenty-five minutes as she was driven further into the Norfolk countryside. Unexpectedly, the driver swung left. At first, Anna thought they were going to crash until she caught sight of a well-disguised entrance.

Once through the gates, the vista opened to reveal immaculately tended grounds and flowerbeds laid out in the formal style. Within minutes, the Bentley came to a stop under a stone portico. A liveried butler waited at the top of a short flight of sandstone steps. He gestured for Anna to follow him into the morning room.

The Duke was charm itself as he greeted his guest. 'Anna. How wonderful to see you again and thank you for joining me at such short notice. Perhaps you'll have a drink?' He turned to his butler who was already pouring two large whiskies into lead crystal glasses, similar to those his heavies had produced at the barn dance. 'How is your aunt, by the way; I do hope she survived the night?'

Anna knew she had to think on her feet. 'Dear Cissy – she's still with us thanks to my father's prayers and the incredible skills of Doctor Brabham.' She worked hard to maintain eye contact with The Duke so as not to raise his suspicions that she was lying.

The Duke lifted one of the whisky glasses from a delicate low-level table and handed it to Anna. 'Ah yes, the good doctor. I know him well. We sometimes do business together, scratch each other's back, you might say. I'll pass on your compliments to him when next we meet.'

Not giving Anna time to respond, a tactic she recognised as one her host liked to employ, the man quickly moved on. 'Now, since you're here, why don't I show you around my little house.'

I hate you.

She followed as he presented room after room filled with expensive furniture and paintings. She tried to remember the layout of the house so that she could make her escape if it became necessary.

'Tell me all about your mother and father. After all, they're an important mainstay of the village, and I like to get to know all the important people.'

Anna's mind raced as she tried to second-guess what he was up to. 'Oh, I don't know. To me, they're my mum and dad. Mum does a lot of charity work and Dad does what vicars do. I'm not sure there's much more to say.'

The Duke led his guest into a vast dining room decorated in the Georgian style. 'This used to be the great hall when the manor house was first built. What tales this room could tell if it could talk. Speaking of which, I suppose your father must be told all manner of things from people in pain or despair, or whatever it is that ordinary people have to put up with.'

What an arrogant twerp.

'And you're not ordinary?' Anna worried she'd gone too far. He surprised her by laughing.

'Quite right, Anna, quite right. It's always the case that some float to the top while others struggle through life, to mix my metaphors. I've fought for all I have, Miss Grix. Being a simple man, I live by just two rules. The first is that no one takes what is mine. The second is that I don't tolerate anyone ratting on me. The Duke's smile morphed into a sneer as he narrowed his eyes. 'You see, people tend to underestimate others. I, on the other hand, underestimate no one. Like your father, I like to speak to many people. You might be interested in knowing what they say about you?'

Anna ran her palm over the long oak tabletop and checked for dust.

Clean as a whistle; he must have at least one woman working for him.

'I'm sure you're going to tell me.'

Leading Anna into a well-stocked library, from which she assumed he hadn't read a single title, she gave her host a disarming smile.

'I'm familiar with that look, Anna; you're playing with me, you naughty girl. Remember me asking you the other day if you could be a naughty girl?'

Anna's blood ran cold. 'There's all the difference in the world between naughtiness and politeness. Being the vicar's daughter, I'm polite.'

The Duke roared as he selected a random book from one of several oak shelves, glanced at its spine and replaced it. 'Excellent response, Anna. I can see you are nobody's fool.'

She decided to push her luck again. 'Speaking of which, I need to get back. Doctor Brabham – he was expecting me an hour ago.'

The Duke looked concerned. 'Of course, how remiss of me, your ankle. Does it hurt terribly? Your American friend really must learn to drive on the correct side of the road, or we shall all be in danger.'

How did he know about that?

She glanced at her lower leg. For now, the adrenaline racing through her veins dulled the pain. 'It's kind of you to enquire. Yes, it's horrible. All the more reason to get it seen to, so if your driver could give me a lift back to the village?'

A familiar sneer spread across The Duke's face. 'Please don't mind your pretty little head; you're quite safe, at least while you're with me.'

Anna's anxiety grew as she detected his demeanour changing from polite host to menacing kidnapper.

Striding from the library into a small sitting room, he invited his guest to sit. 'There, that's taken the weight off your ankle. Perhaps you'd like to hear a little about how I spend my days?'

Again, she tried to interpret his actions.

Where is this going?

'As I said, I need to—'

'Yes, you did, didn't you? Anyway, I like to think of myself as a sort of banker. People leave their money with me. Sometimes they get it back with interest. Of course, some take rather than give, and when it comes to money, Miss Grix, there is no more serious a matter. As I said earlier, I fought hard to get where I am today. No one keeps from me what is mine. Such things make me so sad and believe me, Anna, no one should take the risk of making me sad.'

'Do I make you sad?'

The Duke looked surprised. 'You, my dear? Not at all. You bring the greatest joy to me, which, in a time of war, is a great gift. Talking of gifts, you have something for me, have you not?'

Anna tensed, waiting for him to make a move on her. 'A gift?'

The Duke walked over to where Anna was sitting so that he towered over her.

'Information, Anna, information. Now tell me all about your American friend. After all, you don't want me to be sad, do you?'

Chapter 12: Follow My Leader

Relieved but exhausted that The Duke had enjoyed his sport for the day and she was now free, Anna contented herself with nestling into the luxurious rear seat of the Bentley.

He's one dangerous creep.

Her journey back to the vicarage was, as with the outward journey, completed in silence, except this time, it was she who had little inclination to make conversation.

As the immense vehicle stopped opposite the church, neither minder made any effort to help her from the car. Instead, they remained motionless, eyes fixed to the front.

Opening one of the massive rear doors, Anna moved through ninety degrees so that she could put both feet on the narrow pathway to support her ankle injury. Suddenly, she caught sight of Eddie rounding the corner. Gesturing as discreetly as she could, Anna was relieved he got the message and doubled back around the gable end of the old tannery.

Seconds later, the Bentley moved forward as if in a grand procession. This was the signal for the lieutenant to reappear. 'You look as if you've seen a ghost. Anything to do with that car?'

Anna took a minute to explain what had happened while he'd been in London.

'You need a drink. Let's get you to the King's Head.'

Anna gave him a sideways glance. 'You must be joking – I can't be seen in the village pub on a Monday evening, especially not this early. There'd be half a dozen of my father's flock lining up outside the vestry, ready to tell him the world was about to end.'

The American shoved his hands deep into his trouser pockets and shrugged his shoulders. 'I don't get you people. One minute you're saving a few pennies to buy a Spitfire, the next you're quite happy tearing each other apart.'

'It's a speciality of ours. Anyway, I've got a better idea. Horsey Windpump is only about half an hour away, and there's a great spot overlooking the Broad.'

Eddie told Anna to wait while he collected the Jeep, and soon they were heading east. As Lipton Saint Faith receded into the distance, Anna felt increasingly relaxed.

So, what were you up to in London while I was being kidnapped?'

Now it was Eddie's turn to recount events, though he was careful not to give Anna any detail of his real mission.

'That's terribly sad, but brave of you to get involved.'

Eddie shrugged his shoulders again as he crunched the Jeep's gears to pick up speed. 'You'd have done the same. You're walking past something terrible, somebody asks you to help… It's an easy decision, don't you agree?'

'I agree it's a decision many would take. On the other hand, some people would've kept their head down and pretended nothing was happening. You said there was a photograph?'

Eddie kept one hand on the steering wheel while retrieving the grainy image from his breast pocket.

'They look so happy together. Whoever that young girl is, she's lost her mother. I know the same thing is happening all over the world, but still, when faced with an image, it makes the tragedy all the more real.'

The American didn't answer. Instead, he rammed the clutch pedal to the floor and moved the gearstick with such force that Anna thought he might snap it off.

You're a deep one.

With the Jeep bouncing along a ramrod straight road, the site of Horsey Windpump in the distance represented welcome relief for Anna.

'Sorry, it's a bit rough. What did you make your roads from in England?'

Anna raised an eyebrow. 'Are you seriously telling me that every road in America is as smooth as glass?'

'No, but at least our vehicles have a suspension that means you're not shaken to death.'

Not bothering to engage in what Anna considered a ridiculous conversation, she pointed to where Eddie should pull off the road.

'OK, so this is what you call a windpump. Looks like a pretty windmill to me.'

'I suppose you're right; both types look roughly the same, use the same technology, except they do very different jobs. One grinds grain, this one pumps water to drain the land, or move it to where it's needed.'

Anna led Eddie over the wooden staging next to the windpump, which allowed access to the far side of the narrow waterway.

'Looks like some of these boats are in hibernation for the duration. What are those big ones called?'

She pointed to one vessel in particular. 'It's called a wherry. I guess you could say they're the workhorses of the Broads. Years ago, the roads were so bad it was easier to transport heavy stuff around by water.'

'What, you mean the roads were worse than they are today?'

'No, but the Broads are needed more than ever now. Wherries quickly get supplies where they're needed. Anyway, enough of all that history stuff; look, there's the clearing I told you about.'

Sitting on an old wooden bench at the far edge of the clearing, they watched grey herons as they perched and waited for prey to show itself on the silken surface of the Broad. Occasionally a marsh harrier zipped across the sky on the lookout for its next meal.

'It sure is pretty here. Who'd have thought there was a war on?'

Silence fell as they took in the magnificent expanse of water enveloped by a lush green landscape. All that disturbed the flatness of their surroundings was a network of water pumps and church spires.

'Come on, there's a pub about a mile up the road. You can treat me to a shandy.'

'I thought you said you couldn't be seen in a pub on a Monday evening?'

'I did, but no one knows me around here, so I say we should throw caution to the wind. Are you up for it?'

Entering the cosy atmosphere of the Smugglers Arms, their arrival was met with several friendly smiles.

'A bit different from your village pub,' whispered Eddie.

She didn't answer and instead made for the small bar, where the landlord was busy drying glasses with a brilliant white tea-towel.

'Now, you two, what's your poison?' The man's pleasant smile put Anna at ease.

Order placed, she looked around the small space. Her gaze latched on to an elderly couple sitting at a round table with two empty chairs.

'May we join you?'

The old lady smiled. 'Of course, sit you down here. It's nice to have a bit of company isn't it, Albert.' She dug an elbow into her husband's arm as an incentive for him to put his newspaper down.

'As you wish,' he said in a tone that implied they were an unnecessary disturbance. Nevertheless, he folded his newspaper in two and placed it onto the heavily varnished tabletop.

'Anything interesting?' asked Eddie as the pair took their seats opposite the old couple.

The old man pointed to a headline with a nicotine-stained finger. 'I say he should be shot without delay. The man's only out to make trouble.'

His wife gave Anna a wistful look. 'My husband is always the same. Ignore him; everyone else does.'

The old man busied himself by lighting a Woodbine cigarette, then turned his head so the smoke wafted away from his guests.

'Who should be shot?' asked Eddie.

The old man stabbed at the headline again. 'Rudolf Hess, of course. You're not telling me he flew all the way over here without his boss knowing and, no doubt, help from some of our own toffs.'

Anna and the old man's wife continued to exchange exasperated looks.

Can we not get away from the war for one evening?

'By the look of your uniform and accent, you're an American, so will your government round up what you call "suspect aliens" and stick them in internment camps like you did in the last war?'

Eddie fell back on his conservative characteristics before jumping in with a knee-jerk response. 'I guess it depends on what happens. For now, we're not at war, but who can say what the future will bring. I suppose people are frightened and looking for scapegoats. You know, different means enemy, which isn't right, is it?'

The old man tapped his newspaper yet again. 'Oh, I don't know, we've done the same and packed them off to the Isle of Man.'

Anna could feel anger surging but had no wish to embarrass the old man. 'I agree with Eddie that people are frightened, which sometimes leads them to make hasty decisions. Anyway, I think it's time we got going before my father thinks I'm lost. Knowing him, he'll have a search party scouring the Broads for me.' Anna smiled to take the heat out of what might have developed into an awkward conversation concerning internment.

The old man took another puff of his cigarette and again blew the smoke away from his table companions. 'Well, make sure you young people watch out for yourselves. And keep an eye out for those Nazi spies dropping by parachute. My mate Eric says he's seen two in the last week alone.'

Anna watched as his wife shook her head while nudging her husband with her empty glass and pointing at the bar.

By the time the Jeep pulled away from the Smugglers Arms, the light had almost gone, and an eerie mist hung over the Norfolk landscape.

'We occasionally get this sort of weather in Colorado. I guess you could call it atmospheric.'

'I suppose that's one way of describing it. As if the blackout isn't enough to contend with, now we can't see more than ten feet in front of us. This should make for an interesting journey.'

Eddie switched on the windscreen wipers, which proved utterly incapable of dealing with the conditions. He quickly pulled over, undid two securing latches and folded the windscreen forward so that it rested on the bonnet.

'Do you think we can believe what we read in the newspapers or hear on the radio?'

The American was too busy attempting to get the Jeep's gearbox to play fair, forcing her to repeat the question.

'You know, before 1914, people used the term "propaganda" to mean the dissemination of information. That sort of got corrupted during the First World War to mean edited highlights presented in a certain way as determined by leaders. Things are no different now. All we can hope is that our leaders do what they do for the right reason.'

'Does that include that awful Lord Haw-Haw creature?'

Eddie turned to Anna. 'There's a lot of difference between what the government says to its own people and the grotesque bile that sprouts from that traitor's mouth. The trouble is, it has an effect. You repeated his name, which means you'll have remembered some of the lies he spits out in every broadcast he gives. I'm sure Mr Hitler thinks that's a good thing. I doubt Mr Churchill feels quite the same, but I imagine your government gets up to some of the same tricks as our enemies. Wow, what a profound conversation for a damp foggy night in the middle of nowhere.'

They exchanged smiles as Eddie continued to battle the elements. Progress remained slow.

'Hitting patch after patch of dense mist then perfectly clear weather is what makes these conditions so dangerous. One second you can't see a hand in front of you, the next it's clear as a bell. I just hope that…'

Anna was startled by his sudden silence. 'What's the matter?'

Eddie's eyes were glued to his wing mirror. 'I think we're being followed.'

She half-turned to get a decent view of behind the Jeep but saw nothing. 'Are you sure?'

The American began to vary his focus between watching out for the next fog bank and the barely discernible car chasing them. 'Yes, I'm certain, and they're catching up.'

Eddie pressed hard on the accelerator and leant forward to gain a better view of anything that might be coming the other way.

'Listen, Eddie, there's a little track coming up around the next corner. It will be on your right, but you won't get any warning it's there. You have to trust me to turn the second I tell you. Are you OK with that?'

Eddie took another quick glance in his wing mirror. 'Hobson's choice, I reckon, but yes, I trust you.'

As the Jeep rounded the bend, they hit a dense patch of fog, making it almost impossible to see.

'Now, Eddie. Turn right now.'

The American did as she ordered. 'Heaven help us if you're wrong; I can't see a damn thing.' A few seconds later, they found themselves in a narrow farm track with a line of mature trees on either side, forming a dense canopy.

As soon as they came to a stop, Eddie extinguished the Jeep's lights, before hearing the familiar sound of a Bentley roaring past the track entrance.

'Where are you going?' said Anna as she watched Eddie leap from the vehicle.

As he disappeared over a low hedge, he whispered loud enough for her to hear, 'That was the same car that dropped you off. My guess is that The Duke's thugs are under orders to, how can I put it, make our lives uncomfortable.'

By the time Anna started to shake her head in acknowledgement, Eddie had disappeared. Suddenly she felt vulnerable.

Why leave me alone now?

Anna detected the sound of the Bentley again. She thought about hiding but to her horror, found she was rooted to the spot, such was her level of anxiety. Now it was too late; the Bentley had reversed and parked across the entrance to the trackway. Just at that moment, the fog bank began to lift, leaving Anna more terrified than ever.

I've got to get away.

She could now see the car, which meant the two thugs could see the Jeep with her perched in the passenger seat. Anna watched as the two huge men slowly made their way towards her. Walking side by side, they completely blocked the track.

Eddie, where are you?

She watched as The Duke's henchmen quickened their pace. One of them reached into his trench coat pocket and pulled something out. Although Anna couldn't see what it was, she made a reasoned guess it was a pistol. Waiting for the inevitable, she was unable to take her eyes off the thugs. To her great relief, both men suddenly spun on the spot then ran back towards the main road. Incredibly, their car was rolling backwards and soon disappeared.

'Are you OK?'

Eddie's sudden reappearance frightened the life out of Anna. 'Where in heaven's name have you been? I could have been killed.'

Her companion jumped into the driver's seat and fired up the Jeep. 'Fortunately, you weren't, but I reckon we've got about a minute to get away.'

Chapter 13: A Precious Haul

Still shaken from events of the previous evening, Anna set about tidying her father's vegetable patch to distract herself.

On her hands and knees, she didn't see Constable Tom Bradshaw leaning against the vicarage's low boundary wall. 'Last time I saw you doing that, you were using one or two choice words after breaking a nail. It's good to see you've got a pair of gloves on this time.'

Anna jumped at the sudden noise, which broke an otherwise quiet Tuesday morning in Lipton Saint Faith. 'Do they teach bobbies to creep up on people like that at training school?'

Tom Bradshaw made light of the situation. 'Yes, and I was top of the class when it came to creeping.' He winked and offered a cheeky smile.

The constable's disarming manner helped Anna forget her current predicament for a few seconds. 'You always did think that smile and wicked sense of humour would get you out of trouble, didn't you?' She returned her friend's smile.

Carefully removing her father's gardening gloves, she laid them on the ground. Anna limped over to the constable, taking care not to damage any of the crops that were crammed into the small area.

'Seems to work most of the time. It comes in handy when Betty Simpson's trying to get rid of her punters at closing time. Give me a smile and joke over a truncheon and handcuffs any time. Anyway, it saves me paperwork back at the station.'

Anna smiled, but her heart wasn't in it.

'I know you, Anna Grix, something is upsetting you. Let me guess; it's finding Cyril in that trout lake, isn't it?'

Tom's obvious concern took Anna by surprise, even though they'd known each other since childhood.

Don't let me cry in front of him.

'Hey, come on. I didn't mean to upset you, I—'

She forced a smile, blinked and wiped away a tear from each eye. 'I'm just daft. Yes, finding Cyril was horrible, but it's made me think about Ted Fleming as well.' Anna sat on the low wall and half-twisted her body so that she could face Tom.

The constable frowned. 'So you're still looking into Ted's death, are you? What has Cyril having a funny turn, falling in the lake and managing to strangle himself in the process got to do with Ted?'

'It's not funny, Tom. It was horrible seeing him like that.'

Bradshaw began to blush. 'You're right, of course.' Tom broke into a smile again. 'But you've got to admit it, if you saw a film with Abbott and Costello mucking about with a fishing rod and falling in the water, you'd laugh, wouldn't you?'

Anna's demeanour stiffened. 'Tom Bradshaw, you're a horrible person. My father always taught me that policemen are upstanding, kind and considerate people, at least to those who aren't criminals.'

145

Tom gave her a weary look. 'I know I'm only a village bobby, but if you had to deal with the things I do and see, day in, day out, you'd use gallows humour as well. We all do it: nurses, firemen, the people who dig bodies from bombed-out buildings… To be honest, it's a release. Better that than having a fit of the heebie-jeebies or going mad.'

Her friend's candid explanation brought Anna to her senses. 'I'm sorry, Tom. You've made me realise I'm feeling sorry for myself. I guess we all get wrapped up in our own little world. We forget the horrible things other people have to deal with. Am I forgiven?'

The constable offered the faintest of smiles. 'There's nothing to apologise for. The world's gone mad, and I think it's beginning to affect how we all react to events. Heaven knows how long this mess will go on for. Let's hope there's some humanity left at the end of it all.'

There's more to you than I thought, Tom Bradshaw.

Beatrice Flowers, the village busybody, passed by. 'It seems to me that the police have too much time on their hands if they can stand around gossiping with unattached ladies.'

The pair watched wide-eyed as Beatrice passed without looking at either of them or making any further comment.

'She didn't say that when I rescued her cat from that drainpipe. Come to think of it, she didn't say anything at all, apart from shouting at me for swearing when her stupid moggy bit me.'

They looked at each other and burst out laughing.

A few seconds passed before Anna lost her smile again. 'The thing is, Tom; Eddie and I think there's a link between the deaths of Ted Fleming and Cyril Trubshaw. We can't put our hand on it yet, but we know there's something. I know I shouldn't ask, but is there anything you can think of that'll get Inspector Spillers to keep the cases open?'

Tom removed his bobby's helmet and ran three fingers through his bronze-coloured hair. 'The big bosses in Norwich have already made their mind up about Ted. As far as they're concerned, it was an accident and that's that. As for Cyril, we won't know how he died until the autopsy's been done. As usual, there's a delay, so for now we don't know, but you heard what my inspector said when he looked over Cyril's body.'

Anna persisted. 'Tom is there nothing you can do to—'

'If I broach the subject with Sergeant Ilford, never mind the inspector, one more time, I'll get my head bitten off. And they'll have you for interfering in police work. I wish things were different, but there it is.'

Tom placed his helmet back on and adjusted the chinstrap to its regulation position.

Sensing he was about to leave, Anna tried one last time. 'I get that, but there is something else... What can you tell me about The Duke?'

Tom drilled his steely blue eyes into Anna. 'Some advice from one friend to another: don't go anywhere near him. To say he's dangerous is an understatement. We know he's up to all sorts but can never get the evidence to pick him up. It's always his sidekicks that cop for it – and they never talk.'

'Why the sudden interest in Norfolk's wildlife?' Anna had to shout over the noise of the Jeep's engine and creaky suspension as they moved from one location to another.

'It's your fault; you were the one who pointed to all those birds on the Broad. If I'm honest, it kinda fired something up inside me that made me want to see more.'

Anna held on for her life as a rough track caused her to bounce on the hard passenger seat and sway from side to side. 'You may have noticed, Eddie, there isn't any water here. If you'd have asked instead of whisking me away before I had time to think, I could have taken you to Wroxham; there's plenty to see there.'

He smiled and continued to fight with the steering wheel. 'The people who I'm staying with, you know, Hilda and Albert, told me about all the barn owls you can see around here. I thought we should take a look and, if nothing else, it will take our minds off almost being killed last night and Constable Bradshaw telling you to steer clear of The Duke.'

Anna frowned as memories of the previous evening came flooding back. 'Who do you suppose they were after, me or you?'

'I guess we'll never know. Perhaps I spooked them as they came for you. And, of course, I took the handbrake off their car, so when it started to move, they must have wondered if they'd been rumbled.

'If I know one thing about their types, it's that they have a strong survival instinct. Also, I doubt either of them relished the thought of having to explain to their boss how they came to write his car off, had they not caught up with it.'

As Anna continued to be thrown around like a rag doll, she noticed the recent dry spell had caused all the off-road surfaces to set like concrete. 'Well, all I can say is good riddance to them and I'd rather forget last night, thank you very much. So, let's talk barn owls, shall we? First of all, it's the middle of the day, and the sun is beating down, so you're hardly likely to see any. Second of all, I don't see any barns, do you? Other than that, this should be fun.'

Eddie risked taking one hand off the steering wheel to change gear, which almost put them in a ditch as the Jeep caught yet another deep rut.

'Don't you think enough people are trying to kill us without you doing it for them? Where exactly are we heading?'

As she finished asking, the Jeep passed through a large open gate, allowing the vehicle access to a vast ploughed field. Parking on a grass strip running around the area, Eddie shut off the engine, allowing them both to take in the near-total silence of their billiard table-flat surroundings.

'And your plan is…?'

'My plan is to get you out of this vehicle, have a great walk and clear our minds.'

Anna frowned. 'I assume you've forgotten my ankle, you know, the one you ran over last week.' She pointed to her tightly bandaged lower leg.

'There you go again, making me feel guilty. Well, this time, it won't work. I know it sounds counterintuitive, but my grandpa says keeping moving is the best medicine.' Eddie had walked several yards before realising she hadn't followed. 'Come on, lazybones, we've a long way to go.'

Anna scowled. 'If ever I meet your grandfather, I'll give him a piece of my mind. Now come here and give me your arm before I get back into the Jeep and leave you to it.'

Eddie smiled. 'I don't think you and my grandpa would get on. You're both stubborn, opinionated, and you both kick against authority. On the other hand, it'd be fun to watch the two of you fighting with each other.'

Anna grabbed her companion's arm and leant into him as they began to move off. 'So, it's all right for an old man to be independent-minded, but not a woman?' Keeping her eyes firmly fixed on the uneven ground to avoid further injury, Anna burned with indignation.

'I said nothing of the sort, and I refuse to be provoked. You know as well as I do that women now do everything that men do, apart from fighting on the front line. I suppose you really are all daughters of Emmeline Pankhurst.'

He knows his history.

'If you mean that ordinary women over twenty-one in England were finally allowed to put a cross on a piece of paper thirteen years ago; yes, I suppose I am. But don't ask me to be grateful for what should have been my right in the first place. As for the jobs women do now, you know as well as I do that, like after the First World War, we'll be chucked out of work and expected to get back into our kitchens when the men come home.'

A short silence fell before Eddie fired back. 'Don't blame ordinary men for the things politicians do. A case in point is what's happening now with the war. In the end, we all have to do what we're told, and yes, things are tough for women, I get that. But don't lay that injustice at my feet; things are not exactly rosy for any of us right now, are they?'

Anna realised she'd hit a raw nerve and let the matter drop. Instead, she explained to Eddie the range of crops grown in the area and how the landscape developed over time. Her plan to calm things down appeared to be working well until they were rudely interrupted.

'Get you off my land.'

The sudden order jolted both to look behind them. It was the first time Anna had experienced a twelve-bore shotgun being pointed at her.

'Is there something wrong?' she asked politely.

The farmer lifted his shotgun to a more menacing position. 'I said get you off my land. This is private property, and I'm sick and tired of people poking their nose into my business, especially the likes of you.' The burly farmer shifted his shotgun so that it now pointed straight at Eddie.

The American opened his palms to the aggressor. 'Sir, I'm truly sorry if we're on your land without permission. Blame it on a stupid foreigner who doesn't know his way around your customs. Now, please put that gun down.'

The farmer didn't move. 'Why are you here again?'

His accusation startled Anna, who glared at Eddie.

'I assure you, sir, I have not been in this field before.' The lieutenant stared straight at Anna.

Their tormentor shrugged his shoulders, making his gun jump momentarily. 'You all look the same to me. This is my land, and nobody has the right to take it from me, not you, not the Nazis, not the king himself. Do you understand?'

Anna knew the increasingly angry farmer's words were intended for Eddie and not her.

What's going on?

Eddie squared up to the farmer. 'I get it, sir, I truly do. Now, you have a decision to make. You either shoot us or put your gun down and allow us to continue peacefully walking in the countryside. As I said, I don't understand your customs, but I'm guessing this grass strip is here for the public to walk along, am I right?'

Anna watched the grizzled man as his eyes flicked between them. After what seemed like an age, she sensed him relaxing. A few seconds later, he lowered the shotgun and broke it open to reveal the firing caps of two cartridges. Removing the lead shot, he shouldered the gun and grunted.

'I thank you, sir, and promise we shall do no damage to your land.'

Eddie's calming manner impressed Anna.

The farmer gave them one last angry look, before turning and shuffling off into the distance.

'Phew, that was almost worse than those thugs last night,' said Anna.

'Jeeze, who needs enemies when you've got locals like him to deal with. Anyway, let's get going before he changes his mind. Here, give me your arm.'

Anna did as she was asked. Although progress was slow and she winced from time to time, she was, nevertheless, enjoying being out and about in the Norfolk landscape.

Out of nowhere, the sky clouded over, and it started to pour with rain.

'This is another example of your eccentric English weather, is it?'

She released her grip on Eddie and attempted to cover as much of her head as possible to keep the rain off. 'Believe it or not, East Anglia is one of the driest parts of the country.'

Eddie shrugged his shoulders. 'You could have fooled me. Come on, let's head for those trees.'

Difficult though it was for Anna to keep up, knowing the alternative meant getting soaked, she moved as quickly towards a dense thicket of mature elm trees. 'What do people say about not sheltering under a tree in a thunderstorm?'

Her companion took off his cap and placed it on Anna's head to keep her dry. 'Straight choice, lady. Shelter under a tree canopy and risk being hit by lightning or get soaked to the skin. Over to you.'

Anna wasn't quite sure whether he was joking. Deciding not to take the chance and worried her hair would be ruined, she followed him into the dense canopy.

'That's better; at least we're only getting dripped on from the branches rather than a total soaking.'

'So says the American cavalry. Make sure you keep an eye out for lightning. My hair is already soaked; I don't want it singed within an inch of its life.'

He roared with laughter. 'I do love the English sense of humour, even if it's barking mad.'

Eddie waited for Anna to react. She didn't. Instead, she had moved a few feet and was staring at something further on. 'Well, what do you know. Look at that.'

The American did his best to follow where she was pointing. 'Look at what? All I see is trees.'

She tutted. 'There, look over there. Looks like you'll see your owls, after all. It's a barn.'

Eddie concentrated hard as he came behind Anna and looked along her arm as if it were a gunsight. 'Good Lord, what the heck is a barn doing hidden away in here?'

Making their way over rugged terrain, they eventually found themselves in a clearing. The barn was entirely surrounded by giant trees, except for one end where a small track led to a narrow stretch of water.

'Looking at the wear of the barn, I guess it's been here for hundreds of years. Probably before the trees were even planted. After all, barns are used for storing things. It's no use to man nor beast if you can't easily access the thing.'

Eddie nodded. 'What's that thing people say about not looking a gift horse in the mouth? Let's get inside and dry out.'

Her companion easily unpicked a small padlock that guarded the building's entrance, allowing them access to its vast hay-filled interior.

'Cosy in here, isn't it?' said Anna. She watched as Eddie glanced at every nook and cranny of the ancient wooden structure.

'It reminds me of home, that smell. It must be the same the world over.'

Anna waited for the right moment before asking the question that had swirled around in her head for the last hour. 'What is it you do for a living, Eddie? Why was that farmer so angry when he saw you? He knew as well as I did that we were on a public right of way. Why should he have pointed his shotgun at you?'

Eddie stood rooted to the spot. 'You know, sometimes, for whatever reason, it isn't possible to say the things a person would like to say. You can see the uniform I wear; you know I drive a British Army Jeep. You even know I went to London the other day because I told you so. But sometimes one person shouldn't know what the other person does. It can be safer that way.'

Anna observed Eddie's body language. He was perfectly calm, hands, as usual, in his pockets. His facial features were open, and he kept eye contact with her.

'What, you mean safer than having a twelve-bore shotgun pointed at you? Or almost being killed by two thugs working for a criminal who doesn't seem to set much store by a person's life? Is that what you mean by keeping somebody safe?'

Eddie sniffed the air. 'You're confusing two things. The Duke, his thugs, all that stuff is your doing. You're the one who insisted we look into first one death, then a second. As for the farmer, I think he's simply a frightened old man trying to come to terms with a changing world. All I can tell you for now is that the less you know, the safer you'll be. I don't mean from angry farmers or small-time spivs. It's an ugly world we inhabit. If I hadn't been on that road, and you hadn't been on your bicycle in the same spot, we would never have met. The problem is, we did, and we're stuck with each other, at least for the time being.'

What are you, really?

Anna was stunned by Eddie's words and didn't know quite what to do or say next. Looking behind her, she noticed a low stack of hay bales and decided to take the weight off her feet while she thought of what to say to the American. As she began to sit, one of the hay bales shifted. A second began to fall, followed by others as the whole stack began to collapse.

'Watch out, it's coming down.' Eddie pulled her away just in time. For a few seconds, the barn was filled with flying bits of straw and a haze of dust. Eventually, the air cleared, leaving the two of them covered in a thin film of cereal.

'That was a close one.'

He didn't answer. Instead, he stepped forward a few paces. 'Will you look at that – what have we here?'

Anna hobbled forward. 'What are you talking about?'

Eddie knelt on one of the hay bales and peered into a gap caused by the collapse. 'I now know what Howard Carter felt like when he found Tutankhamun's burial chamber. Come and look – there's all sorts of stuff hidden behind this lot.' He got to his feet and stepped back to allow Anna a clear view.

'Good gracious, I bet this is black market stuff. Why else would somebody be hiding a load of cigarettes, chocolate and whatever else is in there? Perhaps our angry farmer had something to hide after all.' Anna fell silent.

Is that what all this is about?

'Is that what you are? Some kind of government intelligence bod, sent to unmask black marketeers? You almost got me killed just so you could take a look in here?'

'What, have you gone mad? I'm an American if it had escaped your notice. Do you think I've got nothing better to do than chase around the Norfolk countryside looking for contraband gear? For heaven's sake, grow up.'

Her nostrils flared and eyes widened. 'I don't know what I'm supposed to think. On the surface you're a perfectly pleasant man who agreed to help me. Or is it a convenient cover for whatever it is you do for a living? You tell me.'

Eddie shook his head, turned and walked towards the barn doors. Hesitating, he looked back to glare at Anna. 'I told you before; stop mixing up your madcap scheme to catch a killer and the fact that we inadvertently met. Whether you like it or not, I've said all I'm going to say, except to repeat that what you don't know can't hurt you. Now, I suggest we get back to the Jeep and I drive you home.'

In frustration, Anna threw the cap Eddie had given her and watched as it disappeared into a far corner of the mediaeval structure.

'Do you feel better for doing that? If you don't mind, I'd be obliged if you'd retrieve it so that I have a complete uniform to wear in front of my superiors.'

Anna regretted throwing the cap as soon as it had left her

hand. Wincing with pain as she scrambled over the haphazard stack of hay bales, she finally managed to get it. Half-turning to make her way back, she noticed something. 'There's a door back here, or did you already know?'

Eddie's face thundered. 'That's enough. How could I know there was a door there? Yet I sense you're not going to quit the barn until you see what's behind it, so go on, get on with it.'

His anger continued to upset her.

Is he my protector, or a spy?

Anna moved towards the door, turned the ancient doorknob and was surprised when it creaked open to reveal another large space, this time filled with metal cans. 'Come and have a look at this.'

'Why should I bother? According to you I already know what's in there.'

Her eyes were drawn to the remnant of a brown paper tag tied to one of the cans.

Dismissing the paper fragment, Anna glanced back at her companion. 'Please yourself. I'm sure the police will be more than interested.'

Eddie hesitated before scrambling over the hay. He stood by Anna's side. 'Let's get out of here, now. With that amount of petrol, this place could go up like a bomb.'

Chapter 14: Bad Blood

Relieved to have finally got to Doctor Brabham's surgery, Anna was somewhat surprised to find a completely empty waiting room. Taking a glance at her wristwatch to check she hadn't left it too late, she suddenly became aware of a muffled sound from behind the door of a small room in which she knew patient records were kept.

A polite cough to alert the doctor's receptionist, Lily Thwaite, of her arrival, failed to raise any response. Crossing the small waiting room, she pressed an ear against the door and listened, not overly concerned that anyone might catch her.

Well, I'll be blown.

She faced a choice. To be the vicar's daughter she'd been brought up to be, or to allow her free-spirited side to come to the fore. She chose the latter. Pressing her ear against the door again, she detected two people exchanging risqué comments, followed by a burst of intimate laughter. As she gave one of the door panels six sharp raps with her knuckle, the muffled sounds from within ceased immediately.

'Doctor Brabham? It's Anna Grix.' Her innocent tone gave

no clue to her devilish intent. She immediately stepped away from the door.

A few seconds later, the flustered doctor appeared and immediately turned back to his companion. 'Yes, that will be fine, Lily, please continue with your work to archive our older patient records.'

Without further reference to what had occurred, the doctor turned to Anna, straightened his tie and beckoned her to follow him into his surgery.

Anna couldn't help glancing into the tiny storage room as she limped past the open door.

Looking at you, it's not just the records that need rearranging.

Lily busied herself with picking up some of the many record cards with one hand while rearranging her hair with her free hand, without glancing at Anna.

The doctor's surgery epitomised a modern clinical environment. Light flooded in from high-level windows on two sides of the room, which off the brilliant white-painted walls, bounced light around like a kaleidoscope.

'I saw that you were limping when we were over to lunch with your parents on Sunday. Why haven't you come to see me before now?'

Anna felt her cheeks flush as she tried to think of a response that sounded halfway credible. 'The thing is, Doctor, what with the war and all, I didn't want to trouble you, knowing some people must need you far more than me and my aching ankle.'

Doctor Brabham glanced down at his patient's lower leg. 'Judging by the amount of swelling, I'm amazed you can put any weight on it at all. As for the war, I know things are grim currently. However, last time I looked, I omitted to find any

Nazis roaming around the village. Come to that, nor have I seen so much as one man with a parachute sticking out of his trousers, speaking in a silly upper-class accent, asking for directions to the nearest army depot.'

Anna's cheeks flushed all the more as she listened to the doctor's gentle reprimand, which made her feel like a child. 'You're quite right, Doctor Brabham; I've been a little too stubborn. It does hurt a lot.' She rubbed her leg to emphasise the point. 'But I'm concerned you're very busy at the moment. I know the waiting room was empty, but I'm sure there are many other things that occupy your time.' She delighted in watching the doctor blush.

'Just so, Anna, just so.'

She smiled sweetly as he hesitated between retrieving his fountain pen from an inside jacket pocket, placing it back again, then looking at her ankle.

If only I had a camera handy.

Point made, she quickly moved on. 'Will I need an X-ray?'

Doctor Brabham gestured for her to move to a narrow examination table on the opposite side of the spacious room. 'Let's get you on here. I can take a good look at your ankle without causing you too much pain.'

She hobbled over to the table, turned around and pulled herself onto the white linen-covered surface, before twisting through ninety degrees so that she sat with her legs stretched out in front of her. Trying not to wince as the doctor began his examination, Anna reached for her ankle more than once in response to the pain caused by his investigation.

'I know. It's clearly hurting you. Then again, you took a long time coming to see me. My manipulation of your ankle will be more painful than it would have otherwise been. I'll try to be as gentle as I can. Now, how does that feel?'

A pain shot from her ankle bone up the back of her leg.

'No need to speak, Anna, I think I know the answer.'

The doctor continued his examination, alternately focusing on Anna's ankle and her facial expression. 'Right, let's get you strapped up.' Turning to a stainless-steel trolley, he opened a pair of small painted steel doors to retrieve a crepe bandage and safety pin. 'Fortunately, I don't think it needs a cast, nor will it require full immobilisation, so I'm going to bandage your ankle and lower leg. I should warn you that it will feel a little tight, but trust me, the necessary blood flow will find its way to your toes, so it will be quite safe.'

Anna waited patiently, wincing only occasionally as the doctor completed his task.

'That should give you some relief. Now, take a seat back at my desk, will you? Careful, we don't want to cause any further damage, do we?'

You're telling me, Doctor.

Doctor Brabham retrieved a fountain pen from his inside pocket, unscrewed the cap and began scratching on a prescription pad. 'Take this to the chemist. I've prescribed an anti-inflammatory, which should help with the pain, and please, do take it easy for a week to give your ankle the chance to settle down.'

Anna took the paper from Brabham. 'Thank you, Doctor. I'll look after myself after all your wonderful work.' She slowly rose from her uncomfortable seat and hobbled to the surgery door, unsure whether the tight bandaging, or a shoe that now did not fit, hurt more. As she opened the door, Anna turned around. 'Oh, I almost forgot, I came across a gentleman called

The Duke. Yes, I know, a bizarre name. Anyway, he asked that I remember him to you when next we met. So, there you are, I've done so.' She observed for any spark of recognition. Instead, he gave her a bewildered look, shook his head, before continuing to write up his case notes.

Hmm, who's bluffing who, I wonder?

Making her way back to the empty waiting room and out onto High Street, Anna wished Lily a good day while risking a sideways glance.

Still blushing, then.

'There you are. I thought you'd got lost.' Anna's father welcomed her into the kitchen and nodded towards the lieutenant. Her demeanour stiffened as she failed to return Eddie's half-smile.

'Dad, I don't want to sound rude, but I wonder if you might leave Lieutenant Elsner and me to it?'

Eddie returned her father's confused look with pleading eyes, and the vicar nodded and left the room, closing the door quietly behind him.

'I've come to apologise for—'

'Apologise for being a self-opinionated, overbearing know-it-all?' Anna remained on her feet just inside the kitchen door. She was in no mood to compromise, a position she displayed to the full in her body language.

'Listen, I think we were both—'

'Don't blame me for—'

'Anna, I'm not blaming anybody, but—'

'But what?'

'If you'll let me finish a sentence, perhaps I can explain why—'

'I'm not sure there's anything to explain.'

The finality of her response led to an angry silence. Eddie looked at Anna, then back at the table. Drumming his fingers on the pine top for a few seconds, he spoke without looking at her. 'It sounds as if you would like me to leave. Say the word, and I'll go.'

Anna's defiant stand continued, her eyes burning into the American. She didn't speak.

Eddie gave her a final look before shrugging his shoulders, getting to his feet and placing his chair noisily back under the kitchen table. As he moved towards the back door, Anna broke eye contact to look at the floor. For a few seconds after Eddie had left, she remained rooted to the spot.

Accepting her father's advice to take a walk, injured ankle or not, Anna willingly accepted a walking stick from him, which had belonged to her grandfather.

Leaving the immediate confines of the village, Anna used the walking stick to good effect as she headed for one of her favourite field walks. Nearing the bus stop, she noticed a young girl, alone but clearly excited.

Ten or eleven, I'd say.

'Hello, young lady, you look happy. Are you all alone?' She found the young girl's smile infectious. 'You're not from around here, are you?'

At first, the girl didn't answer. Nevertheless, her grin shone through as she shook her head and played with one of her pigtails.

Anna noticed the young stranger looking at her ankle. 'Silly me, I fell off my bike. It was quite funny, though.' She mimed the scene, placing particular emphasis on a range of pained expressions.

The young girl laughed out loud and mirrored some of the faces Anna pulled.

'I wonder if we're friends now. I suppose we would be if you told me your name.'

Her new companion looked sheepish, before breaking out into another smile. 'My name is Tilly Smith, and I'm waiting for my mum.'

Anna immediately caught on that the girl was an evacuee. Judging by her accent, she was from London. 'Well, that's wonderful. What time is the bus due?'

She stretched to see around Anna and down the road. 'Soon, I think.'

'And I bet you're very excited, too. Who are you staying in the village with?'

The girl thought for a few seconds. 'Mrs Page. She's very nice and cooks yummy cakes. We live in that little cottage.'

Anna concentrated on where the girl was pointing.

That's good; her guardian can see the bus stop from the cottage.

'Well then, I hope it's not too long before your mum arrives. I'm sure you'll all have a wonderful time eating Mrs Page's scrumptious cakes. You take care of yourself, now.'

Content that the girl was safe, Anna began to make her way to a field gate, before remembering she had a prescription to collect. 'Silly me, I forgot something.' As she retraced her steps, the young girl replied with the broadest smile Anna had seen in a long time.

Well, I'll be damned, I must have just missed them.

She stood forlornly looking into the dispensary's small window display, which comprised several large bottles of iridescent glass containing various remedies. Coming to terms with the fact that standing by the door wasn't going to make it open, Anna used her walking stick to turn around and head back towards the field on the outskirts of the village. A few seconds later, she heard a kerfuffle from the far side of the street.

What's Walter Plowright up to?

She was appalled to see her ex-boyfriend pushing an old man into a narrow alleyway. Glancing from side to side, she realised there was no one to help. As she neared the unpleasant scene, she heard Plowright growling at the elderly villager, having grabbed him by his collar and pushed him heavily against the brick wall.

'What are you up to?'

Anna spooked the old man's attacker, resulting in him running without looking around to check who'd seen him. He sped from the scene more quickly than Anna had ever observed her past love move before. Reaching the old man, she recognised him as one of the regulars at Betty Simpson's pub. 'Are you all right? What was all that about?'

The elderly gentleman's look of terror unsettled Anna. He had several grazes on his neck and head. Realising she had arrived just in time to have saved the man a real beating, she spoke softly to him. 'It's OK now, you're safe. You know me, don't you?'

Shaking with fear, the old man managed to nod.

Taking a clean handkerchief from her pocket, she began to clean the blood away from the man's injuries. He made no attempt to move, but Anna noticed his eyes darting frantically from side to side.

I've got to get him away from here.

'I'm going for help.' As she moved the few feet to the opening of the alleyway, she glanced both ways along the village's main street. 'Thank heavens for that. If ever I've been pleased to see a policeman, it's now. Look at this, will you, Tom.'

The constable quickened his pace. When they got back to the alleyway, to Anna's horror, the old man had disappeared.

After briefing her police friend on what she'd seen and heard, she leant against the old brickwork and slumped her shoulders.

The adrenaline is obviously wearing off.

'Don't worry, we'll catch up with your ex-boyfriend sooner rather than later and will have him. One of my narks tells me he's hooked up with that mob running the betting scam out of the Cock and Sparrow in Three-Mile-Bottom, so I know where to find him.'

Anna wanted to reply but couldn't find the words. She began to feel quite sad, which showed in her posture and facial expression.

'Have you been arguing with Eddie again, by any chance?'

She tried to dismiss his question while acknowledging Tom probably knew her better than any of her old friends. 'It's just that… Oh, I don't know… what's the point?'

A moment of quiet was broken with Tom making an offer. 'Burglars, that's what you need.'

The constable's startling assertion caught her attention. 'Burglars? What on earth are you talking about?'

Tom pointed to a car parked a little way down the road. 'Well, the inspector's asked me to call in on Jack Crossman at Broadside Mill – apparently, he's been burgled again. If you ask me, you need to clear your head. What better remedy is there than a run out into the Broads?'

She looked intrigued.

Why not – who needs Eddie Elsner, anyway?

'Well, your boss' car does look more comfortable than that old Jeep I've been thrown about in all week.'

* * *

'I never get tired of coming out here, do you?' said Tom.

She wound down the window and took in the fresh air of the Norfolk countryside. 'We're so lucky to live in a place like this. To cap it, half an hour's drive and you're smack in the middle of the Broads. Look, can you see the boat sails over there? If you didn't know the area, you'd think your eyes were fooling you into seeing boats gliding through wheat fields. It's wonderful.'

Constable Bradshaw smiled. 'You're right. it's such a shame that some of those wherries are being used for smuggling black-market contraband. It's like we've gone back hundreds of years to when the mill owners and smugglers were in cahoots.'

'What d'you mean? Are you saying that Jack Crossman is telling lies about being burgled? '

Tom sighed. 'It may sound strange, but in this game, until the evidence proves otherwise, we treat everyone as a suspect. You might say it's a cynical view on life, but you'd be amazed the number of times I've been lied to. It's reached the point where I can usually spot someone telling me porkies a mile off.'

'Remind me to watch out for you, then. But you've got me hooked – what have mill owners got to do with smuggling?'

He laughed. 'What part of a windmill do you usually take notice of first?'

Anna looked baffled.

'The sails. The mill owners who were partners with the smugglers would set the sales in a certain position to tell the smugglers if the area was clear of excisemen. A neat little trick, eh?'

Anna slapped her knee, immediately regretting it as her ankle began to throb. 'Of course! As you say, a clever trick. I suppose the Broads are perfect for bringing stuff from Great Yarmouth.'

The Constable nodded. 'You're not kidding, and it's much the same now, except they've got a thousand secluded places to load and unload stuff from lorries on and off the wherries.'

Minutes later, they had parked up next to the windmill. Constable Bradshaw entered the building to interview Jack Crossman, leaving Anna to kick her shoes outside. For the next ten minutes, she wandered around the base of the brick and wooden structure, wondering what tales it could tell from the three hundred years that it had occupied the site. She walked down to the water's edge, from which the mill had got its name, and watched the occasional wherry making its way along the narrow stretch of water.

I wonder whether that one is legit or belongs to a smuggler.

Inwardly thanking her father for the walking stick again, she turned towards the constable's police car. As she passed the mill entrance, a fragment of paper in a patch of longer grass a little way from the structure caught her eye.

Nothing better to do, I suppose.

Intending to retrieve the rubbish for later disposal, she glanced at a strange mark on one side of the filthy scrap. Rubbing the paper on her trouser leg, Anna tried to decipher the shape.

Where have I seen that before?

Soon she heard the heavy latch of the mill's wooden door lifting and quickly shoved the piece of paper into her pocket. Heading the few feet back to the constable's car, Anna overheard Jack Crossman talking. His mill was vulnerable to thieves because they could get his flour down the Broad so quickly without arousing suspicion.

It must be awful when somebody steals your living.

A minute later, Constable Bradshaw fired up the Wolseley and headed down an earth track to the main road. As the car reached the junction, Anna screamed. From her left, a military vehicle sped across their path, just leaving Tom Bradshaw enough time to avoid a crash. Seconds later, a second car, this time much bigger and sounding more powerful, sped past, its engine emitting a low rumbling sound.

Tom looked urgently across to Anna. 'Are you OK?'

She nodded, though her face was drained of colour. 'I think that car was chasing Eddie.'

Chapter 15: Wise Words

'I see you finally made it to Doctor Brabham's.' Helen pointed at her daughter's newly bandaged leg, as she placed a pot of freshly brewed tea on the kitchen table.

'I got a little more than I bargained for.'

Her mother lifted a stainless-steel tea strainer from one cup to the next, before apologising that the sugar ration for the week had been used up. 'Darling, for a grown woman, you can sometimes be a little naïve. The good doctor and Lily Thwaite's relationship has been the talk of the village since shortly after her husband was called up. And before you jump down my throat, it seems their marriage was in trouble a long time before he left for the war. Quite a lady's man, apparently.'

Anna spluttered as she attempted to swallow her tea while taking in her mother's revelations. 'That's awful. I don't care if their marriage was in trouble or not. It can't be right that she's carrying on with the doctor, or anyone for that matter, while her husband's fighting for his country.'

Helen looked at her daughter without speaking as she added milk to her tea.

'Why are you looking at me like that, Mother?'

Helen gave Anna a mother's loving smile. 'And here's me thinking your father and I had done a reasonable job of bringing you up not to judge others. We're all guilty of doing and saying things we later regret. Lily Thwaite and her husband must sort their problems out, without the interference or judgement of others.'

Anna looked into her cup and blew the hot drink, without any intent to take a further sip. 'I know you, Mother. You're not only referring to the doctor's receptionist, are you?'

'And I know when my darling daughter is angry or upset with me when I'm suddenly "Mother". Do you want to talk about the argument you had with Lieutenant Elsner? Please don't look so shocked; yes, of course, your father told me.'

Anna pushed her brightly decorated teacup and saucer away, before fixing her gaze on the crease in the crisp white linen tablecloth and tracing a finger along its length.

'If it's too soon, I quite understand, but you know my mantra: true feelings are better expressed than locked away. Hidden feelings lead to misunderstandings that can lead to unintended consequences.'

Helen got up from the table, all the time keeping her eyes fixed on her daughter.

'It's just… well, I thought he trusted me.'

Helen sat down again and reached both hands across the table to lovingly cup her daughter's extended hand. 'You know, darling, war intensifies every aspect of people's lives. Time moves so quickly; we become more aware of our own mortality and begin to question who we really are. We also tend to be less tolerant of others because we're so wrapped up in our own feelings. It's OK to be frightened, but it does mean we need to make a special effort to understand that others are frightened too.'

Anna slowly shook her head. 'So isn't it better not to get too close to people? Who knows what might happen next? Look outside, Mum, it's a beautiful day. That means the bombers will be back tonight and we could all be blown to bits.'

Helen stroked her daughter's hand. 'Yes, you're right, darling, just as people get ill and die, or run over and terribly injured. The important thing is to plough on. After all, what's the alternative? Staying in bed all day? Not doing what we normally do at home? Some might say you've been running around doing things that are completely out of character…'

Anna withdrew her hand from her mother's embrace. 'What do you mean?'

Helen smiled. 'Writing letters and hiding them might be a good example.'

Anna frowned and leant back in her chair. 'I have no idea what you're talking about, Mother.'

Helen left the table and walked over to the Victorian kitchen range. Reaching up to a high mantelshelf, she retrieved an envelope that had been leaning against one of her favourite family pictures for several days. Retracing her steps, she handed it to her daughter.

Anna scrutinised the envelope, the implication of which suddenly dawned. 'Oh, Mum. What have I done?'

Helen's demeanour changed from one of mild rebuke to concern. 'What do you mean? Is it not yours?'

She shook her head. 'For a start, Mum, the handwriting is nothing like mine. What was that you were saying earlier about judging people?' She glanced at her mother, who was beginning to stiffen. 'I'm sorry, Mum, that was uncalled for. But I've made a huge mistake.'

Anna's apology settled her mother down. 'This is no time for secrets, Anna. What do you mean "a mistake"?'

Attention turned back to the grimy envelope. 'I found this in the same ditch that Ted Fleming died. I promised Lieutenant Elsner I would take it straight to the police. For some reason, I completely forgot. Where did you find it?'

Helen mirrored her daughter's body language and sat back in her chair. 'Remember what I said about people not doing what they normally do? Well, since you hadn't brought any clothes down for washing for a few days, I took a quick look around your bedroom to pick up anything I thought needed a good soak. Those brown trousers of yours were filthy, and you know I always check the pockets before putting them into the dolly tub. Well, I found that envelope and meant to give it to you. As you see, I too, forgot.'

Anna continued to run the ragged envelope through her fingers. 'So it's not only me who's wrapped up in their own world?'

Helen gave her daughter a look only a mother can conjure up. 'I think we'll leave it at that, Anna Grix. I've changed my mind, and it seems there are some things better left unsaid. However, I'll leave you with one thought: you can't solve the problems of the world on your own. If you try, you'll hurt yourself.'

After a restful sleep which helped Anna understand what her mother had been driving at the previous evening, she resolved to make it up with Eddie. Head clear, she chatted happily with her parents over breakfast.

'Are you running your usual Thursday lunchtime get-together

at the church, Dad?' She helped herself to another round of toast, being careful not to use too much butter.

'I am. Would you like to help out? I'm a bit short-handed this week. You see, a couple of my ladies have abandoned me. It seems they'd prefer to help out the thrift shop for Mum's big push for the Spitfire fund.'

Helen slid a frying pan over the cast-iron heating plate on the range with greater vigour than would typically have been the case. 'Dear husband, you know perfectly well we agreed this weeks ago, so you've had plenty of time to draft in new volunteers.'

Anna held her hands wide apart. 'That will be quite enough, you two. I'm quite happy to help out, Dad, but there're one or two things I need to do first.'

Her parents exchanged a rueful smile before breaking out into a fit of laughter. 'Well, child. You certainly put us in our place but thank you for agreeing to join me later this morning.'

Anna teased her father. 'Dad, I'm twenty-five years old; when will you stop calling me "child"?' She caught a sparkle in the vicar's eyes.

'My darling, you could be fifty-five years old, yet to your mother and me, you would still be our little girl. Something for which we make no apology.' He gave Anna a broad smile and offered some of his butter for her toast.

The rest of breakfast was spent with all three exchanging views about what was happening in the village while making a studious effort not to discuss the war. Their flow was interrupted by the sound of the post dropping onto the tiled floor of the vestibule.

'I hope he's got it right this morning. The new postman, bless him, has yet to learn who lives where. Right, let's see what exciting communications we've received today.'

'Don't you think you're being a little hard, Mum? It's only been a week since—'

'I know how long it's been since Ted died, darling. Now, let's see what we have.' A few seconds later, Helen returned. 'A letter from the bishop for you, dear husband. I wonder what you've done wrong this time?' She smiled at the vicar. 'The other is for you. I don't recognise the handwriting.'

Anna too was at a loss to recognise the untidy script. 'A Sandringham postmark. I wonder…'

Her father looked at his daughter. 'You don't think the… the king is writing to you, do you? Perhaps it's an invitation to dinner.'

Anna wagged a finger at her father. 'Somehow, I think His Majesty's private secretary has more important things to do than writing to me. Anyway, the handwriting isn't neat enough, so there.'

All three laughed.

The vicar read the contents of the bishop's letter and let out a moan. 'He only comes when he wants something. I wonder what it'll be this time?'

'Husband, that's not a very charitable thing to say about the bishop, even if it's true.'

Anna's parents giggled like conspiratorial school children. Meanwhile, their daughter had gone quiet.

'Is there anything wrong?'

At first, Anna didn't respond to her mother and instead continued to focus on a single sheet of paper she'd taken from the envelope. 'It's from my friend June, you know; the girl I used to knock around with for a couple of years after I left school. Her parents moved to Sandringham when June was eighteen and she went with them.

'She married a local chap and we've only exchanged the odd letter since. She says her husband's missing in action in North Africa. To cap it all, they're about to have their first child. As you can imagine, June's at her wit's end.'

The levity that had been present vanished in an instant.

'Why don't you give her a ring and see what she needs. If there's anything we can do, please ask.'

Anna shifted her gaze between her mother and father. 'She doesn't have a telephone, so I'll need to write back straight away. Thank you both for the offer of help. I'm not sure what anyone can do, other than being a good friend to her. May I use your office, Dad?'

Knowing her father wouldn't object, she left the kitchen without waiting for his reply.

I hate this war. Why is it always good people that suffer?

Taking a supply of plain stationery from her father's bureau, she sat at his small, tidy desk and picked up his favourite fountain pen. Trying several times to strike the right tone, Anna found herself writing a line or two, before abandoning each effort.

How can I know what she's going through?

Eventually, Anna found the words she'd been looking for and ended her response by taking care to include the vicarage's number.

As Anna licked the envelope to seal it shut, the vestibule telephone rang. Thinking nothing of it, Anna retrieved a tuppence ha'penny stamp from the bureau, licked the gum arabic and pressed it firmly into place.

Her mother's head appeared around the office door. 'It's for you, darling.'

Curious, Anna limped into the vestibule and picked up the handset. 'Hello, can I help?' She froze as she recognised the voice.

'Good morning, Anna. How are you today?'

Unsure how to respond, Anna hesitated. The Duke's tone was polite, but she sensed an edge of menace.

'Well, anyway, I wanted to ask after Lieutenant Elsner. You are still friends, aren't you?'

Anna's mind raced.

How does he know we argued?

'Of course, we're still friends. What a strange thing to suggest. Is there anything I can help you with in particular?'

His response took several seconds to arrive. 'Now that we're good friends, I wanted to see how you were doing. You see, one of my associates told me a strange tale about Lieutenant Elsner leaving the vicarage early yesterday in somewhat of a state. Also, that he hasn't been seen since.'

Oh no, has he got to Eddie?

'How strange. I don't know what that person thought they saw, but the lieutenant's fine. In fact, I shall be seeing him later today.'

The line fell silent for a second time, making Anna wonder whether her tormentor was still there.

'Well, I'm sure your American friend is perfectly safe, which makes me happy, and you of all people know I don't like to be unhappy, don't you, Anna.'

The walk to Three-Mile-Bottom was both slow and tortuous for Anna, even with the supportive assistance of her grandfather's walking stick.

Another twenty minutes should do it.

At that moment, she heard the sound of a car horn. Quickly moving to the edge of the narrow lane, she glanced behind.

'You look as though you could do with a lift, Miss Grix. What was that I said about giving your ankle a rest?'

She was relieved to see the smiling face of Doctor Brabham leaning out of his open car window. 'I think I'm a lost cause, Doctor, but yes, a lift to the next village would be wonderful.'

A minute later, Anna was comfortably seated in the doctor's car as it made its stately progress into Three-Mile-Bottom. 'Drop me off here, Doctor, this will do fine, and thank you so much for your help.'

Brabham closed the passenger side door after helping Anna out of the vehicle. 'And how are you going to get back to Lipton Saint Faith?'

'Oh, I'll think of something, and I promise to take your advice and keep the weight off my ankle.'

Brabham gave Anna a sceptical glance as he got back into the car. He offered a cheery wave and drove slowly away, leaving her feet from the house where Eddie was staying.

She looked around the quiet hamlet for signs of life. All was quiet apart from the occasional man entering the Cock and Sparrow pub, only to remerge shortly later in a routine now familiar to Anna.

Struggling to mount three steep stone steps to the cottage front entrance, Anna raised the cast-iron door knocker and allowed it to fall back with a solid thump.

I'm going to look stupid.

A few seconds later, a beaming Hilda Crossman opened the door.

'Anna, how wonderful to see you again, do come in. I've brewed a fresh pot of tea.'

Hilda instructed her husband, Albert, to move seats so that their guest could occupy the household's most comfortable chair. Smiling, Albert did as he was instructed and gestured for Anna to make herself comfortable.

'And I've baked a carrot cake. Would you like a piece with your tea?' The Crossmans exchanged a fleeting glance as their guest sat down.

'That's very kind of you; yes, a piece of cake would be wonderful, thank you.'

While Hilda made herself busy in the kitchen preparing things, Albert did his best to hold a conversation with their unexpected visitor. 'So, what have you been up to? And how are your mother and father? Hasn't the weather been wonderful for this time of year?'

Anna guessed the barrage of questions said more about Albert's nervousness at being left alone with a woman than his apparent interest in the weather. 'Well, Mr Crossman, I've been busy helping my mother in the thrift shop. Later this morning, I'll be pouring cups of tea at my father's weekly get-together for the community at the church, so all in all, quite busy.' She watched as Albert nodded, his eyes often turning to the kitchen door.

Soon his saviour returned, loaded with a tray of tea and cake. Again, the Crossmans shared a glance as Hilda set the snack onto a small elm table which Albert had made as a wedding present for Hilda.

'Flour, as you remember me explaining, we have plenty of. Sugar is quite another matter, so I do apologise for the tea tasting a little bitter.'

'Of course, it's the same at home,' replied Anna as she took hold of her cup and saucer in one hand and a slice of cake in the other.

She waited a couple of minutes before broaching the question she thought might make her look silly. 'Is Eddie around?'

The Crossmans exchanged furtive glances for the third time.

'He's popped out to do whatever it is that he does. He didn't say when he'd be back.' Hilda broke eye contact with her guest and took a large bite from her cake while glancing at her husband, who was inspecting his slippers.

Something strange is going on here.

'Oh, I see. Well, I expect I'll see Eddie later. Could you tell him I asked after him and perhaps he could give me a ring tonight?' She watched as Albert gave his wife yet another odd glance. 'Is everything all right?'

Hilda nodded as she finished the last of her cake. 'I'm sorry. I suppose Albert and I are a bit worried about Jack. I assume you've heard about the flour somebody's been stealing. It's not fair, you know; he has to account for it all to the War Office. He's worried sick they'll think he's been up to no good. Listen to me moaning when you've walked all the way over here with that poor ankle of yours.'

Anna placed her tea and what remained of her cake on the low table. 'Well, you know how word gets around, so yes, I heard about the break-ins. Listen, I'd better get going or I'll be late for Dad's little get-together at the church. Look after yourselves both of you, and if you do see Eddie, do ask him to ring me.'

There's definitely something going on.

Having taken leave of the Crossmans, Anna cautiously descended the stone steps that had caused such problems when she arrived. She looked up the lane wistfully, knowing how long it would take to walk home.

'It's your lucky day, Anna, I've finished my last call and I'm on my way back to the village. Would you like a lift?'

She watched as Doctor Brabham walked down the narrow pathway from his patient's cottage. 'I'd be a liar if I said I'd prefer to walk. Thank you so much.'

About to close the garden gate at the vicarage, Anna heard her name being called.

'Miss Anna, I've got something for you.'

She turned to see 13-year-old Vincent Timberlake holding an envelope which had her first name written on its front.

'Who gave you this, Vincent?'

The boy looked sheepish. 'A man said he'd give me sixpence if I made sure I put this into your hand. Goodbye, I have to go now.'

Before Anna had a chance to question him further, the youngster had disappeared into the distance.

She ripped open the envelope and withdrew a single sheet of paper. Its contents shocked her:

'I've had to go away for a few days, Anna. Don't look for me, it will be safer for everyone that way.'

Chapter 16: Only Darkness

Thursday afternoons followed much the same routine at Lipton Saint Faith police station as any other day. The odd enquiry about a missing cat, a civic-minded villager handing in an umbrella. On a busy day, the desk sergeant might deal with a reported theft, though such things were a rare occurrence in the small community.

Today was different. Sergeant Dick Ilford looked concerned as a distressed villager entered the small lobby of the old police station. 'Miss Grix, what on earth is the matter?'

Anna hobbled over to the high mahogany countertop behind which the desk sergeant was standing. She leant against the sturdy structure for support. 'Is the inspector available? I need to report a missing person.' Anna worked hard to regain her composure. Nevertheless, she could feel her emotions welling up.

Sergeant Ilford opened an immense incident book, allowing its covering to land heavily on the countertop with a thump. 'I'm sure I can deal with that for you, now, let's have some details.'

Anna watched as the tall, thin sergeant dipped his pen in an inkwell, then positioned its nib on a blank line, ready to make a new entry.

'No, you don't understand. I need to talk to Inspector Spillers on an urgent matter. Please, is he free?'

Sergeant Ilford quietly sighed as he placed his pen back into its holder.

'Anna, what are you doing here?' said Ilford, then, 'Bradshaw, why are you not on your beat? If you think you can slink in here for a quick cuppa you are mistaken, my lad. Now, get yourself off.'

Constable Bradshaw, who had just walked into the station, looked at Anna before turning to his superior. 'I've not come back for tea, Sarge; I need a new notebook.'

Sergeant Ilford gave the constable a sceptical look. 'A likely story, my lad. However, if that's the case, you should have checked before leaving the station this morning. Don't let it happen again, do you understand?' The sergeant's eyes burned into his subordinate.

Bradshaw nodded. 'Yes, Sarge, I mean no, Sarge.'

Ilford flicked a finger to indicate the young constable should get about his business then turned his attention back to Anna.

'Now, Miss Grix, are you sure I can't help? The Inspector is, as I am sure you realise, an extremely busy man. I can't be interrupting him every time a villager, no matter how esteemed, drops into my station and demands to see him.'

Anna felt her frustration rising. 'Sergeant Ilford, please don't treat me as if I were a 10-year-old. I fully understand you are doing your job, but I have made a reasonable request. It's not my habit to demand anything or to waste people's time.'

Tom Bradshaw winked at Anna and smiled without his boss noticing as he made for the exit.

Meanwhile, Sergeant Ilford gave a nervous cough as he picked up his pen before immediately placing it back in its allotted position. 'Miss Grix, I shall see what I can do, but can make no promises. Please take a seat.' The desk sergeant pointed to a rickety wooden chair resting against the cream-painted wall as he made his way down a short corridor.

This place would make anyone feel like a criminal.

Minutes passed as she waited for him to return. In the meantime, Beatrice Flowers bustled into the small space, looked at the deserted counter, then Anna, muttering something under her breath the vicar's daughter didn't catch.

'Sergeant Ilford is checking something for me, Miss Flowers; I'm sure he won't be too long.'

The elderly lady didn't appear to be in the mood for Anna's explanation. 'It's always the same when I have something to report. Why, it's as if the village has no police officers at all. I shouldn't be surprised if Dick Ilford isn't skulking in the backyard as I speak. He is partial to a cigarette, you know.'

Please, Beatrice, I don't feel like it this afternoon.

'Anyway, what brings you here?'

Anna tried to look engaged; it was the least her parents would expect of her. 'Oh, nothing too important.' She was keen to distract attention from herself. 'More to the point, why are you here?'

She knew the spinster liked to hear her own voice.

'Funny you should ask, but Nelly Arbuckle said Janice Townsend told her the milkman had seen something falling from the sky into Lover's Lane. Therefore, I feel I must report such a serious matter to the authorities. After all, you hear so much about spies these days. I have no wish to be murdered in my bed by a spy.'

I've heard everything now.

'Oh, I see. As you say, we all have a civic duty to report unusual occurrences, and I think that poster sums it up very well, don't you?'

Miss Flowers looked to where Anna was pointing. The War Department message was clear: *'Careless Talk Costs Lives'.*

I couldn't have put it better myself.

Before the spinster could respond, the desk sergeant reappeared. 'You are fortunate, Miss Grix. Inspector Spillers will see you. Please go through to his office. It's the second on the right.'

Anna thanked the policeman then fleetingly glanced at an intrigued Beatrice Flowers. Making her way to the inspector's office, she knew the news of her visit would be around the village within the hour.

Giving the translucent glass in the top half of the office door a gentle tap, Anna waited for the instruction to enter, then turned a bright brass doorknob.

Tidy desk, tidy mind.

She was impressed at the neatness of the inspector's workspace, which was not at all what she'd expected, and chastised herself for being too ready to pigeonhole the senior officer.

'Do come in, Miss Grix. Please, take a seat.'

The inspector pointed to an oak-framed chair. 'My desk sergeant said there was an agitated lady keen to see me. For a second, I thought he meant our friend Miss Flowers again. Do you know, she tries to get into this office three times a week on average.'

Thank you.

Anna knew that Inspector Spillers was doing his best to put

her at ease. 'I'm afraid your intuition may be rewarded after you've seen me. That is unless Sergeant Ilford can fend Beatrice off.' Spiller's broad grin further relaxed Anna.

'Now, what's all this about a missing person?'

She could feel her anxiety returning as the thought of Lieutenant Elsner being in danger welled up. 'It's Eddie, or I should say, the lieutenant. He sent me a note.' Anna slid Eddie's short letter across the inspector's empty desktop. 'I know I haven't known him for long, but it's completely out of character.'

Inspector Spillers had his eyes firmly on the notepaper as Anna gave her explanation. Having digested the two lines of text, he placed the paper back on his desk. He took particular care to flatten its creases by holding one corner of the note with one hand, while using the other to iron the paper flat with an open palm.

'But Miss Grix, this is a military matter and nothing to do with His Majesty's Constabulary. I couldn't get involved if I wanted to, which, with all due respect, I have no wish to. You do understand my position?'

Her shoulders dropped as she realised the inspector wanted nothing to do with her concerns. 'Inspector Spillers, he may be an American serviceman, but I fear something dreadful will happen to him. Who knows, it may already have. I'm sure you'd wish to make every effort to keep us all safe, whether in uniform or not.' Anna knew her words had hit a sensitive spot by the amount of fidgeting the inspector began to display. 'I'm not asking you to commit a huge amount of time or police resources, but please, this is important to me.'

The inspector leapt on her words. 'But that's the point, Miss Grix. I have no wish to sound too officious, but what is important to you isn't necessarily a priority for me. Please don't misinterpret my words as a lack of humanity. Instead, see this more as a case of a military man being unaccounted for, one which his superiors will wish to take full responsibility for. They won't thank me for getting in the middle, I assure you.'

Anna was about to give up.

One more try.

'What if I told you we have stumbled across a possible link between Ted Fleming's and Cyril Trubshaw's deaths?' Anna immediately realised she'd made a mistake. The inspector's relaxed features disappeared in a fraction of a second as he placed his elbows on the desktop and leaned forward.

'Miss Grix, I have listened to you patiently and courteously for the last fifteen minutes. I have explained, in detail, why this isn't a matter for the police. Now you tell me that you and Lieutenant Elsner have been interfering in police matters. Explain yourselves immediately, or you'll find yourself in a great deal of trouble. Do I make myself clear?'

She was in no doubt how serious matters had become.

Why didn't I keep my mouth shut?

Her mind spun as a thousand thoughts bounced around her brain.

Only one way to deal with this.

'Inspector Spillers, I've been run over, belittled in pubs, almost stabbed to death, oh, and for good measure, kidnapped for the day. And now Lieutenant Elsner leaves me a note, at least, I assume it's from him, saying that he had to leave. Frankly, I don't care whether you determine such things amount to interfering in police work. From my perspective, we've been doing the things you should have been doing.'

Anna shook with anger. She too was now leaning forward, eyes rigidly fixed on the inspector.

It was Spillers who broke eye contact first. Unsure what to do or say next, Anna wondered if she was about to be arrested. To her surprise, things took an unexpected turn.

'Listen, Anna, under normal circumstances, you would be in one of my cells by now. However, these are not normal times, are they? Before I continue, I want you to understand I meant what I said last week concerning interfering with a police investigation and withholding evidence. Let me speak plainly: that's exactly what you and your American friend have been doing. I have no jurisdiction over Lieutenant Elsner, but I do over you—'

'But Inspector—'

'Let me finish. I'll consider what Peggy Fleming asked you to do – yes, I know all about that. I'm also conscious of how traumatic it must have been for you to discover Cyril Trubshaw's body, so I'm going to overlook your indiscretions in this instance—'

'May I ask—'

'Sometimes, it's better to listen than continuously interrupt. Now, as I was saying, overlooking a past event is one thing; having a duty of care for your safety is quite another. So, if I'm to help you, then you must tell me everything that has happened.'

Anna's words tumbled from her mouth in a torrent as she updated Spillers on recent events.

Spillers sat back in his chair, his cold stare burning into Anna. 'Very well. I'll investigate what you have told me and get back to you as quickly as I can. In the meantime, I insist you do or say nothing further about the deaths of those two men. Now, we shall leave it at that. Thank you for coming to see me, Miss Grix.'

Pondering what to do next, Anna took a roundabout route to the vicarage, her grandfather's walking stick making all the difference between outright pain and an uncomfortable sensation in her recently strapped ankle.

Approaching the village bus stop, which marked the furthest point on Anna's journey before turning back towards the village centre, she glimpsed a familiar figure. The young evacuee from London, sat on the small wooden bench, looking down at the narrow grass verge.

Where has her bright smile gone?

'Tilly, are you OK?'

The young girl kept her eyes fixed on the floor without answering. Moving closer to her, Anna placed an open palm on the youngster's head and stroked her long, curly auburn hair.

Having asked the question a second time without receiving a response, she knelt next to the young girl. However, the youngster continued to avoid eye contact.

'How long have you been here? This morning's bus has already gone, so it'll be a long time before the next one comes along.'

Nothing Anna did seemed to make the slightest difference to Tilly.

She must have already been here at least an hour.

'Come along, young lady, let's get you home for some of that wonderful baking you told me Mrs Page did.'

Anna took hold of Tilly's hand and tried to coax her from the bench. She could feel the young girl resisting. 'We can always come back later. The next bus isn't due for over four hours, so you won't miss it. If you trust me, let me take you back home. It's OK, I'll come in with you.'

She felt Tilly relax. Slowly, the youngster eased herself from the paint-chipped seat and, maintaining a tight grip of Anna's hand, stood without taking her eyes off the grass.

'That's it, you come with me. Let's go and say hello to Mrs Page and see if she has any cakes for us.'

Tilly still didn't respond but was at least walking, her hand firmly gripping the vicar's daughter.

In less than a minute, Anna was knocking on the panelled door of a pretty cottage. She smiled as the door opened.

Mrs Page first looked at her charge with the concern of a caring adult, then at Anna. A half-smile formed.

'Good afternoon, Mrs Page. This young lady told me all about you the other day when we first met. I've come across her again, but she seems to have lost her smile. I wonder whether you might have a cake for us both?'

The woman looked back at Tilly while gesturing for them both to enter. Mrs Page planted a kiss on the young girl's head as she passed by. 'You go through to the kitchen and see what you can find while I have a word with your new friend.'

The young girl did as she was asked, leaving the two adults in the living room, its ancient oak beams blackened by centuries of smoke from the fireplace. The two women stood opposite each other.

'Hello Anna, it was good of you to bring her back. She told me she'd met a nice lady a few days ago. I didn't realise it was you.'

'No reason you should have, Martha, I didn't know you'd taken in an evacuee.'

Martha Page shrugged her shoulders and sighed. 'What with

John away fighting and me stuck on my own here, I thought I should do my bit. The poor girl really is no trouble, and when her mother managed to visit, you should have seen her little face light up.' She began to stare into space.

Anna frowned, trying to make sense of her host's words. 'But she was waiting at the bus stop, so are you not expecting her mother today?'

Crikey, what have I said?

'You all right, Martha?' Anna stepped closer to the woman as tears began to roll silently down the cottage owner's cheeks. 'What's happened?'

'Her mother is dead. Killed in a raid a few nights ago. I've told Tilly as best I can, but she still insists on going to the bus stop. Frankly, I'm at my wits' end.'

Anna caught sight of a movement to her right. It was Tilly.

She must have heard everything we said.

The young girl ambled into the little living room, carrying a tray on which stood three tumblers of orange squash and three shortbread biscuits.

'Bless you, my darling,' whispered Martha, 'what a good girl you are.'

Tilly placed the tray on the small dining table without looking at either woman.

Anna felt tears beginning to well and tried hard to stem the flow.

Stop being selfish, get a grip.

Tilly sat down on one of the dining table chairs and stared blankly at the stone floor.

'Do I stop her waiting for the bus for a parent who will never come, or do I let her carry on?' whispered Martha.

Anna looked at the young girl, then Martha. 'I'd let her carry on. You can see the bus stop from the window, so you know she'll be safe. I'll also keep an eye out for her.'

It wasn't often that Anna felt the need to be alone in the church with her thoughts. Today was different.

What's happening? Villagers are being murdered, daughters are losing their mothers, and others disappear, leaving only a scrap of paper and a few words by way of a supposed explanation. Why can't things be like they used to be? And while all this is going on, I'm limping around the place playing catch-the-killer. I hate myself.

'You know, Anna, I remember being a short distance behind the front line in 1917. Shells were going off all around, and the gunfire sounded like a thousand firecrackers. Yet I felt strangely peaceful, lost in my own thoughts, feelings that nobody could take away from me, knowing that in the blink of an eye, one of those shells or bullets might have done for me.'

Anna was shocked at the sudden arrival of her father, who was seated in the pew behind. 'I'm… not sure… I don't understand you, Dad.'

The vicar placed a comforting hand on his daughter's shoulder. 'Sometimes, darling, it seems as if things are utterly out of control. However, what you *do* have control over is how you choose to react: the decisions you make and the impact those decisions may have, both on you and others. All the fury in the world, all the pain that can be inflicted, must be endured. In that endurance, you can regain a measure of control, especially concerning your own thoughts and actions.'

Anna began to cry uncontrollably. Head in her hands, she felt the comforting arm of her father around her shoulders as he sat next to her.

'That's it, my darling, let it out. You're safe with me, and you're loved so much. Most of all, you are in God's presence. He hears, He sees, He loves unconditionally.'

Her sobs began to wane, and she gratefully accepted her father's handkerchief. Anna looked to the brightly coloured stained-glass window above the altar, the sun's rays causing multicoloured shafts of light to radiate around the holy place.

'It's just… Oh, I don't know, everything is going wrong, and I don't know what to do.'

The vicar held her close. 'Some things you can do nothing about. I find concentrating on the things that can make a difference helps me to feel as though I'm contributing.

'When all is said and done, isn't that the important thing? Making a difference, no matter how small. This allows one to help others and feel better about oneself. The question is, Anna, how best can you contribute?'

By the time she'd fully absorbed her father's words, the vicar had released his comforting hold and quietly slipped away. Left with her own thoughts, she tried to answer her father's question.

Feeling the need for fresh air, she left the church to spend a little while wandering around the ancient headstones of the old graveyard. She took notice of the age at which people had died.

He was ninety-two. That poor little boy, only one day old.

Anna realised no matter how grand the headstone, or age of the deceased, all had enriched those who loved them.

Life must go on. I'm determined I'll make a difference.

Chapter 17: A Busy Day

'Good morning, Helen. Is Anna about?'

'Hello, Tom, you're up and about early this morning. I'll give her a shout; come in and help yourself to a cup of tea.'

Constable Bradshaw smiled as he entered the vicarage kitchen and headed straight for the teapot. Meanwhile, he could hear Anna's muffled response to her mother's call.

'My lazy daughter will be down soon. It's 8.15 already, and still she's combing her hair.'

'I suppose that's the advantage of being a bloke; within twenty-five minutes of getting out of bed, I've got my uniform on, toast eaten, and out the door.'

'Hmm, perhaps you could have a word with my husband. The older he gets, the more he seems to hate mornings. I'll swear he's nocturnal.' Helen smiled at Tom as she poured herself a cup of tea and joined him at the kitchen table.

'Who's nocturnal?' asked Anna, walking into the kitchen, rubbing the sleep out of her eyes.

Helen wagged a finger at her yawning daughter. 'I was talking about your father, but it seems it applies equally to you. Sit while I get you some toast and marmalade.'

Anna frowned as she studied Constable Bradshaw. 'What are you doing here?'

'Good morning to you, too, Anna. Funny you should ask that. Helen dragged me off the street with the promise of a good breakfast.'

Turning to her mother while shrugging her shoulders, Anna wondered if she was still dreaming. 'Is that true, Mum?'

Helen laughed as she placed two rounds of freshly toasted bread on her daughter's plate. She then pushed a half-empty jar of homemade marmalade to within easy reach of her confused daughter.

'Honestly, you're as daft as a brush sometimes. Anyway, I want to get an early start at the thrift shop, so I'll leave you two to your tea and toast. See you, Tom.'

Anna kept her eyes fixed on Tom as she spread a knife full of marmalade onto her toast.

'Why are you looking at me like that? I haven't come to arrest you, you know.'

She took a large bite of the crispy bread, causing excess marmalade to congeal around her mouth.

'In fact, it's quite the opposite. Now, are you going to share some of that or not?'

Anna looked at her plate then back at Tom. 'What, you want some of my breakfast? Dream on, cowboy.'

Constable Bradshaw continued to stare at her plate. 'It's only a piece of toast, not the crown jewels. Anyway, as I was saying—'

'You were about to tell me Inspector Spillers has dispatched you to warn me off. I expect you heard about yesterday?'

Before Anna could take defensive action, Tom nabbed a slice of toast. 'I heard that you kept interrupting him if that's what you mean.' Tom took a massive bite of the bread before Anna attempted to retrieve it.

Having failed to rescue her breakfast, she tilted her head to one side. 'That means he *has* told you what happened.'

Pausing for a few seconds so that he could swallow a mouthful of toast, Tom grinned like a Cheshire cat. 'I don't know what you said to him, but he's given you three days of my time to see what you can turn up.'

Tom's news almost caused Anna to choke on her tea. 'You mean you haven't come to warn me off?'

'As I said, just the opposite. We have until midnight on Sunday to give my inspector the evidence he needs to make an arrest. After that, he says you're to drop the amateur sleuthing stuff.'

Anna couldn't quite comprehend what she was hearing. 'So, you think he believes me about Ted Fleming and Cyril Trubshaw?'

Tom's smile slipped. 'No, I don't think he does. But he's astute enough to know you won't leave things alone until you unmask the culprit – or make a complete fool of yourself.'

It took several seconds for Anna to take in the full enormity of what her friend had told her. 'And it's your job to spy on me, is it?' She squinted at Tom.

Taking a second, smaller bite from his toast, which allowed him to eat and speak simultaneously, Tom shook his head. 'Don't you trust anyone? For sure, he wants an eye kept on you. You can't expect him to be pleased that you seem to know more about Tom and Cyril's deaths than he does. But the inspector also wants you kept safe.'

The kitchen fell silent as he finished his toast, while Anna digested the opportunity she'd been given. She then got up from the table and left the room, leaving Tom confused. Within a minute, she returned holding an envelope.

'What's this?'

'It's something I meant to give you last week. I forgot, which isn't something I'm proud of.'

Constable Bradshaw took hold of the envelope by one corner between a finger and thumb and placed it on the table. 'Where did you say you found it?'

Anna looked sheepish. 'It was in the same ditch that Ted Fleming died.'

Tom inspected each side of the envelope without touching the artefact, other than using a clean knife to flip it over. 'What is it you think you've got here?'

'Let me show—'

'No, don't touch it. It will have to be dusted for fingerprints.'

Anna recoiled at Tom's stern command. 'But don't you want to look inside?'

Constable Bradshaw peered down at the envelope, then at Anna. 'According to police procedure, this should go to forensics.'

Anna smiled at Tom. She knew it was wrong, but also knew he always gave in to her.

'I know what you're doing, Anna Grix, and it won't work this time.'

Her smile broadened. She purposely opened her eyes wide. 'Aren't you curious what the letter says? After all, the inspector has lent you to me for three days. You could always say I'd already opened it before giving it to you.'

He frowned. 'Well, the inspector did tell me to give you any assistance you needed… Anyway, as you say, I can always blame you if he starts shouting. But from now on, we do things properly, agreed?'

Anna poured Tom a second cup of tea. 'You are a good sport. Right, let's get it open.'

The constable held out an open palm as if directing traffic. 'I said we have to do things correctly. Have you a letter opener?'

In the thirty seconds it took Anna to retrieve one from her father's office, Tom had his notebook on the table to make a record of the evidence.

'Do you want to do it, or shall I?'

Tom raised his eyebrows. 'I think you know the answer to that. Please give me the letter opener.'

Reluctantly, she complied with the constable's request. Sitting down again at the kitchen table, Anna watched in fascination as he held the envelope tight to the table with his notebook, while slitting its top edge open.

Picking the envelope up from the table between finger and thumb, he delicately withdrew a single sheet of paper with a minimum of finger contact, before laying it on the table.

Anna had honed her skills at reading upside down from assisting at her father's Sunday school classes. 'Money trouble, then?' She looked at Tom to gauge his reaction.

He nodded. 'If you read between the lines, it seems he was being threatened by someone.'

'I bet The Duke is behind this – he's a real thug.'

Tom continued to read the short note. 'This instruction to contact the police about a man with shiny shoes in the event of his sudden death is odd. Assuming the letter was addressed to his brother, and the man knew who Ted was referring to, why didn't he tell him?'

'The Duke is always spotlessly turned out; I'm sure this is about him. Can you get hold of your inspector's car again?'

'You don't half push your luck. What's that about giving somebody an inch and they'll take a mile? Anyway, what do we need the car for?'

'We need to go to Norwich.'

'I've been expecting the police; what's taken so long? Anna Grix, isn't it? Peggy rang and told me all about you.'

Constable Bradshaw removed his police helmet and ducked to navigate the low entrance of Billy Fleming's narrow terraced house.

'We didn't know you existed until Miss Grix found an envelope addressed to you.'

Anna detected Billy's distrust of the police. 'I asked Constable Bradshaw to bring me. He's seen the letter, and I thought it'd be a good idea if we came together. He's an old mate and one of the decent coppers.'

Her explanation relaxed their host. 'Come on in, then. Do you want some tea?'

She looked at Tom, who shook his head. 'That's really very kind, but no thank you. May I ask you to take a look at your brother's letter?'

Constable Bradshaw carefully removed the contents of the letter from an evidence bag and placed both on one arm of an upholstered chair. He made sure to put the paper on top of the bag to preserve its integrity.

'Please don't touch the letter, Mr Fleming, I hope you understand.'

Billy leant over to read his brother's words. 'It's not the first such letter I've had from Ted. I'm afraid he was a heavy gambler and always short of money. I've helped out in the past even though I knew it just encouraged him to bet more, but what do you do; family is family.'

Tom returned the paper to the evidence bag, then took out his notebook.

'Is this a formal interview?'

Anna sensed Billy was about to close up. She glanced at Tom.

'No, no. I'm sorry if I've alarmed you, Mr Fleming. It's routine to make sure I don't forget anything we've spoken about.'

She needed to move the conversation on. 'Did Ted ever mention a man called The Duke?'

Billy shifted his gaze from the policeman to Anna. 'Yes, I know all about that little weasel. If ever I get my hands on him, I'll give him a pasting he won't forget in a hurry, I tell you, and I don't care if your policeman friend writes that down or not.'

Tom smiled. 'I suspect you'll have to join quite a long queue, Mr Fleming.'

Billy acknowledged the constable's remark with the nearest thing he'd come to smiling since his visitors arrived.

'Ted was frightened of that creep, there's no doubt about it. He told me once that he had information on the thug as an insurance policy. I never saw it, and he didn't tell me where he kept it.'

Constable Bradshaw's ears pricked. 'Do you think it might have had the opposite effect and got your brother killed?'

Billy shrugged his shoulders. 'To be honest, I thought Ted had got himself into a situation he couldn't control.'

'What do you mean, Billy?' Anna's question had an urgent edge to it.

'Let's just say Ted delivered more than letters. He said he

could get them anything they wanted, and what better cover to get away with it than being a postman?'

'Courtesy of The Duke?

'I think so.' Billy turned to Constable Bradshaw. 'So if you need any help in catching that piece of dirt, count me in.'

Thanking their host for his help, Anna led the way out from the small townhouse, turned and waved to Billy. 'As soon as we have anything new, I'll be in touch. For now, just make sure you stay safe.'

'Don't you worry about me; I can look after myself,' he replied as he smiled and waved back before retreating behind the front door.

Clambering back into the police car, Anna urged Tom to get a move on. 'We need to get to Walsingham. With a bit of luck, the spivs will be doing good trade and I'll be able to track down the one who pulled a knife on me. Let's hope he can shed any light on what's been going on.'

Friday in Walsingham meant market day. This, combined with a swell in pilgrim numbers visiting the shrine, resulted in the town centre heaving with people.

After taking some time to find a parking space, Tom turned to his passenger. 'There's one obvious flaw in your plan, Anna. You won't get anywhere near your friendly spiv if they see you with a policeman.'

Oops, I hadn't thought of that.

Getting out of the car, she quickly looked around the jammed market square to see if any spivs had spotted them.

He might already have run for it.

'I tell you what, Tom. Let's split up so we're not seen together. I'll take a look for my spiv and—'

'I'll call in at the station to see if the local beat-bobbies have picked anything up.'

Working her way through a mass of people, Anna struggled to catch sight of any of the spivs using their patch.

I would've thought a square crammed with punters was the perfect cover for them.

She searched for a full twenty minutes without success. About to give up, she noticed a figure slouched on the floor in an alleyway. The man sat slumped, his back leaning awkwardly against an old brick wall.

I wonder?

Apologising several times for having been bumped into by over-enthusiastic shoppers, she neared her target. Entering the narrow passageway, Anna carefully approached the young man. She could see he'd taken a severe beating.

'Can I help you?' Her words were spoken softly as she crouched next to the sorry figure. 'You can trust me; I'm not the police.'

At first, the young man ignored Anna. Instead, he continued to rest his crossed arms on folded knees, his head leaning back on the grime-covered wall.

He's in a terrible state.

Slowly, the young man half-opened his eyes.

'Is there anyone I can get hold of for you?'

The injured man raised his head to look at Anna. 'Who… Who are you? What do you want? I've got a knife and I'm not afraid to use it.'

Anna retrieved a handkerchief from her jacket pocket and dabbed some congealed blood from the injured man's eyes. 'One of your mates said the same thing to me last week. Is it a standard response from men with suitcases in Walsingham?' She offered the man a gentle smile. He failed to reciprocate.

'You… You were the one that gave Stan all that cheek.'

Thank goodness he heard about that.

'So, his name was Stan, was it. Well, it's him I was looking for when I came across you. What in heaven's name is going on?'

The young man winced as he tried to move. To compensate, he held a grubby hand to his ribs. 'You need to get away, lady. The word is out that Stan spoke to someone and let slip our trade secrets. It must be you.'

His words hit Anna hard.

This really is getting serious.

'Your friend didn't say anything, other than telling me quite firmly he wouldn't answer any of my questions.'

The young man moaned again. 'That's not what I heard happened. Anyway, he hasn't been on his pitch for days. The boss man's had him dealt with, if you know what I mean.'

Anna wiped some blood from the young man's cheek. He offered no resistance. 'The boss man? Does he have a name?'

'You must be joking, lady, none of us knows who he is. We only deal with his sidekicks, and they're bad enough.' The injured man tried to laugh, but instead, the pain caused him to cough as he again held his ribs.

'And you? What happened?' Anna watched as the young man struggled to his feet.

'I told you; his sidekicks are a rough lot. They accused me of short-changing them – as if. They said I got off lightly and if they had to come back, I'd never walk again.'

Anna steadied the young man as he wobbled from side to side. 'Are you sure there's nothing I can do?'

'You can leave me alone. If anybody sees me talking to you, I'll be for it.'

She knew there was little point in pressing things. Instead, she passed her bloodied handkerchief to him and began to turn. 'Look after yourself. If you do see – what's his name? – Stan, tell the man I was asking after him.'

Within seconds, Anna had exited the dark alleyway without looking back. Shielding her eyes to protect against the sudden burst of sunlight, she set off for the inspector's car.

Tom was already sitting in the vehicle. 'Thought you'd got lost. Anything interesting?'

Anna slid into the passenger seat and shook her head. 'I got a name but couldn't find him. I did come across a young lad who'd taken a heck of a beating.'

Tom gave her a concerned look. 'If he's a spiv, it's something he'll have come to expect. It's a rough game and not for the fainthearted.'

Anna shook her head. 'All the same, it's still awful.'

Constable Bradshaw turned the ignition key and slowly edged the inspector's car out of its confined parking space. 'The lads at the station didn't have much information, either. It seems there's a team of four spivs work the town and they rotate around the best pitches to avoid arguments. Right, I've a man to see about some flour before we do anything else.'

'Why on earth do you need to call in at Broadside Mill?' Anna was pining for her lunch and couldn't understand why they needed to make a detour.

'I said earlier that the inspector had leant me to you until Sunday night. Unfortunately, that doesn't mean I've been excused of my other duties. I've been asked to check up on Jack Crossman, what with all these break-ins he's been having.'

It took less than forty-five minutes to reach their destination, but as they parked up next to the old windmill, alarm bells began to ring.

'That's strange, Tom, why's that door hanging off its hinges?'

He was already halfway out of the police car when he answered. 'You wait here; I'll check what's going on.'

Twenty seconds later, Constable Bradshaw came out of the mill. 'I need your help. Jack's been hurt.'

Anna moved as quickly as her ankle strapping would allow. She entered the ancient structure to see Tom leaning over a barely conscious Jack Crossman. 'What on earth has happened?' Anna helped Tom get the injured mill keeper onto a chair. 'You've certainly been in the wars. Who have you been upsetting?' She hoped her attempt to lighten the atmosphere might help calm Jack down.

Rubbing the back of his head, Jack shrugged his shoulders. 'I get on with everybody. My family have owned this place for generations; everyone knows we play fair.'

Tom spent several minutes looking around the mill, while Anna tended to Jack's injuries.

'Is anything missing?' asked Tom.

The mill owner began to nod before wincing in pain. 'What do you think? There were two tons of flour in twenty sacks in that corner. A full week's production and they swiped the lot.'

Anna traced a trail of flour dust, which she assumed the thieves caused when dragging each sack to the mill entrance. 'They chanced it while you were here?'

Jack grabbed for a glass of water from a nearby table. 'After last time, I knew they'd be back, so I've been staying overnight to catch the blighters. Well, early this morning, I thought I heard a noise, and sure enough it was them.'

Constable Bradshaw walked back to Jack. 'Why did you get involved?'

The mill owner took a sip of his water before placing the glass tumbler on the table. 'It was getting light, and I saw there were only two of them, so I thought I stood a fair chance. You should have seen them jump when they realised I was here.'

Anna checked the back of Jack's head to see if the blood had stopped oozing from a nasty wound. 'It looks as though they soon recovered their senses. Did you recognise them?'

'Not a chance; both were wearing balaclavas. They were big lads though; I don't know how long I was unconscious, but they got a move on to shift two tons of flour by hand down to the Broad.'

Constable Bradshaw made his way out of the mill before returning a few seconds later. 'You're right, I can see a trail of flour dust down to the water's edge. The thieves could be anywhere by now.

Chapter 18: Hit and Run

'How old did you say that thing is?'

'If you mean my father's wonderful Austin Seven, he bought it in 1932, and it was second-hand then. Dad swears it will go anywhere at twenty-five miles an hour.'

Anna squeezed herself into the tiny two-seater. Tom stepped onto the running board, cocked a leg over the small door and dropped into the driver's seat.

'I don't want to be unkind, but there's more rust than metal in this old banger. It hasn't even got a roof.'

Tom sighed indignantly. 'It has a perfectly serviceable canvas roof, should it rain. It fits almost perfectly. Anyway, it's forecast to be sunny today.'

After several attempts, he finally managed to get the engine going. However, a passer-by began to cough violently as she walked into a wall of blue-grey smoke from the car's exhaust.

'I think we'd better get going.' Seconds later, the old car finally responded to Tom's request for more speed.

'Twenty-five miles an hour, you say. And how long will it take this thing to go that fast?'

Although Tom ignored Anna's taunt while concentrating on keeping the Austin in a straight line, she nevertheless sensed his pride in managing to avoid stalling the engine.

'You wait until we're speeding downhill, then you'll see what she can do.'

I dread to think.

'Why aren't we in the inspector's car, anyway?'

'He said he needed it for police business. I don't believe him for a minute, though, because he told me the other day that he intended on taking his wife to Wells-next-the-sea. Anyway, Dad's been saving his petrol coupons. He said as long as I didn't drive too quickly and waste the stuff, he was happy.'

Fat chance of that.

As the little car drove further into the Norfolk countryside, Anna's troubles evaporated. 'Do you remember when we used to have bike rides around here as kids? It seems like another life now.'

Tom wrestled with the inadequate breaks as he navigated bend after bend in the narrow roads. 'You were the one that always wanted to see what was around that corner or down a particular track. Given what you've been up to for the last week or so, you haven't changed one bit, have you?'

Anna smiled. 'And you were always the sensible one. That's something else that hasn't changed.'

The two friends continued to reminisce as they neared Hickling Broad.

'How many wherries do you think are still in use?' asked Anna.

'Well, I can say for sure there aren't hundreds and hundreds. Nevertheless, the one we're looking for will still take some finding. I double-checked the map, trying to work out where our flour thieves are most likely to have sailed. Hickling is as good a place as any to start.'

Tom eventually managed to bring the old car to a stop. He applied the handbrake so tightly that Anna was convinced he'd snap it off. 'Let's head for the staithe. You never know; someone might have seen something,' suggested Anna.

Having watched Tom step back over the driver's door and onto the car's running board, Anna copied his technique in getting out of the vehicle.

That was a mistake.

They were soon standing on the timber staging of the staithe, looking for signs of wherries. Admiring the gentle landscape in which the extensive Broad sat, Anna revelled in the peace and quiet of the surroundings.

'Can I help?'

The stranger's voice snapped Anna back into the present and she realised she stood alone next to a stranger.

Where's Tom disappeared to?

'Oh, hello. I'm admiring how wonderfully peaceful the Broad is. Do you have a boat moored here?'

The elderly gentleman, his face creased and cracked from a lifetime working outdoors, puffed on a cigarette as he pointed to a small craft tied to one of the mooring posts. 'It's a lot quieter than it was before the war. Not many tourists now. Anyway, that's mine. Doreen, I call her.'

Anna looked at the boat while glancing around for her erstwhile friend. 'She seems like a lot of fun to sail. To tell you the truth, I'm looking for one vessel in particular.' She sensed she'd triggered the old man's curiosity. 'I'm looking for a wherry that's been transporting flour. Don't suppose you've seen it, have you?'

He took another puff from his cigarette and picked a piece of tobacco from his bottom lip. 'Flour, you say?'

Sounds promising.

'Let's see, there's only one mill anywhere near here that produces the stuff these days, and as far as I know, all his flour goes the other way into Norwich.'

Anna's disappointment was palpable. 'Oh, I see. It's just that a friend of mine told me sometimes the odd sack found its way up here.' Anna keenly observed the stranger's reaction.

He's either a good actor or hasn't a clue what I'm talking about.

'I see. Important, is it?'

She shrugged her shoulders. 'Not really. I heard the wherry was on Hickling Broad, and since I was close, I thought I'd see if they had any flour for sale. We all like a bit extra, don't we, what with the rationing and all.'

At that moment, Tom reappeared. He shook his head to indicate he hadn't found anything without letting the old man see what he was doing.

'Never mind, and thank you for your company,' said Anna as she breezed past the elderly gentleman and joined Tom walking back to his father's car.

Further disappointment followed at Barton Broad and Wroxham. Fed up and hungry, Anna suggested they head back to Lipton Saint Faith for lunch at the vicarage.

'I tell you what, why don't we try Breydon Water? I know it's a bit out of our way, but it sits next to Great Yarmouth. Thinking about it, isn't that the natural place the thieves would've offloaded their ill-gotten gains?'

'That's one way of looking at it, but don't you think it's a bit conspicuous?'

He shook his head. 'You might say hiding in plain sight. So what if the black marketeers have to double back on themselves to distribute the stuff – what better place for a working wherry to offload its cargo than in a port? It's got to be worth a look.'

Anna spotted a wisp of steam rising from the radiator. 'And do you think this thing will get us there, then all the way back to the village?' She pointed at the front of the car.

'I'm certain of it. Dad's car may be temperamental and blow her top sometimes, but a little steam is nothing to worry about, I promise you.'

We'll see.

An hour later, Tom navigated the car to one of the quieter spots on the impressive stretch of water. 'That's strange, why has the mast been taken down?' He pointed to a wherry. Partially hidden from sight, its poor condition gave the impression it had been abandoned.

Pressing the brake pedal and simultaneously applying the handbrake, he eventually managed to bring the temperamental car to a stop. 'Come on, let's take a look.'

Not so fast.

'Shouldn't we be careful? It's not as though you're in police uniform. If it's the boat we're looking for, the thugs that beat Jack Crossman up might still be on board.'

Tom smiled at his companion. 'Now who's the cautious one?'

Before she could respond, he'd scrambled onto the boat and disappeared into the wherry's interior. Seconds later, she jumped aboard to see Tom beaming like a naughty schoolboy.

'This is the one.'

'Since you look like a ghost covered in all that flour, you may be right.'

* * *

Lunch was hardly over when a frantic knock at the front door of the vicarage boomed around the tiled vestibule.

'Sounds as if someone requires your father,' commented Tom as Anna quickly exited the kitchen and hurried to the door.

'Thank heavens you're in. Billy's been run over, and I don't know what to do. I've already lost my husband; please, God, not my brother-in-law too. Will you go to him? I can't face seeing Billy injured.'

Hearing the woman's distressed tone, Tom sped into the vestibule.

'Which hospital is he in? We'll get over there straight away.'

Peggy continued to shake as she tried to get her words out. 'The Norfolk and Norwich. Please tell me he's going to be all right.'

Tom ran back into the kitchen to retrieve his car keys.

'I know it's hard, Peggy, but try to stay calm. We'll be back as soon as we can. I'm sure your brother-in-law is in safe hands.'

By 1.30 pm, they were speaking with Billy's doctor.

'Do you know what happened?' asked Anna.

'We've put him in a side room. He's quite poorly. It seems he was crossing Ipswich Road and a car came from nowhere, hit him, and sped off. We've done all we can for now. He's slipping in and out of consciousness. We must now wait to see if there's been any brain damage.'

Anna exchanged solemn looks with Tom. She turned to the doctor. 'Can we see him?'

The medic hesitated before beckoning the matron over to confer. 'I doubt he'll know you're here, but we can see no harm. It may well be that he'll react to a familiar voice, but please, he must be kept calm.'

Once inside the tiny room, all was quiet. With the curtains closed, Anna pondered how peaceful things were.

Hard to believe Billy might be dying.

They sat, one on each side of Billy's bed, both willing him to wake. Time seemed to have stopped. The only movement to be observed was a liquid slowly dripping from a transparent bag into a clear tube attached to Billy's arm.

'This is looking bad. Billy is in a heck of a state.' Her words were whispered as if breaking the code of silence in a library.

Her companion nodded. 'When a doctor says it's touch and go, I guess we've got to accept he might not pull through.'

Anna's attention was drawn to a slight movement in one of Billy's fingers. Seconds later, the stricken patient half-opened his eyes.

'I'm not dead yet, and I've got steak and kidney pie in for tea.'

Before either could respond, Billy slipped back into unconsciousness.

'Isn't the human body an amazing thing?' mused Anna.

'If you mean it can get itself crushed by a car and still function, it most certainly is. Billy's problem, as the doctor made clear, will be if there's any lasting damage to his brain.'

Anna took hold of Billy's hand. 'But he spoke, having clearly heard us. That must be a good sign.' She felt Billy's hand move.

'And I've got some tasty vegetables to go with it.'

She gave Billy a broad smile as his eyes opened wider.

'You've certainly been in the wars. Can you remember what happened?'

She watched as Billy tried to shake his head but was unable to move it more than an inch or so. 'Stay still, Billy; you need to rest.'

His eyes moved between each of his visitors.

'I think he recognises us,' said Tom.

'I think you're right.'

'And you look like a copper, even out of uniform.'

Anna smiled as she continued to hold Billy's hand, giving him the occasional squeeze to offer what comfort she could.

'Then you must be on the mend, young man. Is there anything you can tell us about what happened?'

His began to drift off again.

'What happened, Billy?' whispered Anna as she leant over the bed.

His eyes closed. Billy gave a one-word reply. 'Tuffsmen'

Anna moved closer so that her face rested a few inches from Billy's. 'Tuffsmen? Who is Tuffsmen?'

'He's out of it good and proper this time,' said Tom.

She looked across the iron-framed bed. 'Do you know the name?'

Tom looked at Billy and shook his head. 'It could be anyone. I don't recognise it as being on our books, but I can check Norwich headquarters to see what I can turn up.

The old Austin began to spew steam again as they made their way back to the village.

'Are you sure this thing will get us home?'

Tom patted the steering wheel as if it were a living thing. 'She runs like clockwork.'

'Then I hope you've got the key to wind the blessed thing up, then,' replied Anna.

For the rest of the journey, the pair grappled with the implications of the hit and run.

'Why do you think the driver failed to stop when he ran over Billy? The man must have known he hit something.'

Tom gave Anna a wistful look. 'You wouldn't believe how many times I've come across this. Drivers panic. Perhaps he didn't have insurance or his car tax was out of date. The only thing I would say is that it's unusual when it happens on a busy city street. The culprit runs the risk that somebody took his car registration number.'

She put a finger to her bottom lip. 'Of course, there could be another reason. Perhaps whoever—'

'Ran him over, meant to. Then you think it was more than an accident?' said Tom.

'I don't know, but perhaps someone thought he was getting too close to them. Who knows, they may have seen us, with you in uniform, going into Billy's house yesterday.'

Tom murmured something she couldn't pick up as the car reached Lipton Saint Faith.

'What did you say?'

He shrugged his shoulders. 'Something I'd rather not admit to myself, because if you're right, it means somebody's been watching every move we've made since yesterday… Of course, it may all be entirely innocent, and Billy was simply in the wrong place at the wrong time.

'All the same, I think we both need to be careful. Remember, something, or some*body*, caused Lieutenant Elsner to leave quickly. Perhaps whoever it was has turned their attention to us.'

Mention of Eddie hit Anna like a stone.

Where are you?

Overcoming her guilt for not thinking about the American for a few hours, Anna hardened her resolve. 'Then we'd better get a move on, hadn't we? Drop me off at Peggy Fleming's place. You might want to see if you can trace this Tuffman chap, then find out who owns the wherry we came across on Breydon Water.

'How is he? Please tell me he's going to be all right.'

Peggy showed her guest into the small living room and looked at her for hopeful news.

Anna tried to look cheerful. She knew how important it was for Peggy's wellbeing that she retained at least some hope. 'It's quite a nasty injury, Peggy. The good news is that we managed to speak to him. That's got to be a positive thing, hasn't it?'

Peggy gave her guest a nervous smile as she continuously turned her gold wedding band between a finger and thumb. 'I can't bear to think about losing him too. He and Ted were so close. I know brothers are supposed to be, but they really were. It's not fair.'

She began to cry and stood motionless like a lost child weeping in a sea of strangers.

Anna pulled Peggy close. 'Billy is still alive. That means there's hope. I know it's hard, but all we can do is wait.'

Anna felt Peggy shaking with emotion as she placed her arms around the widow. She stroked Peggy's hair and urged the widow to give her feelings free rein.

A full ten minutes passed before Peggy began to regain her composure.

'Why don't you sit down? You look exhausted. Shall we have a nice cup of tea?'

Anna disappeared into the kitchen and returned a few minutes later with two steaming cups of the soothing drink.

There were questions she wanted to ask but thought it prudent to wait a while. Instead, Anna spent her time looking around the small room filled with a lifetime of memories.

I can't begin to understand how hard this must be for her.

As the minutes passed, Anna grew more confident; the time was right to raise what she knew would be a delicate subject.

'Do you think Billy knew anything about Ted's gambling problems?'

Peggy hesitated. 'Since they were brothers and close to each other, I suppose he might have, but my husband never mentioned it. Neither did Billy.'

You don't need to know the trouble Ted had really got himself into for now, either.

Chapter 19: A Wanderer Returns

I hope Billy survives for Peggy's sake.

Anna was deep in thought as she took a meandering route back to the vicarage to avoid speaking to anyone who knew her.

The last thing I want is to talk about the weather and village gossip.

Making her way along a twisting track, its surface rutted from millennia of horse and cart traffic, Anna soon realised she'd made a mistake. Even with her grandfather's walking stick, it was hard going.

A little way into the distance, she noticed the welcoming sight of an old tree trunk that had lain in the same position for as long as she could remember.

That'll do.

Eventually managing to sit down in a measure of comfort, Anna placed the walking stick beside her and took in the peaceful surroundings. As a child, the horse paddock, now hidden behind a line of maturing elm trees, served as a safe play area, which had the advantage of being close to home yet far enough away from meddlesome parents.

Anna closed her eyes and tilted her head slowly back to catch the warming sun and enjoy the solitude.

Suddenly, she heard the crack of a small branch snapping. Momentarily, the disturbance brought Anna around from her self-induced stupor before she once more drifted off into childhood memories.

A second branch snapped with a sharp crack. This time, nearer. Anna placed a hand on the fallen tree to support herself as she looked behind her. All seemed normal. Nevertheless, there was part of her that was beginning to regret taking such an isolated track.

'All on your own now your American boyfriend has done a runner, are you?' She recognised the voice immediately and turned to see Walter emerging from the trees.

'Have you nothing better to do than follow me around? I told you what I'd do if you kept on.'

'You haven't got a copper or the Yank around you now, so I wouldn't be so cocky if I were you.' Plowright smirked as he sat uninvited on the fallen tree next to Anna.

You make my skin crawl. What did I ever see in you?

'What is it you want from me, Walter? I've told you a dozen times it's over between us. Why can't you just move on?' Plowright edged closer to Anna, forcing her to shuffle to her right. 'What are you doing?'

'You always did think you were better than me. Well, I'm the bigshot now. I have money and powerful friends. You've even met some of them.'

Has he got himself mixed up with The Duke?

'Listen, Walter. We're not teenagers anymore. Time to be honest with each other. Do I still hold a candle for you? The answer is no. Do I care what happens to you? Yes, I do; so if you've got yourself tangled up with betting scams or the black market, you can tell me.'

Walter laughed. 'What, so you can go running off to Tom Bradshaw? Thanks for nothing. Don't you worry about me; it's you and your new fella that need to worry.'

I've had enough of this.

'Don't make idle threats or you really will be in trouble.'

Plowright inched to his left again. 'Who said they were idle threats.'

Anna sensed his breath on her neck. 'Back off, Walter. You're not the only one who knows The Duke.'

Plowright let out a belly roar.

What's he up to?

'The Duke? Don't make me laugh. I said I knew *powerful* people, not a greasy bloke in a posh suit who thinks he owns the place. You've no idea what I'm talking about, have you?'

She could see Walter was enjoying the moment.

He's not clever enough to be bluffing.

'To be honest, I don't care who you are, or are not, in cahoots with. As long as you don't hurt me or mine, you can do what you like. I can tell you this: if you think people stuffing money into your pockets for heaven knows what in return are your friends, think on, sunshine. There's a world of difference between friendship and being taken for a fool.'

Plowright put a hand on Anna's knee. 'There you go again with one of your little lectures. Who I do business with is none of your concern, and I've got a lesson for you to take in. The day is coming when I'll have more money than I know what to do with, then I'll—'

'Do what? And get your hand off me.'

Plowright smirked as he squeezed Anna's leg.

That's it.

Without further warning, Anna grabbed her walking stick and brought it down hard on Plowright's shoulder blade. He cried out in pain and fell backwards.

The thwack as she landed her blow reverberated amongst the trees, causing several birds to take flight. 'And this is for getting fresh with me. Don't ever try to touch me again.' Anna pulled her arm back. Suddenly a voice rang out.

'I can't let you hit him a second time, Anna, much as I would like you to. The law must take its course. I'm sure you don't want to give his solicitor any excuse to claim he was the one being attacked.'

Tom's calm yet authoritative explanation snapped Anna out of her rage. Instead, she glowered at Plowright as he lay prone amongst the long grass and nettles.

Constable Bradshaw gestured for Anna to move aside. 'Do you want to press charges?'

Tom's question threw her into confusion.

What would my father expect me to do?

As she pondered the point, Anna looked on as Tom restrained Plowright, who was now sitting up, rubbing his shoulder blade.

'Stay still. Don't move. Or else.'

Impressive.

'Right, Anna. I'll get this toerag to the station. Are you OK making your way home or should I call your father?'

She shook her head. 'No, don't do that, you'll only alarm him. I'll be fine. Besides which, that idiot isn't worth it.'

As Constable Bradshaw began to lead Plowright away, he turned back. 'Oh, by the way, the thing I said I'd check out. Well,

I've come up trumps. I'll pop round to the vicarage when I've finished the paperwork on this one. I think you'll be interested to know who owns it.'

Having spent the remainder of Saturday afternoon quietly recuperating from the day's excitement, in her father's office, Anna felt better. Although she told her parents what had happened, she played down the extent of Plowright's threats.

'Anna, you have visitors. Do you want to see them or are you still resting?'

Her mother's reassuring tone reminded Anna of a happy childhood surrounded by loving parents. 'Tom said he'd be calling. Is there someone with him?'

'I think you'd better come and see for yourself.'

Having limped across her father's office, she leant on the doorknob to support her weight as she opened the door and peered down the vestibule towards the front door.

'This chap says he needs to speak to you. Oh, by the way, he also says he hates coppers and hopes the Germans drop a bomb on me,' announced Tom.

The stranger, who had been severely beaten, shrugged his shoulders, yet had a twinkle in his eye for Anna.

'Yes, we know each other. I'm assuming you didn't do that to him?'

Tom smiled as he helped the injured man down the vestibule. 'As if. More than my job's worth, anyway.' The constable redoubled his efforts to support the man as he winced in pain.

'Let's get him comfortable.'

Minutes later, Anna's mother brought refreshments, before asking Tom to give her best wishes to his parents and withdrawing.

'I'm guessing by the way your friend is dressed that he's not a bank manager.' Tom pointed to the injured man's loud suit, trilby and pencil moustache.

He raised his eyebrows at the constable.

'This is my friendly… err, spiv. So sorry to use that horrible term, but when we last met, we didn't get as far as exchanging names. What is it, your name, I mean?'

Anna knew the man was reluctant to reveal anything, but he eventually responded.

'Fred will do.'

You know I know it's Stan.

'Well, that's a very nice name, isn't it, Constable Bradshaw?'

Tom gave the merest of nods.

'The thing is, miss, that boy you helped in Walsingham the other day… Well, he's my brother, and before you ask, let's call him Joe.' Fred tried to smile but held his rib cage, letting out a cry of pain.

'Take your time, Fred; there's no hurry. Would you like something to eat?' Anna noticed mention of food galvanised the man's attention, despite his injuries. 'I'll be back in two shakes of a lamb's tail. I assume I can trust you, Constable Bradshaw?'

Tom's weary smile convinced her he knew what she meant.

Several minutes later, Anna reappeared. 'I'm sorry it's only a little bread and cheese. It's the rationing; you understand, I'm sure.'

Fred smiled as broadly as he was able and reached for his food.

'A bit ironic, don't you think?'

'What are you talking about?'

The constable pointed to Fred. 'You're talking about rations, or the lack of them, and there's him probably able to get you anything you want. As I say, ironic.'

She shook her head and instead concentrated on how Fred was faring. 'Why have you come all the way from Walsingham?'

The spiv struggled to eat his crusty bread, courtesy of his cut lips and bruised cheeks. Having taken a small bite, and the time to slowly chew his food, Fred responded. 'People need us, miss, but they despise us. Not many people show the kindness you did, so I'm here to help you.'

'Help me?'

Fred attempted to take a second bite of his bread before thinking better of it. 'My brother told me what you said, you know, about wanting a name.'

Anna's excitement grew. 'You mean you're going to tell me who beat both of you up?'

Fred shook his head. As he shifted his position, he again held his ribs and let out a grunt of pain. 'I think you mean the person who arranged for us to be clobbered. They never get their hands dirty.'

Tom glanced at Anna, urging her on.

'You mean someone got his thugs to do his dirty work for him?'

Fred nodded. 'I can't give you his name. Taking a beating is one thing; he's arranged for this to happen many times. Naming him, well, if he found out, he'd finish my brother and me off for good, if you know what I mean?'

The Duke and his thugs?

'I'll say this, miss; some people are fireproof. If you decide to go after him and he finds out, he'll kill you, but if I can help you, I will.'

Anna's frustration began to show. 'But Fred, if I'm—'

Several hard knocks on the front door interrupted Anna's

flow. Seconds later, her mother showed a familiar figure into the room.

Her face turned purple with rage and, despite her strapped ankle, Anna rushed forward and slapped his face. 'You dare to disappear and pay a young boy a few pennies to deliver a cryptic message. Now you turn up again as if nothing's happened. What are you playing at?'

Lieutenant Elsner didn't flinch as the blow struck home. 'I'm not going to apologise. I meant what I said in that note.'

She was suddenly aware Tom and the spiv both had looks of incredulity plastered across their faces. 'At least Fred has an excuse, Tom, he doesn't know who my American friend is.'

Constable Bradshaw looked at Eddie, then at Anna. 'Whatever's going on between you two, I don't want to know, so don't have a go at me, Anna Grix.'

The American offered one of his trademark schoolboy smiles.

'And don't you think that silly grin is going to get you out of trouble this time, Eddie Elsner.'

Fred busied himself, trying to eat more of his sandwich, while Tom tinkered with his policeman's whistle and chain.

'There's a couple of things you need to know. If you calm down, you might begin to understand what I've been doing and how the information I have may help, or are you still determined to solve these murders on your own?'

After twenty minutes of sharing what each had discovered, Anna knew what she had to do.

'We haven't much time to get this organised. However, if we get our ducks in a row, we'll have proved who murdered Ted Fleming and Cyril Trubshaw by ten o'clock tomorrow evening.'

Constable Bradshaw looked across to Anna. 'Remember,

you only have until midnight tomorrow before you promised to drop your amateur sleuthing if you don't crack the case.'

Eddie gave Anna a quizzical look.

'Don't ask. I'll explain later. Now, this is what we're going to do.

'Hello, I thought I'd give you a ring. I need your help.' Anna knew stroking The Duke's ego would play into her hands as she spoke into the vicarage telephone handset.

'Dear Anna, always a pleasure to hear from you, and if I can help, so much the better. Has your boyfriend's car broken down again?'

Anna wanted to scream at the man who had kidnapped her, but knew she had to turn on the charm. 'Oh, that was funny, wasn't it? The thing is, Mum has arranged a singsong and prize-giving at the Memorial Hall tomorrow to thank those villagers who have been doing the most for our Spitfire fund. Nothing grand, but it's a chance to let go of our war-weariness for a couple of hours.'

A short silence followed before The Duke responded. 'A singsong… So you want me to do a turn?'

His response took Anna by surprise. 'I didn't know you sang. Well, certainly I can arrange that. The thing is, we want you to present the prizes. After all, everyone knows you.'

The phone once more fell silent for several seconds.

Have I pushed him too far?

'Are you serious? We both know what I do for a living.'

It was time for her to think on her feet. 'Exactly, so isn't this an ideal opportunity to show that you can give a little back? We all like people to like us, don't we?'

Come on, Mr vain.

'One question. Why have you left it so late? Forgive me for being cautious, but you must admit, it all sounds a little odd.'

He's rumbled me.

It was then that Anna noticed her father, who was gesturing for the handset.

'Ah, just the man. Do let me apologise. I'm Anna's father and helping her mother arrange tomorrow's celebration. Yes, I caught the conversation. I'm afraid it's all my fault. You see, I asked my daughter to ring you. Why? Well, yes, a fair question. It's about pulling the community together during difficult times.

'Some of the villagers have suffered so much. As for the rest of us, well, we are all depressed by what we read and hear every day… yes, of course, you're… I understand. So, as vicar, I feel I have to bring all sides together. Short notice? Yes, you're quite correct, but you see, my wife and I were talking a few hours ago about wanting to demonstrate we are all in this terrible thing together.

'After all, we are all equal in God's eyes. Your name came up, and we thought, well, you can only say no. But believe me, sir, you would be paying my wife and I such an honour if you would step in and award our modest prizes to some of the village children.'

The vicar looked at Anna and winked.

'You will? Oh, that's splendid. then I shall see you around eight o'clock tomorrow evening. I know that Anna will look after you. What's that? Yes, yes. Of course, she will most certainly be there now that you are joining us.'

Chapter 20: Prizes and Prisoners

Lipton St Faith Memorial Hall buzzed with excitement as friends from the surrounding area greeted one another and giggled over the latest gossip.

Paper daisy-chains made by village schoolchildren hung in swags from the low wooden ceiling, and Union Jacks adorned the otherwise bare walls.

On the stage rested a square table with a brilliant white cloth hiding its battered surface, behind which sat a row of four faux bamboo chairs.

Anna's father sauntered along the front edge of the small stage, having a few words with one villager, then moving a few feet to speak to another.

Positioned diagonally across the back of the stage stood an old piano. Sat bolt upright, an elderly lady tried her best to coach the out of tune instrument to play 'Roll out The Barrel'.

Away from the hubbub, Anna's mother, Helen, kept Sir Reginald Fischer engaged in conversation. 'May I get you another small sherry? It's so good of you to present the prizes again this evening.' Helen took a small wafer-thin sherry glass from the aristocrat's outstretched arm.

'The pleasure is entirely mine, Mrs Grix. I'm well aware that you and your husband do so much for our little community in these difficult times. Spending an hour with the villagers is, I think, the very least I can do. How many prizes are there this evening?'

Helen handed the replenished glass back to her guest before replacing the crystal stopper on the sherry decanter.

'There are twenty for you to present. Some are relatively modest, while for others, we spent as much as ten shillings. I do hope you don't think we've wasted any of your generous donations. Charles and I thought we should push the boat out this evening to cheer everyone up. After all, it has been a challenging year so far.'

Sir Reginald lazily waved his free hand. 'I try to do the same thing with my employees. Many are women with their husbands away fighting. Let me say again what a pleasure it is to be with you this evening, one which I've been looking forward to immensely.'

The vicar popped his head around the brown-painted panelled door. 'Good evening, Sir Reginald. I do apologise for the delay. We should be ready to begin in about ten minutes.'

Anna was beginning to panic, thinking The Duke had seen through her plan. As she waited nervously in a committee room, she paced up and down, while looking through a window from time to time to see if he'd arrived.

If he doesn't come, I'm going to look stupid.

She smoothed the creases from her aged cotton dress and fussed over whether her hair might look as if she was showing off at a time when everyday life was getting tougher.

What if they think I've spent good money on a new hairdo?

Her concerns were banished as the committee room door swung open.

'Good evening, my darling Anna. I imagine you thought I'd got lost?' The Duke sauntered in as if he owned the place.

He's on his own, no henchmen.

Anna forced a broad smile, although it was the last thing she wanted to do. 'Not at all; I knew you'd come. You told me you are a man of your word, and I believed you.'

Placing his trilby on the corner of a table, The Duke stepped further into the room.

Oh, please, don't say he's going to kiss me.

Her concerns increased as the small, well-dressed visitor closed in.

That cologne smells awful.

'Drink?' Anna slid sideways and made for a tray of alcohol, some of which her father had found in a long-forgotten box in the vicarage stables.

The Duke shook his head. 'I make a point never to drink when I'm working. That way, I keep my senses and don't make silly mistakes. I'm sure you understand.'

I hate that smirk.

As he made a second attempt to kiss her, Anna moved quickly to avoid an embrace she had no intention of encouraging. 'Let me quickly run through the evening. Have you done one of these things before?'

It was enough to distract her unwanted suitor.

'I once gave a speech at a wedding – a distant uncle if I remember. It didn't end well, with the groom and his father-in-law beating seven bells out of each other. I'm sure things will be a little calmer this evening. They will, won't they?'

Anna wasn't sure if he was joking or threatening violence. She realised she didn't know him at all.

What was I thinking? This could go so wrong.

Before she could go through the running order, the door opened again.

'Anna, the vicar said we're ready to start and asks if you might take our guest to the stage.'

Thanking the villager and turning back to The Duke, she smiled.

Thank heavens I'm out of here.

Walking slightly ahead of her guest, she made her way down a dimly lit, narrow corridor. To her right, behind a half-open door, she caught sight of Inspector Spillers, Constable Bradshaw and two other uniformed officers.

If he sees them, I'm done for.

Anna drifted slowly across the corridor as she moved forward and took hold of the brass doorknob, silently closing the door without missing a step. She knew if he suspected anything, now was the time he'd make his move.

'A bit of a labyrinth, this place, isn't it?'

For once, she was relieved to hear The Duke's words.

Ten more seconds and he'll be standing in front of a hundred people.

The Reverend Grix turned to the piano player and nodded as a signal she should stop. Silence from the tuneless piano caused the general hubbub in the hall to subside.

'My lords, ladies and gentlemen, I should like to thank everyone who's contributed to what I know will be a most successful evening. So, without further ado, I ask all present to welcome our two esteemed guests with a generous round of applause.'

The audience erupted in a cacophony of noise.

From one wing of the stage, Helen Grix led Sir Reginald Fischer to a chair. Anna escorted The Duke to a second chair.

He's gone pale.

She took note of how nervous he suddenly looked.

Not quite so confident after all. How exquisite.

Meanwhile, Sir Reginald looked a picture of confidence as he leant across to shake The Duke's hand. The aristocrat sported a self-assured smile and, from time to time, acknowledged various people in the audience by giving them a friendly, regal wave.

Helen took centre stage. 'May I add my thanks to our guests for giving up their precious time to be with us this evening.'

The two men nodded, Sir Reginald still by far the most relaxed of the pair.

'I'm pleased to announce that, by our villages joining forces, the total amount raised towards our Spitfire now stands at £350.'

A chorus of cheers rang out. Helen felt a tap on her arm. She turned to see Sir Reginald holding a small oblong piece of paper.

Realising it was a cheque, and the value, Helen squealed. 'May I make a correction; due to yet another most generous donation from Sir Reginald, our Spitfire fund now stands at an incredible £500.'

A second, louder cheer thundered through the building.

Anna looked at her crestfallen guest.

You have no idea what's coming.

It took the best part of a minute for the excitement to die down. In the meantime, the vicar removed a black cloth from a second table, which revealed an array of prizes.

Catching sight of the display, a more sedate round of applause rippled through the audience.

'Well, wasn't that exciting? Now, if I may invite our two guests to take their positions at either end of the prize table, we shall begin. First of all, I—'

Here we go, too late to back out now.

Anna, who had remained in one wing of the stage, stepped forward. 'Mother, do forgive me for interrupting, but I have a few things I want to say.' A low rumbling erupted as villagers began to murmur to one another. 'This evening is about celebrating our achievements as a community. Although we shall enjoy songs; we all love to sing after the intermission, there is a more serious side to our celebration.

'Most of you know, over the last ten days, we've lost two dear friends. Both stalwarts of our community, who provided invaluable services that made our everyday lives that little easier.'

Anna's father appeared from the opposite wing of the stage. 'My dear, are you sure that this is—'

'The right time to remember absent friends?' Anna looked at the two principal guests. As before, the aristocrat exhibited a confident smile, seeming not in the least perturbed by the turn of events. She noticed that The Duke, however, nervously looked at his watch and then at the exit doors of the Memorial Hall. 'Father, I think it's absolutely the right time.'

The murmuring increased as the villagers turned to each other in confused conversation.

'Ted Fleming, our wonderful postman, was minding his own business as he cycled to the post office to sort, then deliver, the first post last Saturday. Except, he never made it to work. Instead, he died in a ditch like so much roadkill.'

'My darling, is this necessary?' The vicar gestured for his daughter to withdraw.

Anna ignored his pleas. 'Then a few days later, Cyril Trubshaw, the man who provided every one of us with bread for over twenty years, died in what appeared to be a tragic accident.'

Once more, she glanced at the two guests. The Duke stared at a large round clock on the far wall of the hall. Sir Reginald, on the other hand, adopted an empathetic demeanour, nodding at Anna's words from time to time.

'But what if I were to tell you that neither man's death was an accident? In fact, they were closely linked.' As quickly as Anna had appeared on stage, she slipped back into the wings.

Before the villagers had time to react, a man stood from the rear of the building. 'The strange thing about living in a small community is that we all think we know each other when, in fact, each of us has a separate, secret life. We try to hide this other life from our family and friends. Sometimes we succeed.' Lieutenant Eddie Elsner stood out as his smart uniform separated him from the greyness of wartime civilian clothing. 'Ted and Cyril had secret lives, known only to those closest to them.' The hubbub increased as the crowd speculated as to what the American was referring. 'Like drinking that gets out of hand and turns a social event into a prison sentence, so betting can have the same result. The prison I speak of is one of shame. Unable to stop what they do, unable to afford what they've turned into.

'Previously perfectly civil and helpful men morph into withdrawn, moody individuals who begin to keep secrets. Their loved ones notice these changes and try to put things right. However, they're as helpless as the victims of addiction.'

As the hall fell silent, waiting for the lieutenant to reveal more, a muffled sound projected from behind the stage.

'It's a sad fact of life,' continued Eddie, 'that for every addicted person, there is someone who is more than willing to feed that habit. Isn't that true, Mr Albert Root?' A general look of confusion spread around the audience at mention of such a strange name.

Anna looked towards the centre of the stage where Sir Reginald was finding it hard to stifle his laughter. The Duke, however, had a face like thunder.

To everyone's amazement, the vicar's daughter reappeared. 'Mr Root doesn't quite have the same ring to it as The Duke, does it, Albert?' She sensed the embarrassed man beginning to move before he checked himself. 'Do you remember telling me that nobody takes from you what is yours? Well, you may be many things, but you are most certainly a man of your word, are you not?

'I have no doubt your humble beginnings drove your determination to amass as much money as possible and hang onto possessions as if your life depended on it. But that doesn't mean you have the right to make other people's life a misery, does it, Albert?'

The Duke's cheeks flushed with rage, his hands curled into fists clenched so tight that his knuckles turned white.

'Then again, other people's lives don't have much value to you, do they, Albert?' Heads swivelled as the lieutenant took up the onslaught. 'At least, not unless they're the means through which you make even more money. But what if the opposite happens?'

By the time The Duke had gathered his wits, Anna had disappeared again.

'You see, for some people, the problem with money is that they can never get enough of it. You've been making a good living off the ill-gotten gains of your illegal betting ring.'

Wives looked at husbands accusingly as the audience reacted to the lieutenant's assertion.

'But some of those men inevitably lost more than they were able to pay. I imagine for someone like you, that can be quite useful. After all, who better to get your dirty work done than desperate men who will do anything to clear their debts.'

Finally, The Duke took Eddie's bait. 'I have no idea what you're talking about. I'm a legitimate businessman. I have no police convictions, and I often help out by lending people money on reasonable terms.'

The lieutenant jumped on Albert Root's defence of his livelihood. 'And there we have it, ladies and gentlemen, as well as running an illegal betting ring, Albert has just admitted he's a loan shark. I'm sure the police will be most interested to hear that.'

The Duke looked nervously around the room at mention of the police.

'But then you got greedy.' Anna's reappearance looked like a Wimbledon tennis final. The audience turned from Eddie to Anna, then back again as the pair took turns in heaping derision on Albert Root.

'Betting can be lucrative, but this is a small community, and the menfolk don't have that much to gamble away. I'm sure you soon realised that the future of your betting business remained limited. So, you began to look towards the black market. After all, the opportunities there are limitless, are they not?'

Anna began to slip back into the wings. This time the audience knew the drill and, as one, twisted around to look at Lieutenant Elsner.

'If only you'd have stuck to betting, you'd have made a steady, if seedy, living off the backs of other people's misery. But you wanted a piece of the black market, and somehow you found out Ted Fleming and Cyril Trubshaw were involved. After all, what better cover to take orders and make deliveries than two trusted villagers who could hide their side-line into a normal day's work.'

The Duke shook his head. 'You're talking rubbish. I've never had anything to do with the black market. Betting is an honourable business; the black market depends on stolen goods sold at an inflated price. I'm no thief.'

'I agree, Mr Root.' Lieutenant Elsner's admission stunned the audience into silence. 'That's not to say you haven't been tempted, though, is it? Except that when Mr Big heard about your ambitions, he found out Ted and Cyril were in hock to you.'

The Duke looked utterly confused. 'You've agreed I'm not a thief, so what's this nonsense all about?'

Lieutenant Elsner began to walk from the back of the hall, his pace steady as his eyes moved from a bewildered Albert Root across to the Honourable Sir Reginald Fischer.

'You ordered the murder, didn't you, Sir Reginald?'

The hall descended into pandemonium.

'Not only did you arrange the postman's murder,' shouted Eddie to make himself heard above the noise, 'you also arranged for a letter to be forged. It purported to be from Ted, and you cleverly had it addressed to his brother, saying he needed help with money and laying a trail back to The Duke.'

Sir Reginald's demeanour remained unaltered as he continued to hold his hands behind his back, his head tilted to one side as if listening to village gossip.

'Unfortunately for you, that letter, although discovered in the ditch, wasn't finally opened until a couple of days ago. That was after your second victim Cyril Trubshaw's body had been discovered. To misquote the wonderful Oscar Wilde; to find one body is unfortunate, to find a second is beyond a coincidence.'

By now, Eddie had reached the foot of the stage with his back to the enthralled audience.

Sir Reginald stepped forward to look down on him. 'I think my history as a generous benefactor to our community is on record as fact. My family has lived at the manor since 1665. What use have I of the black market? The mere suggestion is preposterous.'

A ripple of applause rang out with several people cheering.

This is slipping away from us.

Anna stepped back onto the stage. 'Before we go any further, there is someone we should hear from. Fred, can you join us, please?'

Heads swivelled as a man began to hobble into the body of the hall. His injuries still obvious from his beating, the spiv rested against a wall.

'You had my brother and me beaten up. You know who I am and that I get my stuff from your people. I've told the police everything because I'm sick of the way people like you do what you like, when you like, to who you like. I don't care what happens to me. All I know is that the likes of you have to be stopped.'

A further gasp rattled around the room as heads turned back to Sir Reginald.

'My dear man, I have never seen you or your brother in my life. I have nothing to do with the black market, and if you would like to get in touch with me after this evening's little charade, I'll see if I have any work for your brother and you on the estate. I have to say I'm a little surprised that neither of you has signed up to fight for your country.'

Mention of war service caused the villagers to jeer at the injured spiv.

Got to move things on.

'One of the things I like most about our wonderful Norfolk Broads are all those sleek wherries gliding effortlessly up and down its silken waters.' Anna's lyrical statement served only to confuse her audience. 'But seeing isn't always believing. What looks like a traditional Norfolk boat going about its lawful business to one person is a smuggling opportunity for another.'

Sir Reginald began to fidget. 'Really, this is too much. Vicar, please do control your daughter. Have I not been a good friend to the church and the village? I say again, this is preposterous. I'm not used to being treated like this. It must stop, now.'

Eddie didn't wait for the vicar to respond. 'Moving on; you do own a wherry, don't you?' asked Eddie, keen to maintain the pace of his interrogation and keep his quarry on the defensive. 'In fact, you own five.'

'I most certainly do not. I have better things to do with my time than sail up and down old peat diggings.'

'I see, but your wife does, doesn't she? Or rather, one of the companies of which she is chairman owns them. In fact, Lady Fischer runs all your companies. A quite remarkable feat, wouldn't you say?'

The audience's bewilderment increased at the latest revelations.

'Are you saying my wife isn't a capable woman, Lieutenant Elsner? Perhaps you're suggesting women per se aren't as capable as men. Let me assure you, my friend, that this war, like the last, proves women to be our equal. Are you really suggesting that's not the case?'

The women in the room erupted into a roar of support for Sir Reginald's views.

Anna jumped back into the fray.

He's a slippery one.

'I tell you what women object to, Sir Reginald; it's being used as a patsy by men. Being chairman of your companies has nothing to do with your wife's abilities, in fact, I doubt you've ever taken the trouble to find out what skills your wife has. From a personal perspective, I object to men assuming women will do as they're told. Am I not correct, girls?'

The women reacted with a roar of approval.

'But let's not change the subject. Two men are dead, their murders sharing remarkable similarities.' Anna's serious tone subdued the audience.

She turned her attention to The Duke. 'Then again, Albert Root, you also expect everyone to do as you say. As a result of your actions, those men, who should still be with their loved ones, are dead. In that way, you killed them.'

The Duke drained of colour. 'Look, everyone knows I run a betting ring, and your American side-kick tricked me into admitting lending money illegally, but I'm not a murderer.'

Eddie moved a few feet so that he was now standing immediately in front of The Duke. 'Again, we agree. Because although you like to think of yourself as a tough guy, you haven't the brains to murder two men and cover your tracks so well.'

The Duke began to visibly relax, only to be ridiculed by laughter from the villagers.

'But you do, Sir Reginald.' Eddie took two small steps sideways so he was facing the aristocrat, who stood several feet above him on the stage. 'Murder, never mind the black market, is a complex thing. It takes cunning, planning and brains to lay false trails and red herrings to fox those seeking the truth. You either possess or have access to all those things.

'You learned about Ted and Cyril's side business. Why you thought two small-time black marketeers were a threat to you is beyond me. Perhaps you considered they were getting above their station in life. That's how you people think, isn't it? So you ordered they be got rid of. Who knows, in your paranoia, you may have assumed Cyril and Fred and his brother were thinking of cutting you out and buying their stuff direct, so you had them taught a lesson.'

Anna noted that Sir Reginald enjoyed the higher elevation the stage afforded him as he looked down with contempt on her friend.

'I think we are all aware that our American friends have a tendency to use ten words when one will do. It seems you have embraced your countrymen's habit with aplomb.' Sir Reginald gave a superior grin.

This time the villagers failed to respond.

'Do you know, I've been talking to an angry farmer. He said he was sick and tired of some people thinking they could ride roughshod over others. In fact, he gave me a concrete example of a barn on his land he needed to use, but somebody told him to keep away from it. Do you know it, Sir Reginald? It's the one that backs on to the Broads. Astonishingly, it turned out to be full of cigarettes, liquor, ladies' stockings. In fact, you name it, and it was there.'

Anna pressed home Eddie's line of attack. 'The trick is to cover your tracks, something you took seriously, except one

241

or two of the people you employ to move goods around got a little slapdash. A few days ago, I found a scrap of paper outside Broadside Mill. Nothing much on it apart from a partial design I didn't recognise. Then, when Eddie and I were in the barn, I came across what was left of a label on a can of petrol. That, too, carried a design, a sort of crest. Suddenly it all made sense – it was the same design as the paper I picked up at the mill.'

She looked across to her co-interrogator. Eddie required no further prompt.

'And that design forms part of your family's coat of arms. A pretty basic mistake, or do you consider yourself above the law?'

Sir Reginald turned to the vicar. 'I've had quite enough of this, so I offer you my apologies for not fulfilling my duties this evening but trust you'll understand.'

The bewildered vicar looked at his daughter.

'We won't keep you much longer, Sir Reginald,' said Anna. 'What my American friend failed to say is that he also found a couple of other things, like the remains of some wire, and a dirty pair of black patent leather shoes.'

Sir Reginald erupted. 'I don't know what you're talking about. Although it's none of your business, I don't possess such a pair of shoes.'

Eddie began to search his pockets. 'Then how is it that your London shoemakers think different?'

A gasp shimmied around the hall as Eddie held up a piece of paper. 'It's a copy of a sales receipt. I'm sure the police will find the original at the manor.'

The aristocrat smirked at Lieutenant Elsner, then the audience. 'You silly little people. Do you not understand the new order that is coming? It is families of my class who will lead,

242

just as we have down the centuries. Those two fools thought they could cheat me. Well, you now know what happened to them. I tell you this, when my kind rule, no one will dare get in our way.'

It was possible to hear a pin drop as he bolted from the stage. However, his escape attempt was abruptly halted by Constable Bradshaw.

It didn't take long for the police to clear the hall of villagers as Inspector Spillers ordered The Duke and Sir Reginald handcuffed and removed to the station. 'Make sure you keep them apart.' The inspector's tone left his subordinates in no doubt of their orders.

Standing to one side, Anna and Eddie were deep in discussion.

'Am I forgiven for telling you fibs by sending that letter, Anna? I meant what I said about it being safer you not knowing what I was up to. I had to get to London and do some digging.'

Anna maintained a stern look, before breaking into a beguiling smile. 'What made you suspect Sir Reginald?'

'Up until a few days ago, I really did think The Duke was responsible for both murders. It was only when I put two and two together and realised he and Sir Reginald were beginning to cross paths that I thought London might provide the answers. Let me tell you the Honourable Sir Reginald Fischer is very, very well connected. However, he isn't held in such good esteem by his peers. It didn't take long for one of them to dish the dirt.'

Anna moved to one side so she could see out of the window to glimpse The Duke and Sir Reginald being frogmarched across High Street and into the village police station. 'The odd thing is that Tom and I were on the same trail. Once he found out who owned the wherry, some of the pieces began to fall into place. But why didn't you tell me you'd been back to the barn?'

Eddie looked at the floor as she walked back from the window. 'We gave each other such a hard time in that barn. The last thing I wanted to do was broach the subject again. I also knew if anyone found out what I was up to, you'd have been first in the firing line.'

The tension Anna had felt all evening began to evaporate as she looked into the lieutenant's sparkling grey eyes.

Constable Bradshaw ambled over. 'You know what, Anna, I've realised what Billy Fleming meant when we left him the other day. It wasn't Tuffsman, it was toff's men.' Tom Bradshaw smiled as he looked at a confused Eddie Elsner.

'And I eventually realised what Fred the spiv meant when he said some people are fireproof. He meant Sir Reginald, but it was still brave of him to turn up tonight, even if he didn't need to offer us a name thanks to Eddie's investigations. Although we caught the murderer, people will say that Fred spilt the beans. I hope he stays safe.'

The emerging friendship between three people who seemed to have little in common a few days before was evident as they exchanged comfortable smiles.

Inspector Spillers joined the group. 'Although it pains me to say it, we'll keep an eye out for the mysterious Fred the spiv so that he doesn't end up in a ditch.'

Anna leant forward and placed a friendly peck on the inspector's cheek. 'You are a softy, really, aren't you? We'd never have caught them without your help, so thank you for believing us.'

Inspector Spillers blushed, then turned to his constable. 'Well, I don't know about that, Miss Grix, but what I do know is that this young fellow acquitted himself well. Not only have we caught a murderer, but we've also shut down an illegal betting ring and moneylending operation. Not bad for a week's work, eh, Constable Bradshaw?'

'I…err, I couldn't really say, sir.'

'Admirably modest, Constable, but no more so than I would expect of my staff. However, perhaps it's time you put in for your sergeant's exam, don't you think?'

Tom beamed with pride.

'Quite right, Inspector, quite right,' added Anna before closing in on the constable and planting a kiss on his forehead.

Anna then turned to Eddie. 'I have an admission to make, Lieutenant Elsner. You said a few days ago that I was determined to solve the murders on my own, and I know you didn't mean it as a compliment. I've come to realise we all need help. So, does that mean you'll stick around or hightail it back to London?'

Eddie gave her a stern look. 'You can't be trusted—'

His searing assessment cut Anna to the bone. 'But—'

When she finally found the courage to look at Eddie, he was smiling. 'There you go again, interrupting me. What I was going to say is that you can't be trusted to keep yourself safe, so I think I'd better hang around, don't you?'

Epilogue

'Come with me.'

Anna looked perplexed as she followed Eddie out of the Memorial Hall and down High Street before it became apparent where they were headed.

They knocked on the door of a thatched cottage and it didn't take long for it to open.

'Come in, she's in bed, but I've told her she can read until you've come and gone.'

Anna first looked at Martha Page, then Eddie. 'What are you two up to?'

'You'll see, come on,' replied Eddie.

Eddie had lifted the Suffolk latch of the slatted timber bedroom door and gently opened it. Inside, the excited youngster was sitting up in bed with an open book resting on the eiderdown.

'Hello, Tilly. I imagine you're quite excited?'

The young girl fizzed with anticipation as the three adults neared her bedside. Martha sat on one edge, while Anna positioned herself on the opposite side.

Eddie undid the silver button on his uniform breast pocket,

246

withdrew a small card-like object and showed it to Anna, who understood immediately.

Tilly's eyes focussed on the small square of paper. He gazed at her with a kindly smile, then handed over what she'd waited so patiently to see.

Silence fell as she concentrated on a black and white image.

'My mum had this taken in our backyard last summer. She's so beautiful, isn't she?' Tilly fell quiet as a tear began to trickle down her cheek. 'I mean… she was…'

Eddie knelt and gently dabbed her cheek with a handkerchief. 'Have you seen what's on the other side?' He spoke with a gentleness Anna hadn't heard before.

Tilly took the handkerchief from Eddie and turned the photo over.

'My special girl, Tilly. How lucky I am to have such a beautiful daughter.'

2 June 1940.

'Listen to me. Your mother loves you very much and will always be there for you. You may not be able to meet at the bus stop anymore, but she'll be watching over you. If ever you need to talk to her, she'll be listening. Do you understand what I'm saying?'

Tilly looked at Eddie, her tears replaced by a beaming smile.

English (UK) to US Glossary

ARP: Air Raid Warden in WWII. A civilian volunteer who patrolled the streets checking no lights showing during a blackout (to prevent enemy bomber planes seeing their target).

(A) Turn: Old term for performance, e.g., song, dance or tell a joke. Often used in an informal setting like a British pub, 'Give us a turn, Bill'.

Austin Seven: A relatively inexpensive British car manufactured from 1923 until 1939

Bobby: Slang name for the British police derived from its founder's name, Sir Robert Peel in 1829

Broad: A stretch of shallow water formed from old peat diggings. Common in Norfolk and Suffolk regions of the UK. Can take the form of narrow stretches of water like canals or open water like small lakes.

Car boot: Trunk

Chemist: Pharmacy

Clapped-out: Something that is ready to break, 'Your car is clapped-out.'

Come a cropper: Slang term for getting yourself into trouble or minor harm, 'If you don't watch out, you'll come a cropper'.

Cuppa: Shortened form of the phrase 'a cup of tea'.

Dolly tub: A zinc-plated tub used for hand-washing clothes. The 'Dolly' was a hand-held wooden pole with a handle and a domed or three-pin end to agitate the clothes.

Dressed up to the nines: Of smart appearance

Isle of Man: A self-governing British Crown dependency situated in the Irish sea between the British mainland and Ireland.

Jack-the-lad: British slang word for someone flashy and too sure of themselves

Lav: Shortened British form of the word, lavatory.

Lummox: Old British (East Anglian) name for a fool, said in a light-hearted way, 'You are a daft lummox'.

Marsh harrier: A bird of prey often seen on the Norfolk Broads

Mushy peas: Marrowfat peas soaked for at least eight hours. A traditional side dish to go with fish and chips

Naff: Of low value, 'It's worth naff-all.' Alternatively, 'That car is naff.'

Nark: Old English name still used to describe a police informer

Settle: An old wood chair or bench with a high enclosed back to keep the wind off a person. Were often used in old British pubs.

Shandy: A mixture of roughly fifty per cent or more of beer and fifty per cent lemonade.

Shilling: A UK coin used until 1971 worth approximately four US cents today, the cost of a pint of beer during WWII.

Sixpence: A UK coin used until 1971 and worth about two US cents today.

Staithe: A landing stage for loading and unloading boats.

Thrupenny bit: A British coin used until 1971.

Toe-rag: A slang term of derision, 'You are a toe-rag for doing that, it was an awful thing to do'.

Toff: Slang word for an upper-class or wealthy person generally seen to be looking down on other people.

Two-shilling piece: A British coin used until 1971, worth ten per cent of one British pound sterling.

Wherry: A traditional sailboat used for carrying goods and passengers on the Norfolk & Suffolk Broads.

About the Author

Keith Finney grew up in the North West of England listening to two distinct sounds: Brass band music and a loud hooter calling employees to work at the town's cable making company.

Discovering construction sites involved working in foul weather, which he hated, so Keith opened a joinery business soon after completing his apprenticeship, and ran this until entering teaching in his early thirties.

Over the following twenty years, Keith steadily rose through the ranks, ending up as an Assistant Principal at a large college of further & higher education in Norfolk, England.

Now retired, he divides his time between writing mystery stories and helping mind his two youngest grandchildren. However, his wife calls into question Keith's definition of 'helping'.

Keith Finney is the author of the successful self-published Norfolk Cozy Mystery series, together with Lume Books, Lipton St Faith Mysteries.

Keith loves hearing from his readers and you can email him at keith@keithjfinney.com.

Lightning Source UK Ltd.
Milton Keynes UK
UKHW010049050521
383134UK00001B/91

9 781839 012228